feels like home

Feels Like Home

This book is a work of fiction. Names, characters, places, and incidents are the product of the author's imagination or are used fictitiously. Any resemblance to actual events, locales, or persons, living or dead, is coincidental.

Copyright © 2023 by Melissa Grace

The scanning, uploading, and distribution of this book without permission is a theft of the author's intellectual property. If you would like permission to use material from the book (other than for review purposes). For more information, contact at: www.melissagracewrites.com.

First paperback edition: June 6, 2023

Cover art by Elle Maxwell

Cover copyright © 2023 by Elle Maxwell

ISBN: 978-1-7355646-8-5

ASIN: B0BVRQG8GC

www.melissagracewrites.com

feels like home

MELISSA GRACE

Also by Melissa Grace

Home Is Where You Are
Home Again
Long Way Home

Author's Note

Dear Reader,

This book contains a storyline involving chronic illness, which some might find troublesome to read. I have been chronically ill since 2004, and though our main character Katie and I have different issues, there is a lot of overlap. You'll find some of my own journey tucked within these pages.

While Katie gets a definitive diagnosis fairly early in her journey, it's important to note that many women go years without getting an accurate diagnosis. I am one of them.

If you find pieces of yourself inside this story, and you're one of the many still waiting for answers, it's my hope that you won't stop searching. There are medical professionals out there who will listen, who will see the bigger picture. You are worth the fight it takes to find them.

Love Always,
   Melissa Grace

For Kate
None of this would be possible without you.

"You'll never do a whole lot unless you're brave enough to try."

—*Dolly Parton*

ONE

Katie

My patience was wearing thinner than the wire rims on Dr. Lowe's tiny spectacles. The lenses were no bigger than a couple of circus peanuts. *Can he even see out of those things?*

"Your thyroid and white blood cells look good, so let's focus on increasing the amount of exercise you're getting and put you on an anti-inflammatory diet." Dr. Lowe didn't even glance at me over the top of his small black laptop. "And I can recommend the name of a good therapist. Dr. Schafer—he's up on the third floor. He's great with meditation and visualization."

If it wouldn't have hurt me more than him, I would have launched myself off the table and punted his tiny computer into the air like a football before connecting my fist with his annoyingly square jaw.

It was barely nine a.m. on a Monday, but I was already spent. This was the fourth doctor's visit I'd had in two months, and with every appointment I was growing more and more agitated.

"Hold on." I stared at him from where I sat on the exam

table. "Do you have any clue what might have caused my white cells to spike a couple months ago?"

"Probably some sort of infection." He squinted as he typed, and I was even more convinced those glasses were just for show. "Whatever it was, the antibiotics must have sorted it out."

"Right." I pressed my lips together. "But is it possible there could be something more going on? Something we're missing?"

"Katherine, I see this often." Dr. Lowe made eye contact with me for the first time since I'd been there. "Chronic pain in women is almost always associated with anxiety and depression, inflammatory Americanized diets, and not enough movement."

"But I'm not depressed or anxious, and I've already been following a mostly anti-inflammatory diet." I folded my hands in my lap. "I don't exercise regularly, but I *am* on my feet all day at work."

Dr. Lowe raised his dark caterpillar brows at me, then lifted his phone out of his jacket pocket, tapping out something with his thumbs.

"I would really like to explore more options," I said, digging my nails into my palms. "Could we—"

He held up a finger to silence me before continuing to type on his phone.

My blood turned to boiling-hot lava, and I was certain I'd melt right through the table. *You have* got *to be kidding me. No, no. Take your time. Really.* I wanted to snatch the phone out of his hand and toss it in the biohazard bin. *How's that for visualization?*

"Did it ever occur to you that people might be anxious or depressed *because* they're uncomfortable and totally exhausted?" I blurted out the words before I could trap them inside my mouth.

Either way, he kept on texting.

"I guess I don't understand how eating more broccoli and doing Pilates is going to help with the pain I'm in," I said. "Let alone the vertigo I've been having."

"The body is like a car, Katherine." He flashed me a toothy smile, finally tucking the phone back inside his pocket. "Exercise is the oil, and our diet is the fuel. You can't let your oil run dry or fill a Camry with diesel and expect it to function properly."

I massaged my temples in an attempt to assuage the headache building behind my eyes, feeling personally victimized by the poster on the wall of a monkey hanging from a branch with the words 'hang in there' printed at the top.

"I apologize, but I'm running late for my tee time." He snapped his laptop shut. "I can give you prescriptions for a couple of mild muscle relaxers and some Tramadol."

"But what about the vertigo? I don't think you understand. Sometimes it's so bad I can't work."

He plucked the prescription pad off the counter and scribbled on it before tearing off the sheet and handing it to me. "I really do think you should make an appointment with Dr. Schafer. You'd be surprised at how emotional stress can manifest itself physically."

I bit down on my lip so hard I tasted blood. "Fine."

I can barely stay awake as it is, and now he wants to give me shit that's designed to make me even more tired. But I also wasn't any closer to getting answers, and there were days where I needed *something*. I mumbled a thank you as he started for the door.

"They'll check you out up front," he said with a wave as

he exited the exam room, leaving me with nothing but my prescriptions and a nagging sense of self-doubt. What if this really *was* all in my head?

I pushed the thought away as I hoisted myself off the table, the crinkly white paper sticking to my thighs. With a heavy sigh, I grabbed my purse and headed toward the checkout.

"Katherine Kelley?" An older woman in navy scrubs asked from behind the desk, and I nodded. "You have a fifty-dollar copay."

Fifty freaking dollars to hear that I needed to eat better and exercise from a guy more worried about his golf game than his patients. I dug inside my purse for my wallet, pulled out my credit card, and handed it to the woman.

"It's gonna be a hot one," she said, making small talk as she swiped the card in the machine and passed it back to me. "The high is ninety-four today."

"Yeah, I heard that." I forced a smile as I twisted my honey-colored waves into a bun on top of my head and secured it with the scrunchie on my wrist. It was bad enough that my day was already off to a crappy start, but it was made worse knowing I had the early June Nashville heat to contend with. Over the course of a year, I'd discovered that my body no longer knew how to operate in extreme temperatures. In the cold, my muscles became rigid, and my bones turned to glass. But the heat caused my vision to blur, and my limbs to grow so heavy it was as though I'd put on soaking wet clothes. The only thing I could do to remedy it was lay down in a cool, dark place and try to sleep it off.

The receptionist handed me the charge slip, which I quickly signed.

"Do you need to set up another appointment?" she asked.

I'd go to a veterinarian before I'd come back here again. "No, thanks."

I exited the office and strolled out the automatic doors, grateful for the slight breeze that blew across my face when I stepped into the sunshine. Soon it would be the heat of the day, and I wouldn't be able to tolerate being outside for more than ten minutes, so I planned to enjoy the short walk to my car. I might even get crazy and roll my windows down on my drive to work. I laughed at how completely absurd it was that *that* had become my definition of living on the edge.

Not that I'd ever led an especially exciting life to begin with. But there had been a time when I did more than go home and crash on the couch while Netflix lulled me to sleep. My heart ached for that version of myself—the one who could dance with friends till two a.m. or even just go for a walk without feeling utterly depleted.

I climbed in my VW Bug and slid behind the wheel, clamping my phone in the holder attached to the air vent. Rolling down the windows might be pushing it when I already didn't feel great, so I called my best friend instead.

Jo answered on the second ring, her voice crystal clear through the Bluetooth. "I was about to call you. How'd it go?"

"Back to the drawing board," I muttered as I pulled out of the medical center parking lot.

"*What?*" Her voice was razor sharp. "You have *got* to be kidding me. He didn't give you *anything?*"

"Just some mild painkillers and muscle relaxers," I answered. "Oh, and he told me to clean up my diet and exercise more."

"How are you supposed to work out when everything hurts and you feel like garbage?" she asked. "That's baloney.

What about the bloodwork he ran last time? Did that show anything?"

"Nope. It was all normal." I slowed to allow someone in the next lane to merge in front of me. "He also gave me the name of a therapist because apparently depression and anxiety can be linked with chronic pain."

"He *what*? This is bananas. There's clearly *something* wrong. And it has nothing to do with your mental health or what you're eating or your stupid BMI."

"Ugh. Don't remind me." Those three little letters were enough to make me flinch. Dr. Lowe had been quick to let me know my BMI was on the high side of normal at my first visit and that it 'wouldn't hurt to lose five pounds.'

"Where did this bozo go to medical school?" Jo let out a groan. "Everyone knows that BMI is a total joke and literally means nothing."

"Clearly not everyone."

She huffed. "Well, anyone who doesn't know that is dumber than a box of rocks, and their medical degrees aren't worth the paper they're printed on."

"I don't know, Jo. Maybe it really is all in my—"

"Don't say it," she cut me off. "Don't you dare say this is in your head, Katie. It's not, and there's a doctor out there somewhere that will confirm that. In fact, I have an appointment with my OB next week. I'll ask if she has any recommendations."

"I don't know what I'd do without you. Honestly, I'd probably never step foot in another doctor's office."

"I'm not letting you give up. I'll hound you until you get so annoyed with me that you make an appointment just to shut me up."

"I know you will," I said with a chuckle. "How are you feeling, by the way?"

"Emotional. I now understand why Ella cried when Sonic ran out of nuts for her fudge sundae when *she* was pregnant." Jo laughed. "Literally everything makes me cry, which is a little inconvenient when you do nothing but cover feel-good, inspirational stories. It's a wonder I'm not dehydrated from all the waterworks, and I'm only two months in."

"Speaking of work, where are you guys now?" I asked. Jo and her boyfriend Derek were part of a weekly segment on the *Today Show* called "Tell Me Something Good."

"Philly," she replied. "We're spending the day with a couple who's been married for seventy years, and I'm getting all weepy even *thinking* about it." Her sniffle came through the phone, and it made me smile. "Speaking of, we just got here."

"Okay. I'll let you go."

"I'll check in tomorrow," she promised. "Love you."

"Love you too," I said before ending the call.

When I pulled into the lot behind Livvie Cakes Bakery and Cupcakery about ten minutes later, I was surprised to see my friend Liv's car there. Liv Slade was the owner, but she didn't come in often. Her music career had taken off nearly four years ago, and she'd left her best friend Ella and I to run the show.

I cut the ignition and went inside before grabbing my apron off the hook by the door and replacing it with my purse.

"Hey." McKenzie greeted me without looking up from piping buttercream on a white cupcake.

"Those are gorgeous," I said, leaning over her shoulder to take a peek at the intricate floral designs she'd created. "Your technique is incredible, McKenzie. It's hard to believe you've only been doing this a little over a year. This is expert-level stuff."

It had taken me a while to get McKenzie to begin to open up, but I really liked the parts of her I'd gotten to know. It was like peeling away the layers of an onion, and I still had a long way to go, but at least her somewhat standoffish demeanor had softened over the past several months.

"Oh, um, thanks." Her cheeks flushed, and she swept a piece of her milk-chocolate hair off her face with her forearm. "Ella and Liv are in the office waiting for you."

"They are?" I wrinkled my brow. Did we have a meeting on the books that I'd forgotten about? "Do you need anything before I step in there?"

She shook her head. "I hope everything is okay."

"What do you mean?" I asked. "Why wouldn't it be?"

McKenzie shrugged, not taking her eyes off the cupcakes in front of her. "I dunno. Ella was crying, and Liv looked all somber, like somebody died or something."

The hairs on the back of my neck stood on end.

"I'm sure it's fine," she added quickly. "You know how Ella can be."

I did, in fact. But Liv being there and knowing she'd seemed off too sent alarm bells blaring in my head.

"I'll be back," I said.

The office door was slightly ajar, but I knocked anyway before sticking my head in. Panic shot through me when I got a look at Ella's tear-stained face and Liv's gloomy eyes as she leaned over the desk, her hand on her best friend's arm.

"What's going on?" I asked. "Is everything okay?"

Liv gave me a sad smile and motioned for me to come in.

"Hey, Katie Bug." Ella reached into her pocket and pulled

out a tissue so she could blow her nose. "Do you mind closing the door?"

I did as she asked and took a seat beside her. "Okay, you guys are freaking me out a little bit."

Were they letting me go? Was Livvie Cakes going bankrupt? No way. Business was booming, and I was an integral part of the team. This place was my life. Sure, I'd been having issues with my health, but I did everything in my power not to bring those troubles to work. And when things *had* been especially difficult, Liv and Ella had always understood… hadn't they?

Liv's eyes were misty as she and Ella had an unspoken conversation in the span of a single glance.

McKenzie's words returned to the front of my mind. *Had someone died?*

I gripped the seat of the chair, bracing for my already shitty day to get worse. "What's this about?"

Finally, Liv faced me, her posture slumped and her voice solemn. "We need to talk."

TWO

Dallas

"Thanks, man," Brandon, the sound engineer, said as I exited the booth late Monday afternoon at Blackbird Studios after laying down some beats. "You were great today."

"Yeah, no problem." I twisted the cap off my water bottle and took a gulp.

"Sucks that Midnight in Dallas broke up, dude. You guys were one of my favorites." He leaned back in his chair, his hands behind his head.

I gave him a nod. "I appreciate that, brother."

"What's everyone up to now?"

This was a question I wasn't sure I'd ever get used to. Since we'd played our final show together two months ago, other industry professionals and even fans on the street often asked about the members of the band I'd been a part of for my entire adult life.

"Jax is recording his next album with Liv," I answered. "Luca is… doing whatever it is Luca does, and Derek got out of music entirely. He's working with his girlfriend on the *Today Show* now as a photographer."

"And what about you?" He leaned forward, resting his elbows on his knees. "What are you doing these days?"

It was the very same question I'd been asking myself for the last two months. The truth was I didn't know. I still felt a little... lost.

"I mean, I know you're doing sessions and shit now." He gestured at the booth. "But do you have any other projects coming down the pipe? Any plans to start up another band?"

"Nah, man. I'm just taking it day by day right now." I crossed my arms over my chest, which made the vines tattooed on them intersect like an interstate overpass. "Enjoying a little time off, picking up some sessions here and there so I don't get rusty."

That was my bullshit answer. The truth was a lot less glamorous. I wasn't doing jack.

"I hear you, man," Brandon said. "Sometimes we just gotta take a step back and, like, reevaluate."

That was all well and good, except my step back wasn't voluntary. It was forced.

"I know everyone has a hard-on for Jax since he's the lead singer," Brandon said, "but I always felt like Luca was the real star of the show."

Fuck this guy.

"And you too, of course," he tacked on quickly.

"Right." I tightened my grip around my water bottle. The plastic cracked, and I kind of wished it was Brandon's stupid face I was squeezing beyond recognition. "Well, I gotta get going."

"Yeah, dude." He gave me a flimsy salute. "Good to see you."

"You too," I said as I pushed out the door, weaving my

way through the bowels of the studio and out the front entrance.

I polished off my drink and chucked it in the recycling bin outside. Logically, I knew that Luca had been a big part of Midnight in Dallas. He and Jax had always been the members people gravitated to, even though it was *my* name that was in *our* name. Even though the band had made up so much of my identity.

It made me think about Tracii Guns, a guitarist I'd always respected. He'd been the Guns in Guns N' Roses but had left before the band got signed. Before they rose to meteoric fame and everybody lost their minds over Slash and his top hats, while Tracii experienced just a small fraction of that success with his new band, LA Guns. I mean, I liked the Guns N' Roses that everyone came to know, but no one ever remembered that it was Tracii's name on the band. He appeared happy enough from my occasional scrolling on Instagram, and he'd still had an incredible career. But stories like his made me wonder why some people stuck out inside the minds and hearts of the masses, while others were quickly forgotten.

The inside of my black Mercedes felt like an oven set to at least four hundred degrees. It was only early June, but the mid-south was already experiencing a hellacious heatwave with no sign of rain in sight. I turned the air on as high and cold as it would go and drove out of the lot.

My fingers drummed against the steering wheel, tapping an erratic beat. I was wound tighter than the ass of a pair of skinny jeans on an East Nashville hipster. Too restless to go back home and try to find a way to pass the time, I found myself cruising the familiar side streets of Nashville from the Berry Hill neighborhood over to 12 South where my friends' bakery was. Though Liv wasn't there much anymore, Ella and Katie often were.

Katie. Just thinking about her was enough to make the muscles in my shoulders loosen.

I pulled into a spot behind the bakery and went to the back door, a privilege I'd earned after jumping in to help at the bakery on a few occasions. Katie had taught me how to make and decorate cupcakes when we'd met nearly four years earlier. I'd never be as good of a baker as she was, but because of her, I wasn't half bad.

"Knock, knock," I said as I stepped inside the humid space, the AC straining against the heat of the ovens that were always in use. Katie's back was facing me as she hovered over the center island with her coworker, McKenzie.

"Hey, Dal," Katie said without turning around. Her tone had an edge to it. Anyone who didn't know her, who didn't hang on her every word, would probably never have noticed. But I did.

McKenzie nodded in my direction. "Tommy Lee." I wasn't sure if she knew or cared what my real name was. After finding out I was a drummer covered in tattoos, she'd taken to calling me by the name of the notorious member of Mötley Crüe.

"How are you ladies doing?" I asked, ambling over to where Katie and McKenzie were swirling icing over cupcakes.

"Fine. What are you up to?" Katie glanced up at me. Her eyes were red and puffy, and her skin was slightly pink, like she'd been crying.

"I was in the neighborhood after my session." That wasn't entirely true, but she didn't need to know that. "Thought I'd drop in and say hi. See if you want to grab a coffee."

McKenzie looked at her, her eyes softening as she nudged Katie with her elbow. "Why don't you take off early and let me finish up?"

"I have too much to do," Katie said. "Lots of prep for tomorrow."

"Are you sure? If you tell me what needs to be done, I can help," McKenzie answered. "Sydney and Jacob are up front. I can always pull one of them back here if I need to."

"No, that's okay. I'll do it." Katie moved to the sink to wash her hands. "I'm gonna step out for a bit, but I'll be back within the hour to finish up."

"Okay," McKenzie said with a nod.

"Want to pop over to Frothy Monkey?" I asked.

"Sure." Katie grabbed a couple of paper towels from the dispenser and dried her hands before taking off her apron and hanging it on the hook in place of her purse.

"Can we bring something back for you?" I asked McKenzie.

"No, thanks." She peeked at me over the table, a flicker of something resembling concern in her eyes.

I followed Katie into the parking lot.

"Hey, are you okay?" I asked once the door snapped shut behind me.

She turned and collided into my chest, her arms wrapping around me as she wept.

"Whoa, Katie." Seeing her cry was a punch to the gut, like that time I'd taken a hit while attempting to break up a bar fight Luca had found himself in at some dive bar outside of Tulsa. I didn't know what had caused her to feel like this. All I knew was I'd do anything to fix it. "Hey, what happened? Talk to me."

She let out a ragged breath, and I held her closer, cupping the back of her head with my hand. "Shhh." I murmured. "I've got you. I don't know what's going on, but whatever it is, it'll be okay."

Katie sniffled and pulled away so she could wipe beneath her eyes with her fingertips. "I'm sorry. It's been a really shitty day."

"It's okay. You never have to apologize for the way you feel." I kept my hands on her shoulders and squeezed them gently. "What's going on?"

Her bottom lip trembled, and her hazel eyes filled with fresh tears. "I think the bakery might be closing."

THREE

Katie

"I can't believe it," Dallas said as we sat in a booth near the back windows at Frothy Monkey. "I know Liv isn't as involved in the business now, but I never imagined she'd consider closing it."

It was late afternoon, and there weren't many other patrons in the coffeehouse, but that didn't mean Dallas went unnoticed. I caught a young woman tugging on the shirt of the guy she was standing with, nodding toward Dallas in what I'm sure she thought was a subtle gesture. Before I'd become friends with him and the rest of the band, it was something I wouldn't have picked up on, but now, I could almost sense the curious stares.

"Honestly, I should have seen this coming." I swirled the iced lavender latte in front of me with my straw. "Liv has this whole new life now, and Ella and Cash are getting married in September. Plus, they have the baby, and Cash's work at the label has been taking him out to L.A. more often, especially now that the band broke up. It makes sense they'd move out there, but I can't shake this feeling of being… left behind."

Dallas's expression was pinched as he took a sip of his coffee.

"And maybe it's not entirely rational, but I'm hurt. We did those renovations a couple years ago, and added the coffee bar. I put in all that work to expand the menu. But for what? For Liv and Ella to realize it didn't suit their lives anymore?"

I sucked in a breath and blew it out. "I mean, I get it. They have new lives and growing families. But that place is home for me, you know? It's where I feel most like myself."

We locked eyes, and my chest tightened. I was preaching to the choir. Of all the guys in the band, Dallas had taken their split the hardest. He knew what it was like to watch everyone else move forward, while his life was stuck on 'pause.'

"I'm sorry." I reached across the table and placed a hand on Dallas' arm. "I know you understand this feeling all too well, and you're going through your own shit. I shouldn't be dumping this on you."

"You're not dumping anything on me," he said. "I care about you. I *want* to be here for you."

He focused his amber eyes on me and covered my hand with his, causing a familiar shimmer of electricity to pass through my body. For a second, I wondered if he sensed it too. I'd had this feeling since I'd first met Dallas, and it had only gotten stronger as our friendship grew. It was like my heart was trying to reach through my body to hold him close. The air stilled, and dust particles glittered in the space between us like stars suspended in a night sky.

He dropped his gaze and moved his hand, lifting his mug to his lips. And just like that, the spell was broken.

Dallas cleared his throat and placed his cup back on the wooden table. "So, is closing the only option they're considering?"

I shook my head. "They also mentioned the possibility of selling it, but there's no guarantee the buyer would even keep it the same. They might have an entirely different vision that changes everything I know and love about the place. They could even bring in their own staff."

"How soon is this happening?"

"Luckily, I have some time. They're not going to make any major decisions until Ella and Cash move, which won't be until later this year or early next."

He nodded. "So, do you want to stick it out and see what happens or start thinking about finding another job?"

I didn't even pause to consider the question. The answer was easy. "No, I'm married to that place. I'm gonna be there till the end, if that's what it comes to. Of course, if they do decide to sell or if it turns into a place I no longer recognize, I'll be forced to make a change. And that comes with a whole host of worries for me."

The corners of his eyes creased. "What do you mean? You're Top Chef Katie. Other places would be beating down your door to hire you."

My cheeks pinked. It still made my limbs go tingly anytime he called me by the nickname he'd given me the first day we met.

"It's not so much that I'm worried about getting a job as I am about keeping it." I ran my finger along the rim of my plastic cup and tilted my head. "Most jobs aren't going to be as considerate of my health as Ella and Liv are. If I'm having an exceptionally tough day, they don't even ask for an explanation. They tell me to take all the time I need, and they pay me for the time I'm not there, which I've told them repeatedly they don't have to do. It's not something I do often, but it's nice to have the option if I need it."

"Katie, I'm so sorry." He pushed his hand through his shoulder-length hair. I secretly loved when he let it hang freely instead of tying it up in his usual haphazard bun. "Has your doctor been able to help you?"

"Nope." I sighed. "He tells me to just change my diet and exercise more or see a therapist. Like I'm making up these symptoms for attention or something."

He jerked his head back. "Who the hell is this guy? Dr. Oz?"

I choked on a laugh. His ability to make me smile was unmatched.

"It's frustrating, and it's starting to make me question my own sanity," I admitted. "I'm to the point where I wish for one of these symptoms to manifest in an obvious way. Like if you break your wrist or have a rash all over your body, people can *see* that. Doctors don't doubt that someone like that needs help. But with me, there's no fracture or tear making my body hurt all over, no flu making the room spin or my head ache. What I feel is invisible to everyone but me."

His Adam's apple bobbed as he leaned closer across the table. "You are *not* invisible, alright? That doctor is a clown, but we'll find someone who can help. I promise."

My heart fluttered. "Thank you. I talked to Jo about it this morning, and she's going to ask her OB if she has any recommendations when she goes next week."

"Good. If not, we'll find the right doctor. Even if we have to go to another state," he promised. "You don't have to go through this alone. I know you have Jo and Ella and Liv, but you have me too."

I wanted nothing more than to live inside the velvety depth of his light brown eyes, held safe within his gaze. He didn't have to say it—I knew I could count on him. Over the years, he'd become a great friend, which was almost a consolation for the fact that I'd never be anything more than the ever dependable Top Chef Katie. But even as grateful as I was for the bond we shared, it would never be enough to dull the ache that appeared whenever I was in his presence. Or when I'd been without his presence for too long.

From the second I met Dallas, I was all heart eyes. He was handsome, charming, talented, and completely out of my league. As our friend groups merged, my feelings only grew deeper. But by then the dynamics were already established, and it wasn't worth upsetting the equilibrium of our little found family or risking our connection on feelings that would probably never be reciprocated. Even if they were, Dallas was a musician, and up until a couple months ago, being on the road a lot came with the territory. It wasn't the best start for any budding relationship.

"Thank you, Dal. You're such a good friend." My breath nearly caught on the last word, attempting to give me away.

A flicker of something passed over his face like a shadow. Was it disappointment? Sadness? Regret? Whatever the feeling, it was quickly replaced with his broad, beaming grin.

"Ditto, Top Chef Katie."

A COUPLE WEEKS LATER, I WAS SITTING IN THE LOBBY OF YET another doctor's office, leafing through an old issue of *Women's Health*. I'd been lucky enough to snag a cancellation at Dr. Brower's office, the person Jo's OB had recommended, and I was anxious. What if this visit was yet another let down, leaving me with more questions than answers? My chest squeezed as though my apron had been tied too tight. It was a feeling I got often, but with the stress of trying to figure out what was wrong with me, it was no wonder my body was reacting so strongly.

The door separating the waiting room from the rest of the clinic opened and a tall blond guy in black scrubs appeared, glancing down at the chart in his hands. "Katherine?"

I laid the magazine on the end table next to me and started toward the open door.

"Actually, you can call me Katie," I said as I fell into step beside him.

"Oh, sorry." He circled something at the top of the page. "We're just going to stop by the scale over here on the way to the room." He pointed to the physician's scale that stood alone in the hall next to a single office chair. "You can set your purse down there."

The very sight of those stupid scales was enough to make my blood pressure go up because I knew whatever they said might cause the doctor to look no further than the number that appeared. But not wanting to make waves before I'd even met Dr. Brower, I stepped on anyway.

"How tall are you?" he asked, scribbling down the number I wouldn't dignify with a glance.

"Five foot five," I answered, stepping down.

More scribbles. "Alright, follow me." He led me down the narrow corridor, stopping in front of an exam room with the number three just outside it. "We're going to be right in here. You can have a seat wherever you like."

I crossed over to one of the two chairs against the wall and sat, depositing my purse onto the other. He made small talk about the Nashville heatwave while he took my pulse and blood pressure.

"Alright, Katie, the doctor will be in shortly," the nurse said before exiting the room.

My eyes bounced from wall to wall, glancing at the various posters and brochures. One poster touted the benefits of the Mediterranean diet and another listed the warning signs of diabetes. Among the brochures were ones about family planning and mental health resources.

At least the reading material is well-rounded.

There was a knock on the door, and a man with thick dark hair entered the room. He wore a button down and slacks beneath his white lab coat.

"Hi, Katie." He reached out to shake my hand. "I'm Dr. Brower."

"Hi," I said. "Nice to meet you."

"So, what brings you in today?" Dr. Brower asked as he sat on the stool beside the small counter, glancing over the chart the nurse had been making notes in.

"I've been having some pain issues for a while now, and I've seen a couple of different doctors about it, but so far I've not found any real answers."

The doctor nodded, glancing up at me. "Can you tell me what the pain feels like and where it's located?"

"It kind of depends," I explained. "Sometimes it's in my legs or my arms, especially my hands. Sometimes it's in my back. It can feel like a stabbing, sharp pain, but it can also feel sort of like pins and needles."

He jotted something in the chart. "Like when your foot goes to sleep?"

"Yeah, but a little more intense than that," I answered. "I also get this kind of tight feeling around my chest."

"Are you experiencing that now?"

I nodded.

He wrote down something else. "Are you feeling anxious at all?"

"A little, I guess."

"That can be caused by anxiety, and in patients who are dealing with some sort of chronic pain, that's not uncommon," he said.

Here we go again.

"But that doesn't explain the pain you're experiencing."

My mouth fell open. Was he actually *validating* how I felt?

He tapped his pen on the counter. "Tell me, Katie, what is it you do for a living?"

"I'm a pastry chef," I replied.

"Hmm." He pursed his lips. "Has anyone ever diagnosed you with carpal tunnel?"

I shook my head.

"I think that might be worth exploring given your profession."

"But how would that explain the legs?" I asked.

"I take it you're probably on your feet a lot?"

I nodded.

"It could have something to do with that." He sat up straight, crossing his arms over his chest. "I think it would be beneficial for you to invest in some supportive footwear. I'll have the nurse write down the name of a store in town that sells orthopedic shoes," he said. "And I'd like to set you up with an orthopedist to get you tested for carpal tunnel if you'd be on board with that."

"Sure." It was the closest thing I had to a plan, and it planted a seed of hope in my chest.

"Your last doctor faxed over your most recent bloodwork, and I didn't see anything of concern. But I'd actually like to run a couple more tests they didn't do." He wrote something on the chart, circling a couple of spots on the page in front of him. "I'd like to check your B1 and B6 levels and your antinuclear antibodies. Basically, I just want to rule out any sort of autoimmune conditions."

"Okay," I said. "I've also had major fatigue—the kind that makes your bones ache. And I've had some vertigo episodes."

He tilted his head. "Do those seem to be triggered by anything specific?"

"Not that I can tell. It just comes out of nowhere."

"Sounds like we could be dealing with multiple unrelated issues." He propped his elbows on the counter in front of him and leaned forward. "These vertigo episodes—do they happen often?"

I nodded.

"Let's also set you up with an ENT specialist," he said. "I'd like to get you tested for Meniere's disease."

"What's that?"

"It's an inner ear disorder that can cause some dizziness like what you're experiencing. Have you had any ringing in your ears or felt any pressure in them?"

"Nope. Just the vertigo."

Dr. Brower made a couple more notes. "In the meantime, if you have any more of those episodes, you can take some over the counter medication like Dramamine to help. If that doesn't do the trick, there's something stronger I can call in for you."

"Okay," I said, annoyed the last doctor I'd seen hadn't suggested these things.

"I know I've just thrown a lot at you, but let's take it one step at a time. The most important thing is we have a plan to move forward and hopefully get you feeling better." He rose to his feet. "I'm going to do a quick exam before I send the nurse back in to draw some blood, and then she'll call and set up those appointments for you. Sound good?"

"That sounds perfect." Actually, it was music to my ears. Someone was finally taking me seriously and helping me find some answers once and for all.

"I'M GOING WITH YOU," JO ANNOUNCED ON THE PHONE ONE night about a week before my appointment with the orthopedic doctor.

"You don't have to do that," I said, flopping on my couch, too exhausted for this conversation. I'd been at work from seven a.m. until a little after nine p.m. My mind and body were in shambles like they'd been through a paper shredder.

"You need moral support," she argued, through ragged puffs of air. "And I'm in town, so it's perfect."

"Are you okay? Did you take up mountain climbing or something?"

"Going up stairs while pregnant should be outlawed."

I snorted. "Listen, I appreciate your concern, but I've got this."

I'd gone to the other appointments on my own, and that was how I intended to continue moving forward. I preferred to do most things myself, and I was happy that way. At work, I liked being the one doing prep, designing cakes, and generally, running the charge. As long as I remained in control, nothing could slip through the cracks or go wrong, because I wouldn't allow it. Not on my watch.

"That's not the point," Jo said. "Obviously you're capable of going on your own, but it's also okay to accept support."

"Nobody's a bigger champion for me than you, and I love you for it. But I can handle a few measly tests on my own."

"Did the point buzz off the top of your hair when it flew over your head?" she asked with a laugh. "What I'm saying is that it's okay to let people take care of you too. Like you did for me last year when I turned up on your doorstep with nowhere to go."

"That was different," I insisted.

"It's not, though. That was you showing up for me, and this is *me*, doing the same for *you*."

"Okay. Fine. Come with me," I said through a yawn. I didn't stand a chance of winning this argument, so I acquiesced, eager to move on. Besides, I enjoyed spending time with my best friend. I just preferred for it to be under circumstances that didn't involve me being tended to like some high-maintenance plant.

"Thank you." Her chipper tone told me she was pleased. "You sound tired."

"I am," I admitted. "We got a last minute request for a birthday cake tonight, so I stayed late and worked on it."

"By yourself?"

"Well, yeah. There's no sense in anyone else staying late to do what I can manage on my own."

Her heavy sigh came through the phone. "Katie."

"What?"

"You've got to stop pulling these late nights. At least let McKenzie or one of the others stay to help so it won't take as long." Her voice turned soft. "I'm sorry. I'm not trying to be bossy or overbearing. I just care about you and want you to feel better."

"I know," I assured her. "It's okay, but I'm pretty zonked. I'm gonna take a shower and get in bed."

"Call me tomorrow?"
"Of course."
"Sleep well," I said. "Remember, you're busy growing a human, so you need your rest too."
I can almost hear the smile in her voice. "I'm hitting the hay now. Promise. Love you."
"Love you too," I said, ending the call.
I decided to click on the television to watch an episode of *Gilmore Girls* and unwind.
I fell asleep before the opening credits.

FOUR

Dallas

I WAS IN HELL. It had been three weeks since my last drum session. I'd gotten called for another one at Blackbird for some up-and-coming pop star called Prose Gold whose music, if you could call it that, sounded like what would happen if you put bubble gum and a dying cat into a blender and turned that sucker up as high as it would go. The lyrics were about things like day drinking and doing lines off library cards. I liked to think I was pretty open-minded when it came to music *and* day drinking, but this was not my bag.

The prose is definitely not gold. Or maybe I'm just gettin' old. Fuck, that was more clever than anything Prose had ever written.

And it was just my luck that the sound engineer on this hell-coaster with me was none other than my ole buddy Brandon. It was the last week of June, *and* the AC had just gone out at the studio thirty minutes earlier. I was sweating my fucking balls off to record the most boring album in existence for a nineteen-year-old whose nails were long and pointy like the claws of a honey badger. Maybe I wouldn't have been so annoyed if she hadn't had to do the same part *twenty-seven* times, especially when all the girl had to do was sing *yeah, yeah, yeah*. There wasn't enough autotune on the planet to fix that shit, and I would have felt a little bad for Brandon having to run take after take if I didn't hate him.

The stupid thing was, I didn't even have to be there. I didn't need the money. My career with the band had been successful enough that I didn't have to work another day in my life. But I kept taking these jobs anyway, chasing a feeling —anything that might help me remember who I was without Midnight in Dallas.

My mind had turned to mush because I wasn't creating anymore, and every single session I did was more soul-crushing than the last. Just being in the studio made me feel like I had a fifty-pound amp on my chest. I'd become nothing more than an instrument in the background of other people's music.

"Listen, guys," Brandon said, wiping the sweat off his face with the collar of his T-shirt. "We're going to have to reschedule. It's way too hot in here."

"Okay." The tarantulas that Prose Gold had sacrificed for eyelashes were sweating off, the outer corners hanging down. When she blinked, it was as if they were waving at me. "I really need to take a few days to practice and, you know, get in my zone. I need to capture the *essence* of the moment."

I stifled a laugh, my thumb and forefinger tracing along my jawline. "The essence of the yeahs?"

Her eyes widened and she let out a little gasp. "OMG, that would be such a great song. 'The Essence of Yeah.'" She held her hands up as though she were framing the words before turning her attention to the woman whom I assumed was her assistant. "Libby, write that down. That's *such* a vibe."

I stared at her, blinking slowly.

Completely misreading my expression, Prose added, "And you'll get writing credits too, obvi."

"Oh, that won't be necessary," I said, doing my damndest to keep a straight face. "It's all yours."

"Thanks, man," Prose said. "Let's reconvene after the Fourth of July. I'm leaving for The Hamptons tomorrow and won't be back till after the holiday."

I tugged on my shirt, fanning my chest, desperate for some sort of air flow. Between the heat and Prose Gold, all the oxygen had left my brain.

"That's fine. Brandon, just text me when you have a date set," I said.

Prose made her way over to me and air kissed my cheeks. "Thanks so much, Dalton. You were amazing today."

"You bet." *For fuck's sake. I'm already a has-been.* I didn't bother to correct her—I just wanted to get out of there as fast as I could.

I exited the studio and ambled down the hall until I pushed out the entrance, going from the pot to the frying pan. It was nauseatingly hot. I checked my phone as I crossed the lot to my car and saw I had a text from Katie's best friend Jo, who happened to be my cousin's girlfriend.

Jo: Can I ask a favor of you?

I'd grown to really care about Jo, even though we'd gotten off to a rocky start. When Derek announced he was ready to quit the band in March, I'd gone off the rails and blamed her, but I quickly came to my senses and realized she was the best thing that ever happened to him. I even flew all the way to New York to apologize to her in person. We were a lot more alike at the time than I wanted to admit—both a little lost, caught somewhere between who we thought we were and who we had the potential to be.

I waited until I reached my car, climbed inside, and turned on the AC before replying.

Dallas: I pretty much owe you till the end of time, so yeah.

A few seconds later, her reply came through.

Jo: True. :) I have a feeling you won't mind doing this favor.

The little dots appeared to signal she was still typing.

Jo: I was going to go to the doctor with Katie tomorrow for moral support while she's getting some tests done, but Derek and I have to fly to New York for a last minute meeting. I hate that I can't go, but I was thinking maybe you'd be willing to go in my place. :)

A smile formed on my lips as I wiped the sweat from my brow with the back of my hand. If I wasn't already burning up, a flush would have crept down my neck. Spending time with Katie was far from inconvenient.

Dallas: I'd be happy to. Anything for Katie. And you too, I guess.

I added the emoji with its tongue sticking out. I didn't have any sessions scheduled, but even if I did, I'd cancel them all to be there for Katie.

Jo: I thought you'd say that.

More dots.

Jo: Be at her place tomorrow at three. I'll send you the address of where you're taking her. It's Tennessee Orthopedics. I'm not planning to tell her you're coming. Thought it could be a fun surprise?!

I hadn't seen Katie since we'd gotten coffee together a couple weeks before, and just knowing I'd be spending time with her the next day made the stress of Prose Gold melt away.

Jo: Oh and Derek says hi!

I smiled. I may not have had a clue what I was doing with my life, but it made me happy to know Derek had found Jo.

Dallas: Hi to Derek. I hope this will be a good surprise?

I found the emoji that looked like it was gritting its teeth and sent the text.

Jo: It will. Promise. :) Talk soon.

My fingers hovered over the screen.

Dallas: Thank you. For asking me.

Jo sent back a pink heart, and I tossed my phone onto the center console.

As I pulled out of the parking lot, my chest already felt lighter.

I GOT TO KATIE'S JUST BEFORE THREE THE NEXT DAY AND sauntered up the steps of her back patio. If you knew Katie, you never went to the front door. I rapped my knuckles against the wood three times. A few seconds later, she moved the curtain on the other side and peered out. Her eyes widened when she saw me, and she flung open the door.

"Dallas, hey!" She smiled so big it made my heart swell. "I'm actually on my way out to a doctor's appointment."

I beamed. "I know. That's why I'm here."

I could see the wheels in her head turning as she pieced that information together, and she rolled her eyes. "Dammit, Jo."

I chuckled. "The one and only."

She shook her head, and her cheeks flushed. "I *told* her I would be fine. Really. I don't need anyone to go with me."

"I have no doubt you can do this on your own, but the thing is, you don't *have* to." I leaned my arm against the doorframe. "Look, I know Jo didn't clear this with you, but she did it because she cares. And so do I. If you really don't want me to go or aren't comfortable with the idea, I'll get out of your hair, but I'm taking the iced coffee I got you with me."

Her eyes brightened. "You brought me coffee?"

"I've got an iced lavender latte in the car with your name on it."

She smiled with her whole face, and the apples of her cheeks turned rosy against her golden skin.

"It would be a shame to let that latte go to waste," she teased.

My heart thudded against the walls of my chest. Her honey-colored hair kissed her bare shoulders, and I suddenly wished I could do the same. Thank God she couldn't read my mind. The thoughts bouncing around my head were far from friend territory.

"The company wouldn't be so bad either," I joked. "If you're into drummers with lots of tattoos."

"Well, as it happens, that's my favorite type of drummer." Her voice had the most subtle drawl that was the cutest fucking thing I'd ever heard. "Let me grab my purse."

She disappeared inside for a few seconds and came back with her bag hooked on her shoulder.

"You ready?" I asked.

"Ready."

I held my arm out and did my best impression of a chivalrous bow. "Your chariot awaits, madam."

She giggled. "Why thank you, good sir."

I followed her to my car and quickly skipped ahead so I could open her door.

"Thank you." She tucked her hair behind her ear and climbed in.

I jogged over to the driver's side and snapped my seatbelt in place, while Katie dug her phone out of her bag.

"We're going to—"

"Tennessee Orthopedics," I finished for her.

She laughed, grabbing her latte from the cupholder and took a sip. "Wow, Jo really made sure you were prepared, huh?"

"Would you expect anything less of our girl?" I asked.

"No," she answered. "No, I would not."

I took a sip of my hot Americano, and Katie scrunched up her nose at me.

"I will never understand how someone can drink hot coffee when it's nearly a hundred degrees out," she said.

I held up my cup. "*This* is real coffee." I gestured to her drink in the cupholder. "*That* is a coffee-flavored milkshake."

"Is not," she argued.

"Is so."

"Well, whatever it is, it's *good*." She wrapped her pillowy pink lips around the straw in a perfect 'o', and I realized the hot coffee was, in fact, a bad idea. It was a million degrees outside, and just watching Katie's gorgeous mouth around that damn straw was enough to make me sweat.

"You okay, Dal?" She placed her hand on my bare arm. "You spaced out on me for a second."

I cleared my throat and smiled. "Never better, Top Chef Katie. Never better."

KATIE SAT BESIDE ME IN THE WAITING ROOM OF TENNESSEE Orthopedics, clipboard in hand.

"If I don't have carpal tunnel now, I will after filling out this mountain of paperwork," she joked, writing in the blank spaces on the forms.

"So, what are they doing today?" I asked.

"I think they're going to do some x-rays and then do something called an EMG test," she explained. "I looked it up online last night, and basically, they hook me up to some electrodes and send electrical pulses through my hands to measure the response of my nerves."

My brow creased. "Is that gonna hurt?"

She shrugged. "Google said it could be a little uncomfortable, but at this point I would literally let them cover me head to toe in peanut butter if I thought it might make me feel better."

My mind took that visual and ran with it, turning it into something a lot sexier than she'd intended.

I placed my hand on her shoulder and gave it a squeeze. "I'm sorry, Katie. I can't imagine what you've been going through."

My chest constricted. It killed me to think of her in any kind of pain. I just wanted to fix it.

She took in a deep breath and let it out. "I feel like I have to be close to getting answers, though. The new doctor I've been seeing, the one who sent me here, ruled out a couple of vitamin deficiencies. He said my ANA was positive, but that plenty of people have that without any real cause."

"What's that?"

"Antinuclear antibodies," she answered. "Or something like that. Honestly, I get so overwhelmed with all of this medical terminology. Basically, it can be a marker for an autoimmune condition, but he told me that plenty of people have positive ANAs, so it's probably nothing."

I leaned forward, my forearms resting on top of my legs. "That doesn't sound like nothing."

"It's all just a lot," she admitted. "And it's frustrating. You go to these doctors and pray they know what they're talking about. You hope they know which stones to look under."

"Well, they should look under *all* of them until they figure out what's wrong." I filed the information about the ANA thing away in my mind. If she didn't get any answers from the x-rays or the nerve test, I would bring it back up.

"I also have an appointment with an ear, nose, and throat specialist set up for after the Fourth to look further into the vertigo stuff."

I didn't know a lot about health-related things because I hadn't really had to. Other than the occasional cold or flu, I'd been pretty healthy most of my life. And while I certainly wasn't one to think the worst, I couldn't shake the uneasy feeling that crept into my chest. What if there was something more these doctors were missing?

My gaze dropped to my shoes.

Don't turn this into something it isn't. The doctors know what they're doing.

I studied her face as she continued filling out her paperwork. She was the most gorgeous woman in the world to me, but even her beauty couldn't disguise the shadows that framed her eyes.

Katie looked at me, her lips turned up in a tight smile. I had to push my worries down. This wasn't about me. This was about *her*, and she didn't need someone asking more questions right now. She needed support, a shoulder to lean on, and that was exactly what I was going to be.

"It's gonna be okay," I said. "And hey, maybe when they send those electric pulses through your hands you'll end up with some sort of superpower. Maybe you'll be able to shoot lightning out of your fingers."

She laughed, returning her eyes to the clipboard. "Is it weird that I kind of hope that happens?"

"Um, no. Because I also wish for that. Maybe you can figure out how to give me some of that power."

"Nope," she teased. "That one's all mine. You have to pick one of your own."

"I see how it is. I bring you coffee, and you won't even share your superpowers with me." I nudged her gently with my elbow. "No more lattes for you."

"But if you have your own power, we can team up," she explained, circling various fields on her form. "Like Wonder Woman and Superman. Batman and Robin."

"Ah, I see." I raised my brow at her. "Do I get to be Batman?"

"Absolutely not." She chuckled. "So, what would your superpower be?"

That was easy. It would be making her feel better, making her smile. It would be the ability to take away anything that caused her pain or discomfort, but I couldn't say *that* out loud.

"Hmmm." I rubbed my thumb along my jawline. "I'd like to be able to freeze time."

"Pfft," she said. "That's lame."

"What?" I clutched my chest as though she'd wounded me. "Me freezing time while you take out the bad guys with your lightning fingers is lame?"

"First of all, we're going to have to think of something better to call them than *lightning fingers*." Her mouth stretched into a broad grin. "And second, I accept. That's actually genius."

"I know."

My plan was genius, but not for the reasons she thought. If I could freeze time, it wouldn't be to take on a life of crime-fighting. It would be to hold on to every second with her. The thought made my chest ache because I knew the only moments I'd ever have with her would be as a friend.

I couldn't tell her how I really felt. She meant too much for me to chance it. So many things could go wrong. What if she didn't feel the same? It could alter our friendship forever. She could become reluctant to confide in me anymore, and we would inevitably drift apart. Could friendships even survive unrequited feelings? All I knew was it was more important for me to have her in my life than not at all. But how long could I shove my feelings down before I'd eventually break?

FIVE

Katie

THE NURSE POINTED me in the direction of the exit that led back to the lobby where Dallas was waiting, drumming his fingers on his leg. When he saw me, he immediately rose to his feet.

"How'd it go?" he asked.

I blew out a sharp breath. "More questions and no answers. The doctor doesn't think carpal tunnel is the issue. He already looked at the results from the x-ray, and the EMG was fine too."

"How was that?" His brow furrowed. "Was it painful?"

"Not really." I shrugged. "It just felt weird. Like a super tiny, *super* fast fish was swimming through my arm."

He wrinkled his nose.

"I promise it wasn't as bad as it sounds." My voice was flat and dejected, but that was exactly how I felt. I'd hoped the tests would give me some sort of reason why I felt the way I did, but once again, I was leaving with nothing. "Are you ready to get out of here?"

"Yeah, come on." He placed his hand on the small of my back and guided me out the front entrance.

We walked side by side to his car, our arms touching every few steps, sending an entirely different kind of electricity through my veins.

"I'm sorry I dragged you out here for this," I said as he opened the passenger door for me.

"Hey." He placed both hands on my shoulders, stopping me from getting in the car. "You didn't drag me anywhere. I wanted to be here. And this wasn't a total waste. Even if you didn't get a definitive answer, it still ruled a couple of things out."

I let out a heavy sigh. It was so damn hard not to get discouraged. "You're right."

He winked at me. "Of course I am. It's okay to be frustrated and disappointed. Just don't lose hope because we *will* get to the bottom of this one way or another, okay?"

Even if it hadn't been ninety-eight degrees out, my heart still would have melted. My health wasn't his problem, but he made me feel like it was still one we'd solve together.

"You know you don't have to help me." My cheeks pinked. "I appreciate it, of course, but I can handle it."

He playfully rolled his eyes at me. "I'm going to pretend you didn't say that. I care about you, Katie. That's why I'm here, and I want to help you if you'll let me. But I'm going to need your permission 'cause I don't want you using your lightning fingers on me."

My flush crept down my neck, and I wiggled my fingers at him. He staggered back as though I'd pelted him in the chest, and I laughed, the stress in my limbs fading away.

"Now, get in this car," he said. "Because I'm taking you to get ice cream."

My eyes brightened. "Ice cream *and* coffee? I feel so special."

His gaze lingered on me as I climbed in.

"Good," he said. "Because you are. Besides, that should be the cardinal rule of doctors appointments: treats before *and* after."

He flashed me a warm smile as he closed my door, making his way around to the other side.

"I could get used to this."

He reached his hand over the center console and squeezed my knee. "I hope you do."

DALLAS TOOK ME TO JENI'S ICE CREAM IN HILLSBORO Village near my house, where I got a scoop of Brambleberry Crisp, and he opted for two scoops of Cookies n' Cream. We settled at a corner table, and he made me laugh until my sides hurt. It was the kind of pain I welcomed with open arms—one I hadn't had near enough of lately. If only I could have felt that good after *all* of my doctor visits.

"Do you have plans tonight?" he asked as he stood and gathered our trash.

"Does changing into my pajamas by seven and watching reruns of *Golden Girls* count?"

He chuckled. "It does not, in fact."

I grinned. "Then, no."

"How about you let me make you dinner?" he asked.

My heart did cartwheels inside my chest. "Really?"

His lips quirked. "It would be my distinct honor to cook dinner for you, Top Chef Katie. The ice cream was just an appetizer."

Was this happening? This was the most time we'd ever spent together, just the two of us. My stomach fluttered like a moth going into the light.

"Oooh." I rose to my feet. "Well, count me in."

He guided me out the door, tossing our trash in the bin on the way out. "Let's stop by Whole Foods so I can pick up everything I'll need to wow you with my culinary skills."

"What are we having?" I asked.

"I don't actually know yet." His grin stretched to his ears. "I do better when I think on the fly. But whatever it is, I can promise it will knock your socks off. Whether that's because it's the *best* or the *worst* thing you've ever tasted remains to be seen."

I kicked my sandal-clad foot out. "You can't knock my socks off because I'm not wearing any."

We made the short drive to the store, and Dallas had me listen to some new artist called Prose Gold he'd recently worked with whose music he said he couldn't stand. I swayed slightly to the beat.

"Don't hate me, but I kinda like it," I said once we'd gotten out of the car and started toward the store. "It's catchy."

"Ugh, *nooo.*" He groaned. "You were supposed to agree with me that it's awful."

I laughed. "It's not awful. It's… fun. *Eclectic.*"

"You say eclectic, I say chaotic." He grabbed a cart from the return on the way inside. "Honestly, every single session I've done has been… weird. I don't know how to explain it. It just feels different."

I shrugged as we strolled through the produce section. "Of course it does. It *is* different."

He stopped in front of the tomatoes, grabbing one of the small plastic bags off the roll beside them.

"But it's *music*." He picked out a few tomatoes and placed them in the bag, tying it off. "And that's literally all I've ever done. It shouldn't feel like this."

"Music with *Midnight in Dallas* is all you've ever done." I leaned my elbows on the cart as he reached for some arugula. "I'm not surprised it feels different. You're comparing apples to oranges. Midnight in Dallas was yours, you know? You poured your heart and soul into that band. These sessions are different. You don't have any real creative input or ownership of the project, I imagine."

"I don't." He grabbed a red onion and some fresh oregano. "And it freaking sucks."

Out of the corner of my eye, I spotted a kid who appeared to be about fifteen or sixteen shopping with his mom, and his eyes widened when he saw Dallas. I gave the boy a small smile.

"Would you consider starting a new band?" I asked as we meandered over to the dairy section, where he tossed some sliced mozzarella into the cart.

It was impossible not to let my mind wander for a moment, imagining a life where Dallas and I did everything together, including a Whole Foods run on a random Thursday evening. Being with him like this felt natural, and the more time we spent together, the more I longed for... well... *more*. I'd always buried my feelings for him, shoveling over them with all the reasons why it would never work. He was a freaking rockstar, and I was sure he would find a new band that would take him back out on the road again soon. But even if that wasn't a factor, our friendship meant too much to me to think about messing it up. What if I told him and he didn't feel the same way? It would change our relationship forever.

"I don't know. It just doesn't feel right." He paused for a second, holding up one finger. "You've got flour and baking powder and all that good stuff, right? Actually, that's a dumb question. You're Top Chef Katie. Of course you have that."

I laughed. "I even have salt."

"Good, because I'll need that too." He pushed the cart forward again, turning down the wine aisle. "We'll also need a bottle of red to go with the delicious flatbread pizza I just decided I'm going to make for you."

"Ooooh, that sounds good."

"I'm even making the flatbread from scratch."

I held my hand against my chest. "My culinary heart is all aflutter."

He rubbed his palms together, an excited glint in his eyes. "With a balsamic glaze."

"My love language," I said with a giggle.

His eyes held mine for a moment, and he raised his brows. "Then get ready to fall in love."

My heart wanted to reach for him and tell him it was far too late for that—that I'd already fallen in love with him a long time ago. But I couldn't. Even if I *was* crazy enough to risk it, what would happen if things ended badly? What if he wanted to break up, but I didn't? Would our gatherings with the gang and our frequent Sunday dinners together become awkward? Could I even *go* to a Sunday dinner ever again if that happened? I reminded myself that I was lucky to have him in my life in any way I could get him, and I shoved the other feelings down as far as they would go.

A mischievous smile formed on his lips. "You ready to do this thing?"

I nodded, and he pushed the cart with one hand, slipping his other around my waist, steering me toward the checkout. After we got in line, he kept his arm around me, as though it belonged there. And for a moment, I pretended it did.

DALLAS' TATTOOED FOREARMS FLEXED AS HIS KNUCKLES worked the dough into submission. He chattered animatedly while he walked me through each step of his plan, but he refused to let me help. Instead, he hoisted me onto the counter where I sat with a glass of wine, enjoying the view as he chopped the vegetables and made the sauce before setting them aside to prepare the flatbread. Watching him work was fascinating, like witnessing him play the drums. His hands and arms moved with precision and purpose, his mind running a million miles a minute.

"You know," I said, "you cook like you play drums. That never occurred to me until now."

He divided the dough in half and started rolling one piece out. "How so?"

"When you play, you're *there,* you know? You're in the moment," I explained as he repeated the previous step with the other piece of dough. "It's almost like you're conducting a symphony in your head, making sure each piece is exactly right. You kind of lose yourself in it. You do the same thing when you cook."

"Huh." He tilted his head as he took the discs of dough and placed them in the large skillet that had been preheating on the stove. "Do I really do that?"

I swirled the wine in my glass. "You do. It's fun to watch."

A soft smile played on his lips. "I do enjoy it, and I guess it is a lot like playing drums for me. When I play a song, I know that if I combine certain beats, a marcato or a ghost note or a well-placed high-hat, I'm going to get something amazing. All the beats are like ingredients, and the song is the recipe."

I studied him in awe as he flipped the dough, a perfect char on the side that was now face up. "But it's astonishing to me that you didn't even have a recipe for this. It's incredible how you started throwing stuff together and made it work."

"And that is e*xactly* what I do with music. I see the steps play out in front of me, and I hear them in my mind. With food, I do the same thing, only I don't hear it. I smell it and taste it."

I breathed in and placed my glass on the counter beside me. "That's... amazing."

"It's all because of you, you know," he said, turning toward me. "I didn't play around in the kitchen much until I met you. It all started with you teaching me how to make cupcakes."

"No way." I waved him off. "I'm sure you cooked some before we met."

He shrugged. "I'm serious. Being on the road so much, I never had to. Even when I was home, it wasn't something I did much of when left to my own devices, short of boiling noodles and heating up a jar of spaghetti sauce. But that first time you showed me how to bake, it sort of captivated me." He leaned against the counter, and his firm torso touched my bare knee, causing my breath to catch in my throat. "After that, I started watching YouTube videos and tutorials and started experimenting on my own. I loved watching how focused you became in the kitchen, but also how much it relaxed you, and I wanted that."

My cheeks flushed, a result of the wine and the compliments.

He turned off the stove, grabbed the flatbreads from the skillet and began to gingerly piece together the pizzas.

"Cooking is like music, but it's more personal—more intimate."

"How so?" My voice came out soft, almost inaudible.

"A recorded song sounds the same every single time you play it, right?" He paused, placing the pizzas on a cookie sheet and into the preheated oven before turning his eyes back to me. "And with music on an album, tons of people can be listening to the exact same track at once. But with these pizzas, for example, we're the only two people who will experience these together in the same exact moment."

The heat from my cheeks traveled down my neck and chest. "Damn, Dallas. That's so... poetic."

"With music, we only get a clipped view of how people experience a song," he explained, moving the dirty dishes to the sink. "When you're playing live, you can see maybe the first row or two from the stage if you're lucky, and we don't get to see how people react when they listen to an album in their car on the way to work or while they lay in bed on a rainy afternoon. But with these pizzas, I'll get to watch you take that first bite."

He clicked the oven light on and took a peek at his creations. "In fact, I'll get to do it right now."

He grabbed the potholder, opened the oven, and took out the cookie sheet, placing it on the silicone mats beside me.

"Pizza cutter?" he said, scanning the counter.

"It's in here." I tapped the face of the small drawer below where I was sitting.

I was about to hop down so he could open the drawer, but his strong hands stopped me.

"You don't need to move." His eyes never left mine as he parted my legs slightly and opened the drawer, reaching inside.

There was a four-alarm blaze taking place at my center, and I swallowed hard, praying that my expression wouldn't reveal how badly I wanted to grab his face and kiss him.

"There it is." His voice was low and husky as he carefully extracted the cutter and gently pushed the drawer, along with my legs, closed.

He held the sheet in place with the potholder as he sliced the pizzas into perfect quarters before drizzling the balsamic glaze on top.

"Here we go," he said, taking one of the pieces into his hand and blowing on it before bringing it to my mouth.

I leaned forward and took a bite. The flavors and textures exploded on my tongue. The sweetness of the balsamic, the bitterness of the arugula, the creaminess of the mozzarella all combined in a delicious crescendo.

He watched my face intently as I chewed. "So? How is it, Top Chef Katie?"

"Perfect," I answered. "Simply perfect."

He brought the slice to his mouth and took a bite, his eyes closing for a couple of seconds as he savored the taste.

When he opened his eyes again, he smiled at me. "The perfect bite and the perfect moment."

With the perfect person, I added silently.

"It's amazing, Dallas. Truly. If you ever decide the music thing isn't for you, you'd make a great chef."

He puffed out a breath. "No way. I enjoy it, but I'm

nowhere near good enough for that. Besides, don't you have to go to culinary school?"

I shook my head. "There are plenty of chefs who don't. Some are self-taught, and some do apprenticeships with other chefs." I fixed my gaze on him. "And you *are* good enough. You're creative and passionate and innovative. Everything it takes to be a good chef."

He put the pizza down and pursed his lips as though he'd never allowed the thought to cross his mind.

"Well, that is certainly something to consider." He reached his hands out to me to help me off the counter. "Ready to eat?"

My eyes focused on his lips that were curved into a dazzling smile. "I'm starved."

SIX

Dallas

WE LINGERED at the dining table until well after the sun went down, and the light that peeked around the blinds faded to darkness. Dinner had been devoured and the wine was long gone, but we continued talking and laughing for hours.

I told her stories about the early days of the band, like the time a drunk guy got on stage at one of our first gigs and insisted we play "Sweet Caroline" three times in a row. Katie described life growing up with her Granny in the very house she still lived in. She even showed me the lines on the doorframe in the kitchen where her grandmother had chronicled Katie's height each year until she turned thirteen. Even though we'd known each other for nearly four years, it felt like we were turning over new stones, never running out of things to say or learn about one another.

"Are those all yours or were some of them your Granny's?" I nodded toward the floor-to-ceiling bookshelves in the dining room that were lined with cookbooks. Some looked new, while others were clearly well-loved, the titles worn from the bindings.

"A little bit of both. A few of them belonged to my great-grandmother, and a couple were even my mom's." A soft shadow fell over her eyes. "Before she and my dad passed away."

"I'm so sorry." My arms ached to reach out to her. It was something I knew about Katie's past, but we'd never delved deeply into the subject.

She shook her head and gave me a faint smile. "It's okay. It was a long time ago." She rose from the table and stood in front of one of the shelves. Her fingers trailed over the spines of the books until she found the one she was searching for, then she gently pulled it out and brought it over to me.

"This one was my mom's favorite," she said, pulling her chair closer to mine. She gingerly opened the book, turning the thick, yellow-tinged pages until she landed on the one she was looking for. "See here? She wrote notes on the recipes she loved—adjustments she made that worked and ones that didn't."

The flowery curl of her mom's script looked so familiar. I'd seen it on order forms at the bakery dozens of times.

I grazed my finger over the page, feeling the slight indent of the letters Katie's mom had written. "Your handwriting looks just like hers."

"That's what Granny always said." She rested her head on one hand. "She said we were like two peas in a pod."

"May I ask... what happened to your folks?" My forehead creased as I turned my eyes on her.

She gave me a solemn nod. "They were killed by a drunk driver when I was six. They left me in Chattanooga with my aunt and cousins on a Friday afternoon, and that was the last time I saw them."

"Jesus," I murmured, covering her hand with mine. "Katie, I'm sorry."

"It's okay. Really." She took a breath and tucked a loose strand of hair behind her ear. "Wow, I guess I never told you that, did I?"

I shook my head. "And I never wanted to pry."

"Oh no, it's not like that," she said. "In a way it almost feels like it happened to someone else. I was so young that I don't really remember much about them. I guess I try to focus on what I had instead of what I never got the chance to experience. I mean, I miss my parents. Of course I do. But Granny loved me enough for them both. She gave me the world." She flipped a few more pages in the cookbook until she landed on another recipe with her mom's handwriting in the margins. "And Granny told me about my mom all the time. Between that and my mom's recipes, I feel like I got to know her in kind of a weird way. Granny once said it was my parents' dream to own a restaurant one day. My dad was an accountant, so he would have been the numbers guy, but my mom was the talent."

"So, that's where you get your love of cooking?"

She nodded. "And Granny and my great-grandmother were both amazing cooks too. I guess it's always been in my blood."

"Would you ever want to have your own restaurant one day?" I asked.

Her face lit up. "That would be a dream come true. Not just for me, but for my folks and even Granny. But... I don't really see how it could happen. I don't have the kind of capital I'd need to start one, and until I get some concrete answers about my health, I'm too scared to even think about trying to take out business loans. Besides, I love my job."

But we both knew there were a lot of unknowns with that situation.

"I just have to hope I get to keep on loving it," she said, as though she were reading my mind. She turned a couple more pages, a smile stretching across her face. "This was mom's favorite apple pie. Granny always made it for the Fourth of July. She'd say there wasn't nothin' more American than apple pie."

"I couldn't agree more." I chuckled, leaning forward on my elbows. "Speaking of the Fourth, you're coming downtown with everyone for the fireworks, right?"

"Wouldn't miss it," she said. "Jax and Liv are headlining one of the biggest celebrations in the whole country. Of *course* I'll be there."

There was a dull ache in my chest. I was proud of Jax and Liv, but I had to admit, it felt weird being on the sidelines.

"Would you want to maybe… go together?" I asked. "I could meet you here, then we could head downtown?"

"I'd like that." She stretched her arms over her head and yawned. "Sorry. I promise it's not the company. I just tucker out so easily these days."

I squeezed her shoulder as I stood from my chair. "It's okay. I should probably let you get some sleep."

"I'll walk you out," she offered, and I gave her my hand, pulling her to her feet.

"This was really nice," I said as we made our way to the back door.

"Thank you for making me dinner." Her voice was crisp and sweet, like the apples I imagined went into her favorite pie.

I pushed out the door and onto the back porch, turning back to face Katie. "We should do this more often."

"We should." Her perfect pink lips curved into a smile. God, I wanted to kiss those lips, to know what they tasted like, so fucking bad.

"It's nice to have a friend cook for me," she said, immediately causing the thought to float away just beyond my reach.

"I'm usually the one running the show."

I swallowed hard and forced a smile. That dreaded word. *Friend.* A reminder that she'd never see me as anything more.

"Well, I'm happy I can do that for you."

She stepped closer to me and wrapped her arms around my waist, and I inhaled the sweet scent of her hair. "Good night, Top Chef Katie."

"G'night," she said before disappearing inside and clicking the lock shut, leaving me alone with my thoughts on the porch.

I blew out a breath and raked my hands over my face.

It was better this way—leaving this stone left unturned. Our lives were so intertwined that if things went south it could affect more than just us. If we ever split, it could make things awkward for everyone. Our friend group wasn't just a casual group of buddies. We were a family. It was best to leave well enough alone. If only I could get my heart on board with my mind.

DOWNTOWN NASHVILLE WAS A TOTAL CLUSTERFUCK ON THE Fourth of July—even more so than usual. The bachelor and bachelorette parties that plagued the area had been replaced with locals and tourists alike who had come in droves to see the fireworks display.

That evening, I'd gotten an Uber Black to take Katie and

me as close to the action as we could get, which admittedly wasn't all that close. We still had to walk about a quarter mile in ninety-five degree heat to get to FGL House, where a local radio station was hosting a private party. The space was decked out in red, white, and blue, and wait staff flitted about the throng of guests, passing out themed cocktails.

"Are you okay?" I asked Katie once we finally made it inside. Her skin was flushed, and she already looked exhausted.

Still, she smiled. "Yeah, I'm good. Just hot."

I snagged an icy blended cocktail from one of the passing trays and handed it to her. "Let's find you some water too."

She waved me off and took a sip of the bright red drink. "This is perfect. Let's just find everybody else."

I agreed and led the search for the rest of our crew. She held onto the back of my shirt, damp with sweat from our walk to the club. As we maneuvered through the crowd, I prayed to God I didn't smell. The thin cotton fabric was nearly plastered to my chest, but somehow, Katie still looked gorgeous. She'd woven a red bandana into her braid and had on a navy-blue tank top with cut-off jean shorts that showed off her legs.

We snaked around the bar, passing the DJ booth, until Jo caught my eye and waved.

"Over here," she said, motioning us toward the far wall of the club.

"Hey." I greeted her as Katie looped around me to hug her best friend, while Derek and I clapped each other on the back.

"How long have you guys been here?" Katie asked.

"Not long," Jo answered, fanning her face with her hand. "I know I'm only three months along, but I'm already too pregnant for this heat."

"I don't envy you one bit," Ella said as she approached, cocktail in hand. "I'm sweating my tits off."

Derek gave her a hug. "How's Betty?"

"She's good." Ella took a drink. "She really is the sweetest baby, but I'm kinda glad to get a break tonight. With Cash gone, I feel like I'm burning the candle at both ends."

"Wait, what?" Katie asked. "I thought everyone was coming tonight?"

"They were supposed to." Ella heaved a sigh. "Sam got offered an endorsement deal by Apple Music, but they wanted to meet with him right away. I think it's because they also want to do this big livestream concert with him this summer. So, Sam, Cash, and Grace are all hanging out in LA, leaving me and Betty girl to our own devices again."

Now that Midnight in Dallas was no more, Sam Corbyn was the star of Cash's label, Carrie On Records. Ella's daughter, Grace, worked for the label, but she was also Sam's girlfriend, much to the dismay of his legions of fans.

"He's out there a lot, isn't he?" Derek asked, propping himself against the wall.

Ella blew out a breath. "All the time. It seems like every one of his new bands are based there. It's been… challenging."

Katie shifted beside me, and I gave her shoulder a squeeze. While she empathized with Ella, I knew it was also a painful reminder that her job at the bakery could be in jeopardy.

"Where are Antoni and Nate?" I asked about our former manager and his husband.

"They're in Nebraska visiting Nate's family," Ella answered. "What about Luca? Is he coming?"

"He should be here soon," Derek answered.

Katie took a sip of her drink. "Have you guys seen Jax and Liv yet? Did they bring the kids?"

Ella shook her head. "They're with the nanny. Liv felt so guilty leaving them at home, but it's too hot for them to be out in *this*." She looped her finger in a circle. "I got to see Jax and Liv for all of two minutes until they were whisked away for some press."

"I don't miss that stuff one bit," Derek said, and I flinched.

He didn't miss it, but *I* did. I wasn't used to experiencing shows from the side of the stage. I was used to being the one interviewed and playing for the masses. Now, I was just another face in a sea of people.

Katie touched my arm and gave me an encouraging smile. The simple gesture made my heart soar. Even though the music and stage lights had faded, she still saw something special in me.

"What kind of lame party is this?" Luca asked, joining us.

"Luca!" Ella cried. "You made it! I feel like I haven't seen you in ages."

"It's only been three months." He pretended to be put out, but allowed her to hug him anyway before pulling a small flask from his back pocket and taking a sip. "It's hotter than Satan's ballsack."

I eyed the flask, and I wasn't the only one. Derek and Ella noticed it too, but we all chose not to say anything. This wasn't the time. Luca'd had a tendency to overindulge over the years, but when the band split, he'd said he hadn't had a drop in months. I assumed that streak was over.

My relationship with Luca was complicated. The guys and I were like brothers, but that meant we fought like brothers too. Things had been dicey between the two of us since the band had broken up—largely because I'd been a massive dick when it happened, and Luca was just a massive dick, period. It wasn't personal, that's just how he was. We'd never really talked things out after the split, instead opting for some sort of silent truce.

Katie swirled her straw in her drink, and Luca wrinkled his nose.

"What the fuck *is* that?" he asked, nodding his head toward the red concoction. "It looks like a Slurpee."

"I believe this one was called the 'Let Freed-rum Ring.'" Katie held the drink out for his inspection.

He immediately pulled his head back once he got a whiff. "It smells like every memory I have from high school."

Ella tilted her head. "Like cheap wine coolers and disappointment? Or was that just my high school experience?"

Luca tucked his flask back in his pocket. "Where's Cash?"

Ella explained the whole ordeal again and frowned. "It feels weird, doesn't it? Without him and Grace and Sam here? And Antoni and Nate. Then we've got Liv and Jax running around somewhere busy being celebrities."

"It does feel a little different," Katie admitted. "It seems like everyone's being pulled in different directions."

"That's because they are." Luca's voice was flat as he kept his focus on the toe of his black Converse. I couldn't help but notice his use of the word *they* instead of *we*. Was it possible he was feeling just as lost as I was?

"Oh hey, is McKenzie coming?" Ella asked. "I meant to touch base with her this morning."

Katie shook her head. "She said she already had plans."

"That's too bad." Ella grimaced and wrinkled her nose. "It smells like ass in here."

"What do you guys say we hit up the buffet?" I asked.

"The line is a mile long already anyway," Jo said. "We may as well go ahead and get in it."

She started in the direction of the food as Ella, Derek, and Katie trailed behind her.

"We were literally just saying how it smells like ass in here, and naturally, your first thought is food. *Always* with the food." Luca smirked and crooked one eyebrow at me. Over the years, we'd forged a friendship out of mostly good-natured ribbing and annoying the ever-loving shit out of each other. It was how we communicated, so his teasing me about my voracious appetite, like he'd done many times before, centered me in a weird, fucked up way. It was a shred of normalcy on a day that felt anything *but* normal.

A grin spread over my mouth. "I guess some things never change."

He shrugged. "Guess not."

Katie turned around, looking for me to follow her. "You coming?"

"Yep," I said, catching up to her with Luca on my heels.

It's true that some things never change, I thought as Katie beamed up at me. *But I really hope some things do.*

SEVEN

Katie

I PRESSED my palm to my forehead and took a deep, steadying breath. *You are not going to ruin this night. You are not going to ruin this night.* When I'd woken up that morning, I hadn't felt right. My body was off kilter, more so than usual. I'd spent the entire day resting because I knew I'd be on my feet a lot when we got downtown, but it clearly hadn't helped. Even though we were inside, the air conditioner struggled to cool the FGL House, which was crammed with people. But I refused to let how crappy I felt rain on my parade or anyone else's. We'd only been at the club for an hour. I could push through with the best of them—I *had* to.

Dallas had gone to get more food for him and some water for me, while Ella had set off in search of the ladies room. Jo and Derek had run into someone they knew from work, leaving me alone with Luca.

"What's going on with you?" he asked, leaning against the wall beside me. "You look like shit."

I snorted. "Gee, thanks a lot."

He chuckled and nudged my arm. "I don't mean it like *that*. You just don't look like you feel well. Are you still having those... issues?"

His face softened as he looked down at me, and my heart swelled. It was sometimes hard to reconcile the version of Luca I was used to with the kind one who so rarely made an appearance.

"Yeah," I answered. "I am."

Luca was, by all definitions, a complex guy. Last year, Jo had helped host a toy drive and Christmas party for underserved youth in the city, and at the last minute, I'd gotten sick. I was devastated that I couldn't go, and Jo didn't want to leave me by myself. Of course, I wasn't going to let her miss her party, but she refused to budge unless someone came to stay with me. Surprisingly, it was Luca who came, but under one condition: we weren't allowed to tell *anyone*.

He nodded, his lips twisting to the corner of his mouth. "Still don't know what's causing it?"

I shook my head. "Nope. I feel like I'm on a wild goose chase searching for answers. So far we've ruled out some vitamin deficiencies and carpal tunnel. I have an appointment with an ENT specialist, but they're so booked up I can't get in until December." I blew out a puff of air between my lips. "It's just so frustrating. Sometimes I wonder if it's all—"

"In your head?" he finished for me, cutting me off, his piercing blue eyes searching mine.

"Yes," I admitted, taken back. I'd never voiced this concern to Luca before. How could he possibly know that? "But how did you..."

His eyes flitted away from mine. "It's just really fucking easy to feel that way when you can't find a logical reason for what you're going through. It makes you feel like you're going fucking crazy."

"Yeah," I agreed. "It does."

The room swayed along with my stomach, and my mouth was dry like a jar of cotton balls.

"Seriously, Katie, you don't look good." He placed his hand on my shoulder and pointed to where a couple was vacating a high-top table a few feet away. "Come on. You need to sit down."

I allowed him to steer me there, and he pulled a stool out for me.

Once I was settled, he reached for the flask in his back pocket. "Here. Take this."

"Really?" I pushed away his hand. "I highly doubt whatever's in there is going to help me right now."

He chuckled softly and offered it to me again. "It's just water."

My eyes narrowed at him as I took the flask. "It better be."

I brought the bottle to my lips and took a drink. Sure enough, it was water.

"Thank you." I blushed as I handed it back to him. "Sorry."

"It's fine," he said, screwing the top back on.

"No. It's not. But why, though?" I asked. "Why put water in a flask? You know what people will think, what they'll assume."

He shrugged. "Let them. People are going to think what they want anyway. They already think I'm a fucked-up asshole. Why not give them the proof they're looking for?"

If I hadn't already felt terrible, that would have done the

trick. His words, his nonchalance over people believing half-baked mistruths about him, hit me like the oppressive humidity. It was suffocating, and if it made *me* feel like that, I could only imagine how much worse it was for him.

"You're not like that, though," I insisted.

He arched an eyebrow at me. "Aren't I?"

"No," I said softly. "Not at all."

He cleared his throat as he caught the gaze of a gorgeous, busty blonde nearby. "Can I, uh... get you anything? You good?"

"I'm fine," I answered, shaking my head. "Dallas and Jo should be back soon."

"Then if you'll excuse me." The blonde gave him a flirty wave, and he turned to me and smiled, but it didn't reach his eyes. "I have a reputation to uphold."

He approached the woman and leaned in close to her ear. She wore a smoldering stare as she bit her bottom lip. It was only a couple of seconds later when she followed him as he wound through the crowd, but not before he tossed one last look at me from over his shoulder. His eyes were turned downward, a melancholy expression on his face.

The room tilted, and I inhaled, holding my breath for a few seconds before I let it out.

Keep it together, Katie. You're gonna be fine.

"There you are," Dallas said, interrupting my thoughts as he handed me a bottle of water, twisting the top off. His brow furrowed as he scanned my face. "You okay? You look a little flushed."

"Yeah," I lied as I took a sip, relishing in how cold the bottle felt in my hands. I forced a smile. "I'm great."

THE CLOSER WE GOT TO DARK, THE MORE PACKED THE CLUB became. Drinks were flowing, and the volume of the music and the voices struggling to talk over it had grown increasingly louder. The air conditioner strained to cool the cramped space, and the humidity covered me like a wet weighted blanket.

"I'm going to get another water," Derek said. "Anyone else need anything?"

"Nope. If I drink anything else I'll definitely have to pee again before the show starts, and I know we're about to head that way soon." Jo rose from her seat. "Speaking of, I better go ahead and get in line for the bathroom now." She started toward the other side of the club, weaving between the wall-to-wall party-goers.

"What about you guys?" Derek asked, turning his attention to me and Dallas.

"Bring Katie some more water, if you don't mind," Dallas answered.

"Of course," Derek said. "I'll be right back. I'm going to see if I can round up Luca and Ella too." He started to inch his way through the swarm of people.

My vision was hazy like someone had filled the room with a cloud of smoke. And I was so hot, except I wasn't damp at all. I wasn't even sweating.

"I think I need some air," I managed as I got to my feet. "I'm going to step outside for a second. I'll be right back."

Dallas was immediately at my side, his hand gently clasped around my arm. "I'm coming with you."

I was too tired to argue. It was taking every ounce of energy I could muster to put one foot in front of the other, but I knew that if I could just get outside and breathe in some fresh air, I'd feel better. At least, I hoped I would.

Dallas acted as my shield. He held his arm out in front of me to keep people from running me over, which I was thankful for. One small push would have likely sent me to the floor.

"Over there," Dallas said in my ear, pointing at a side door nearby. "Let's go out that way. It's a little less crowded."

I nodded wordlessly. My hands started to tremble when we were a few feet from the exit, but I continued to move forward.

You're almost there. Keep going.

Dallas pushed the door open, and I spilled out into the crowd that milled around on the sidewalk. I took in a shallow breath, but there was no relief. It was just as bad outside as it was inside. The air was still and stale and hot. So very hot.

My head was light, as though it was floating away from the rest of my body like a balloon on a string that had slipped through my fingers. It was like gravity had suddenly grown hands and was using them to pull me toward the ground. Voices around me melded into an indistinguishable roar, as though I was underwater, and they were talking just above the surface.

What's happening to me?

Dallas gripped me by the arms. "Katie, are you okay?"

At least I thought that was what he said. His voice was muffled and far away, even though he was right in front of me.

I tried to speak, but my words wouldn't come out.

There was no panic. There was no asking for help. I was too tired to fight my own body.

"*Katie,*" Dallas said my name again, this time with more urgency. "Talk to me."

I tried opening my mouth again, but this time the corners

of my vision flickered like someone had dimmed the lights. Dallas' lips were moving, but the sound had been turned off, muting everything around me. The next thing I knew, his face disappeared behind a blinding bright light.

EIGHT

Dallas

"Katie!" I slipped my arms around her as she slumped forward, catching her before she hit the ground. My heart raced as I scooped her up, cradling her against me. "Help! I need help over here!"

"What happened?" A woman with gray hair wearing flashing red and blue earrings came to my side immediately, and a small crowd began to gather around us.

"She said she needed some air, and we came outside, and she just passed out." The words tumbled out all at once. "She hasn't been feeling well lately. She…" I couldn't think straight. My thoughts spun like a car out of control, and at any moment, I was certain they were going to hit a guardrail.

"We need a medic over here!" a bystander shouted.

"Jesus, what happened?" I heard Luca's voice before he materialized next to me.

"I don't know," I cried.

"I'm a nurse!" A short woman with a nose ring came rushing toward us. "What happened?"

"She seems to have passed out," the woman with gray hair

answered for me as the nurse reached for Katie's limp hand, placing her fingers on the inside of her wrist. "He said that she needed some air, so they came out here, and she fainted."

"How much alcohol did she have?" the nurse asked. "Has she taken any drugs that you're aware of? Prescription or otherwise?"

"Just one cocktail. She mostly had water." I answered. "And she doesn't do any sort of drugs. I don't know of any medications she's on."

"Her pulse is elevated," the nurse said, moving her hand to feel Katie's arms and then her face. "And she's warm but not sweating, which concerns me. She could have heatstroke. We need to get her to an ambulance and out of here. Now."

"How the hell are we going to do that?" Luca asked. "The streets are packed."

I raised my head and looked around, an icy chill spreading through me despite the heat.

"I don't see an ambulance close by," Light-up Earrings said. "And it will take forever for anyone to get through here."

Luca looked around surveying the scene, then clasped my shoulder. "I have an idea. Come on. Follow me."

"I'm coming with you," the nurse said, not leaving my side. "Just in case."

I swallowed hard as I looked over at her. "Thank you."

"Move!" Luca led the way, pushing through the crowd, parting the sea of people like some sort of foul-mouthed Moses. "Get the fuck out of the way! Fuckin' move!"

We ran down one block and then another, until Luca caught sight of something up ahead.

"Hey!" He waved his hands over his head, running ahead of us. "Hey! My friend needs help!"

The next thing I saw was a uniformed police officer jogging toward us.

"What's going on?" he asked.

"She passed out," Luca answered quickly.

"I think she might have heatstroke," the nurse said, out of breath. "I'm a nurse. She needs medical attention right away."

"Come on," the officer said. "My cruiser is one street over. I'll get you to the hospital as fast as I can."

He pulled his radio from his belt and began barking orders in a code I didn't understand. But I gathered that the basic gist of it was asking for help clearing a path. We followed him, and I held Katie closer to my chest.

Just as we got to the officer's vehicle, Katie's eyes fluttered, her flushed face peering up at me. "What happened?"

"Oh, thank God," I said, my eyes glossing over with relief.

"What's going on?" she asked as the nurse grabbed her hand, checking her pulse again.

"Heart rate is starting to slow," she said, focusing on Katie. "Hi, sweetie. Sounds like you took a little spill, but you're alright. We've got you. How are you feeling?"

Katie blinked slowly. "I… I feel dizzy."

"Yeah, you were out for a couple minutes," the nurse said. "This officer is going to take you to the hospital to get you checked out."

A couple minutes? It felt like an hour had passed.

"I'm fine," Katie insisted, but her voice was weak. "Dal, you can put me down. I can walk—" She tried to raise her head, but instead it lolled against my chest. "Okay, maybe not."

"That's what I thought," the nurse said with a soft

chuckle. "Let these handsome men take care of you, sweetheart."

"Thank you," I said to her. "Seriously."

"Don't mention it," she replied and patted Katie on the arm. "You feel better, hon."

The officer opened the back door of the cruiser, and I eased into the seat, covering the top of Katie's head with my hand. Once we were tucked safely inside, Luca shut the door and climbed in the passenger seat as the officer got in, started the car, and turned on his sirens.

Luca clicked his seatbelt in place. "Riding in the front seat of a cop car is certainly a change of scenery."

"What?" the cop asked.

"What?" Luca repeated before turning to look at Katie and me. "How you doing, Katie?"

"You know, I've been better," she said. "This is my first time in a police car, so I guess that's exciting."

The officer chuckled. "That's one way to look at it."

Katie's eyes widened "Oh God. Everyone is going to be wondering where we are."

"I'll call Derek." Luca pulled his phone from his pocket.

"I think he went looking for you, but I take it he didn't find you," Katie said.

"I had a prior engagement," he answered, swiping a finger across his phone.

"A pretty blonde engagement," Katie mumbled, leaning her head against my chest.

"Listen, Derek, we have a situation." Luca's voice became background music as I focused on Katie who was still nestled in my arms.

She brought a shaky hand to my face and wiped her thumb gently beneath my eye. "Dallas… You're crying."

"I guess I am." I chuckled, tucking a piece of hair that escaped from her braid behind her ear. "You scared me there for a minute."

A shadow fell over her face. "What about Jax and Liv? And the fireworks. You're missing everything because of me."

Flashes of red and blue from the sirens above passed over her face, lighting up her hazel eyes as she gazed at me.

I shook my head. "This is the only place I want to be."

She gave me a soft smile that pulled at my heart. "I could think of a lot of better places than the back of a cop car."

"That's fair." I pressed a kiss to her forehead and closed my eyes for a second, grateful she was conscious and talking—grateful she was safe in my arms. "But there's no better place than with you."

She held my gaze, my mouth just inches from hers. Every millimeter between us shimmered like those Fourth of July sparklers I remembered playing with as a kid, tracing an invisible path between us.

My lips ached to touch hers. I'd thought about kissing her so many times before, but none more than this moment. When she fainted, something had shifted inside me. The fear of losing her had lit a fuse I didn't know existed until it caught fire. I wondered if she felt it too. It was impossible *not* to.

"Katie..." My voice came out in a gravelly whisper. "I..."

"You what?" she asked softly.

I couldn't do this. Not here. Not in the back of a police car with Luca in the front seat. Not on the way to the hospital.

I smiled down at her, pushing my feelings as far below the surface as I could. "I'm just glad you're okay."

The Vanderbilt Emergency Room was packed. Katie had been triaged upon arrival, but she'd stabilized enough that she'd been moved down the priority list. We'd been there for nearly two hours by the time a nurse escorted Katie and me back to a gurney in a hallway deep within the bowels of the hospital. Katie's vitals had been taken a couple of times, but we were still waiting for the doctor to see her.

"You don't have to stay back here with me. I'm fine," Katie said, raising up on her elbows to look at me where I sat in a chair near her feet. "I feel bad that Luca's out there by himself."

"I'm not going anywhere." I rubbed her calf through the thin white blanket that covered her. Though it was hot outside, the hospital felt like the Arctic, which had helped to cool Katie off. "Trust me. Luca can take care of himself. He's been texting to check on you, and he's updating Jo for us too."

The emergency room was so overburdened that staff was only allowing one visitor back with each patient, leaving Luca holding vigil in the waiting room. I had to admit that I was a little shocked by the tenderness he'd shown Katie. While we waited for her to be triaged, he reached for her a couple of different times and squeezed her shoulder with a brotherly familiarity that I'd never noticed before.

"Hey there." A tall bald man in a white coat smiled as he approached Katie's side pushing a small cart with a thin laptop. "I'm Dr. McKinny. I apologize for your wait, Ms. Kelley. Holidays tend to get a little crazy around here. Especially ones that involve pyrotechnics in the hands of drunk people."

"It's okay," Katie said with a laugh.

Dr. McKinny glanced at the computer. "So, I see here that

you fainted tonight. Can you tell me a little more about what happened?"

The doctor nodded as he listened to Katie explain what she remembered feeling before she'd passed out and after she came to, and I filled in the blanks.

"It's not at all uncommon for folks to get heatstroke," the doctor explained as his fingers tapped along the keys of the laptop. "Especially in weather like this. It's been brutal."

Katie sighed. "And honestly, I've been feeling so crummy lately that I'm not surprised a little heat would knock me down for the count."

The doctor stopped typing and looked at her. "What's been going on?"

"Episodes of vertigo, some really bad fatigue, some pain and generally feeling like trash." She shrugged. "I get this tight feeling in my chest sometimes, but everyone I've seen so far seems to think I have anxiety."

The doctor pursed his lips. "But do *you* think you have anxiety?"

"I really don't," she answered.

"What about that ANA thing?" I asked her before turning to the doctor. "Her bloodwork has been good except for that."

"It was positive?" Dr. McKinny asked.

Katie nodded.

The doctor tilted his head. "Have you seen a rheumatologist before?"

"I'm not even sure what that is," she admitted.

"They're physicians who specialize in treating autoimmune and inflammatory conditions," Dr. McKinny explained. "Rheumatoid arthritis, fibromyalgia, things of that nature. What you experienced tonight could have been heatstroke, but there are a number of autoimmune disorders that could make you more sensitive to extreme temperatures. With the symptoms you mentioned, I think it could be worth looking into, if for no other reason than to rule some things out."

"That all sounds... scary." Katie glanced over at me, and I gave her leg an encouraging squeeze. It *did* sound terrifying, but I kept those fears to myself. She needed me to be strong for her, and that was exactly what I intended to do.

"The good news is that in many cases there are lots of different treatment modalities to help with these conditions. Treatments that could have you in considerably less pain." Dr. McKinny pulled his prescription pad out of his pocket and scribbled something before ripping the page, handing it to her. "But let's not get ahead of ourselves. This is the information for Dr. Tara Childers, a rheumatologist with Vanderbilt. We did our clinicals together, and she's excellent."

"Thank you," Katie said, holding the paper like a lifeline. "I appreciate it."

"Okay." Dr. McKinny clasped his hands together. "If you don't mind, I'm going to do a quick physical exam and run a basic blood panel to make sure your kidney and liver values are normal. But if all that looks good, we'll get some fluids in you and get you discharged. How does that sound?"

"That would be fantastic." Katie stifled a yawn. "Sorry. It's well past my bedtime."

Dr. McKinny chuckled, pulling his stethoscope from around his neck. "Then what do you say we get you and your husband out of here?"

Katie's cheeks flushed, and she opened her mouth to speak, but no words came out. Tension exploded in the air like fireworks as we looked at each other. Something had felt different between us since she'd gazed up at me in the back of that cop car. It was as though some invisible barrier between us had shattered.

Was I just imagining things? Seeing Katie like this had caused the already thin binding that held my feelings for her inside to break. I blew out a breath, glad the doctor wasn't checking *my* pulse because I knew it was racing faster than a prized horse at the Kentucky Derby.

I bit back a grin as the doctor examined her, not bothering to correct him either. I was happy to play the part of the man that got to go home with Katie, even if it was just for one night.

NINE

Katie

"I'M FINE," I promised Jo over FaceTime. Dallas and I were still in the hallway at the hospital, waiting on my discharge papers. "They gave me fluids, and I feel a lot better. I'm just going to go home and crash anyway."

"Absolutely not," Jo insisted. "I'm coming to stay with you. You have no business being alone right now, Katie. You passed out."

"It's nearly two a.m., and you need some rest. Besides, aren't you guys back on the road for an interview tomorrow?"

She waved her hand dismissively. "I'll get someone else to do it. This is too important. *You* are too important."

"I could stay with you," Dallas spoke up. "Jo's right. You really shouldn't be alone right now, and I'd be happy to do it. Then Jo can still go to her interview."

"That's really not necessary," I said. Of course there was a part of me that wanted him to stay over, but not because I was some sick charity case who needed a babysitter. I was embarrassed enough about my stupid fainting spell, and all I wanted to do was curl up in bed and pretend it never happened.

Jo pursed her lips, poised in thought, then nodded. "One of us is staying with you, and that's that."

Dallas nodded in agreement, and I sighed. I was outnumbered. They were looking out for me. I just hated feeling like anyone needed to look out for me at all.

"Fine," I conceded. "Dallas can stay."

A smile tugged at the corners of his lips, and my heart did a pirouette. Something had changed since we'd been in the back of that police car. Even in my haziness, I'd had the distinct feeling he was about to say something. Something potentially earth-shattering. But the more time that passed between that moment and the present, the more I wondered if it had all been in my head.

"Now, will you please go get some sleep?" I asked Jo. "You're growing my future niece or nephew, and they need some rest."

"Yes, yes. I'm going." I could tell by the shrill tone of her voice that she was still totally wound up. "I love you. Call me tomorrow after you get up?"

"Yes, Mom," I teased. "Love you too."

She grinned. "Listen, I'm overbearing because I care."

I rolled my eyes and smiled. "I know. Go. Sleep."

"Good night," she said. "Bye, Dallas."

"G'night," he mumbled through a yawn.

I ended the call, plopping my phone on the thin mattress. "You really don't have to do this, you know."

"I want to." His brown eyes had soft golden flecks in them that made his pupils shimmer like topaz stones in fancy jewelry store lighting. "Besides, Jo would kick my ass if I didn't, and don't tell her this, but I'm a little scared of her."

He flashed me a mischievous grin, one that almost made me forget the real reason for our impromptu slumber party.

"I can't believe Luca stayed," I said, pressing my palm to my forehead. "He's probably going out of his mind."

Dallas laughed. "Actually, he texted to let me know he went outside because some old lady named Marge kept hitting on him in the waiting room."

"Is it weird that I kinda want to meet her?" I asked with a giggle.

"If we're not careful he might be bringing Marge to Sunday dinner," he joked.

We were covering our mouths, attempting to quiet our laughter when the nurse approached with a smile. "Okay, Katie. What do you say we get you out of here?"

She went over my discharge instructions, which basically consisted of lots of rest, fluids, and a promise to return if I had any more fainting spells before I set up an appointment with the specialist.

"Any questions?" she asked.

I shook my head. "Nope."

"Alright," she said. "If you two want to follow me I'll show you how to get out of here."

I hoisted myself off the bed, and Dallas held a hand out to steady me as I rose to my feet.

"I'll go ahead and order an Uber," Dallas said as we followed the nurse through the corridors to the door that led to the lobby.

"I hope you get to feeling better," she said. "Let us know if you need anything."

"Thanks," I replied as the automatic doors groaned open.

Dallas placed his arm around my shoulders and steered me out into the warm night air. I loved feeling his skin on mine, but the thrill was dampened by the fact that he was probably only doing it to make sure I didn't fall again on his watch.

Luca leaned against the brick wall outside, scrolling on his phone before glancing up and striding towards us.

"How are you feeling?" Luca asked, his eyes creasing at the corners as he pulled me into a hug. "You scared the shit out of us."

"Better," I answered. "But tired and ready to get the heck out of here."

"I bet," he said, shifting his eyes up to Dallas. "You're staying with her tonight, right?"

Dallas nodded, and I blew a piece of hair out of my eyes. "It's bad enough I've got Jo mothering me, and now you too?"

"Damn right." Luca lifted his chin. "You've got to take care of yourself."

I raised my brows at him. "Hello, pot. Meet kettle."

Luca cleared his throat. "Well, if you guys don't need me, I'm going to get out of here. My Uber just arrived and is trying to find me"—he pointed toward the end of the next block—"somewhere over there."

"Of course. Thanks again for staying," I said. "I appreciate it."

He gave me a faint smile and a wink.

"Thanks, man." Dallas extended his fist to him, and Luca gave it a quick bump before disappearing down the sidewalk.

"Alright." Dallas slid his arm back around me and shoved his phone into his pocket. "Cameron will be here in a black Escalade in three minutes."

I yawned, and he smoothed his hand over the back of my hair, sending an ardent chill through my limbs despite how muggy it was outside.

I peered up at him. "Hey, Dal?"

His Adam's apple bobbed. "Yeah?"

"Thank you," I said, "for, you know… being here."

He pulled me closer and held me against him the entire three minutes it took Cameron and his SUV to pull up to the curb.

Our ride home was mostly quiet except for our driver's greeting and the soft sounds of the music that played through the car's speakers. Dallas kept his arm around me the whole way home, as though he could prevent any harm from coming to me as long as he was there to be my shield.

Something felt different between us. But maybe it was just me. Maybe all the time we'd spent together that night was messing with my head, confusing me. Add to that the heightened emotions and exhaustion from my fainting spell, and my feelings were piled as high as a Jenga tower. It wouldn't take more than a tiny puff of wind or an errant sneeze to send them scattering everywhere.

We thanked the driver when he pulled into my driveway, and I dug in my purse for my key as we got out of the car and slowly climbed the rickety porch steps.

I needed to give Dallas another out—another opportunity to bail. I wasn't sure if that was more for him or for me. Him staying with me was the ultimate tease, and it wasn't hard for my imagination to run wild and wonder what it would be like if this wasn't just a pity sleepover. What it would feel like if we were more than just friends.

"Really, you don't have—" I began before he cut me off.

"I'm exactly where I want to be." He reached out and touched my arm, and a thousand fireflies shimmered inside my chest.

I managed a faint smile, too tired to question him further.

"Okay."

I jammed the key in the lock and pushed it open, flicking on the light over the kitchen sink as I plunked my purse on the counter.

"You can stay in Jo's old room," I said, more to myself so I didn't start getting any crazy ideas.

"There's fresh sheets on the bed. Do you want some tea or water or anything? Something to eat?"

He shook his head and let out a low chuckle. "It really is impossible for you, isn't it?"

"What is?" I asked, suddenly self conscious.

"Letting someone take care of you." He stepped closer to me, and my pulse quickened. "You just got out of the hospital, and you're already in hostess mode."

My cheeks burned, and I bit my lip.

"Now, let's try this again." He cupped my head, smoothing his hand over my hair.

I closed my eyes for a second, melting into his touch. "Okay."

"Can *I* make *you* some tea?" he asked. "Or some food? You didn't really eat anything tonight."

I swallowed hard. "I'm not hungry." All I wanted was more of him. More of feeling his hands on me. More of his time. I just wanted... more.

What was I thinking? I'd *just* gotten out of the hospital. I should be worried about what was going on inside my body because clearly it was *something*. But it was hard to focus on anything but Dallas, especially when he was in such close proximity.

"How about some water?" he asked. "Why don't you go get comfortable, and I'll bring it to you?" He gently grazed my cheek with his thumb, sending a shiver of longing throughout my body.

I nodded and mumbled a barely audible 'okay' before backing away and starting toward my room. Once inside, I closed the door and leaned against it, freeing my hair from its braid.

I needed to text Jo. She was probably still awake, stubborn as she was, and I wanted someone else's insight. Was something actually happening between Dallas and me, or was I imagining it? I reached for my purse on my shoulder and cursed silently the second I realized I'd left it in the kitchen with Dallas.

Okay. I blew out a breath. *This is okay. I'll just go get it. No big deal.*

But for some reason, I remained frozen in place, afraid of making any sudden movements. I needed to pull myself together and open the damn door.

I squared my shoulders and steadied myself before turning and twisting the handle, flinging the door open. I let out a garbled yelp when I saw Dallas standing just outside my door.

"Dallas!" My cheeks flamed, and I couldn't help but laugh at how silly I was being—acting like a teenager with a crush on the captain of the football team. Nobody on any kind of athletic team had ever known I existed, but Dallas... he *knew* me. "You scared the shit out of me."

"Sorry." He smiled sheepishly, shoving his hand through his hair. "I was about to knock. I... You forgot your... I think you got a text." He held my bag out to me, and I hung it on the vintage coat rack just beside the door, extracting my phone to peek at the screen.

"Thanks," I said, rocking back on my heels. "It was just Jo making sure we got in okay."

"I didn't mean to…" Dallas trailed off, and pressed his balled up fist to his mouth. "Sorry. I'll let you get changed."

He started to turn away, and my heart pounded in my ears.

"Dal?" My voice betrayed me, calling after him without my permission.

When he faced me this time, there was a fire burning in his amber eyes. We stared at each other wordlessly for a moment, and I opened my mouth to speak. But before I could, Dallas took my head in his hands, and his lips collided with mine in an explosion of fireworks that glittered against the backs of my eyes. His kiss was a supernova, lighting up the darkest corners of my heart, turning the deepest blues to a blinding white light.

I slid my hands around his neck and pulled him closer, pressing my body against his broad chest. His fingers caught in my hair as a four-letter emotion caught in my throat. It was always there just below the surface, no matter how hard I'd tried to suppress it.

When I reluctantly broke our kiss so that I could come up for air, he pressed his forehead to mine, his breath tickling my lips.

We stood like that for a few seconds, unsure what to say. Or maybe we were just afraid to speak for fear of breaking the beautiful spell we were under.

Finally, he flicked his tongue over his lips and smiled.

"What?" I asked, returning his grin.

"You have no idea how long I've been wanting to do that."

I breathed him in and pressed my lips to his once more. "I think I do."

TEN

Dallas

"You do?" I asked. My heart was pounding so hard I wondered if she could see it through my shirt.

She nodded and bit her lip, her cheeks flushed. "But... I..."

Shit. My excitement was replaced with a sinking feeling. She regretted it. She didn't feel the rush of emotions I did when our lips touched. I braced myself for the impact of what she'd say next.

"I have to ask you something." She blew out a breath as though *she* were the one preparing for the worst. "And I need you to be completely honest with me, even if you think it could hurt my feelings."

"Okay," I said, though I knew full well I would do everything within my power to never do or say anything that could make her sad.

"Did you..." She paused, glancing up at the ceiling like she was asking some anonymous source for strength to get the words out. "Was that a pity kiss?"

I snorted out a laugh, thinking there was no way she could

be serious, but I quickly stopped when I saw the troubled expression on her face.

"A pity kiss?" I asked. "What do you mean?"

"Tonight—or I suppose now it was last night—was a lot. Emotions were heightened, and..." She trailed off and cast her gaze downward.

I narrowed my eyes. "And you want to know if those emotions caused me to kiss you out of... out of pity?"

The question seemed ludicrous, but when her watery eyes met mine again, I could see she really believed that was a possibility.

"Nothing about that kiss had to do with pity. What happened *did* affect me. I'd be lying if I said it didn't, but it wasn't for the reasons you think." I cupped her beautiful face with my hands. "It made me realize that all the reasons I never did it sooner weren't really reasons at all. That if something ever... happened, and I didn't tell you how I felt about you, I'd never be able to forgive myself."

She took in a shaky breath. "How do you feel about me, Dallas?"

I couldn't tell her the truth. That I loved her. That I'd *been* in love with her since I'd gotten to know her all those years ago, and it turned out that for me, knowing Katie was synonymous with loving her. But I couldn't tell her that. Not yet. So I settled for the next best thing.

"I have feelings for you." My voice wavered slightly as though it were toppling over from the enormity of what I was admitting. "Deep ones. I care about you." I kissed her softly. "I don't want to just be your friend, Katie. If I'm being honest, I never have. I've always wanted more."

Happiness and worry collided on her face, and she pressed her palms to her forehead.

"What is it?" I asked.

"You're saying things that I always wanted to hear you say, but…"

"But what?"

She raked her hands through her hair and brought them to rest just beneath her chin, and I didn't know it was possible for her to be even more fucking adorable.

"I don't want to lose *this*." She twirled her finger in a circle between us. "What if things don't work out? What if—"

"What if we decided not to deal in hypotheticals?" I asked, cutting her off. "What if we focus on what's right in front of us?" She studied my face, and I continued. "I waited nearly four years to kiss you, Katie. I'm not in a hurry to mess this up, alright?"

She placed her hands on my chest and nodded, her shoulders starting to relax.

I rubbed a piece of her honey-colored hair between my fingers. "We don't have to have everything figured out right now. We'll take it one step at a time, and the next step is you getting some rest."

She stood on her tiptoes, pulling my face down to hers so our foreheads touched.

"Stay with me? To sleep, of course," she clarified with a grin. "I just… There's no reason for you to sleep in the guest room when there's a perfectly good bed right here."

My entire body hummed with nervous energy. Me and Katie in the same bed. Being close enough to hold her all night long.

A smile crept across my face. "I'd love to stay with you."

I WAS IN A SAUNA. WAS I HAVING SOME SORT OF WEIRD, lucid dream? Why was it so fucking hot? My eyes flew open, sweat dripping down my face. The air was muggy and stagnant, like waking up locked inside a pot of stew.

Katie was still asleep beside me, the covers thrown off her legs. The light that filtered in around the edges of the blinds told me it was well past sunrise. I reached for my phone on the nightstand, lighting it up to check the time. Through bleary eyes, I could see that it was 10:27 a.m.

Maybe the power had gone out while we were sleeping, something to cause the air to turn off? I slid out of the bed, careful not to disturb Katie, as I crept out of the room in search of the thermostat. Sunlight poured through old glass windows, allowing me to maneuver down the hall where I found the thermostat.

My eyes widened when I saw that it read eighty-two degrees. I turned it off and waited a few seconds before clicking it back on, listening for the hum of the air conditioner, but there was no sound.

"Dallas?" Katie's voice came from the bedroom.

"I'm here." I shuffled back to the doorway. "I was trying to figure out why the air conditioning won't turn on."

"Oh God, I thought it was just me," she said, looking relieved. "It's burning up. Maybe a breaker blew?"

She got up and I followed her to the hall closet where she opened the door, the breaker box wedged inside. Once she found the switch she was looking for, she flipped it, waiting a few seconds before resetting it. Then, she repeated the same process I had done with the thermostat and we waited together for some sound that signified it was coming to life.

"Shit," she cursed when nothing happened. "The damn thing has been struggling all summer."

We went outside and checked the unit itself, but neither of us were exactly well-versed in air conditioning repair. From what we could see there was no obvious trauma—it wasn't frozen, and there was no debris on it other than a few dried-up leaves. Despite all that, it was completely lifeless.

"I don't exactly know what I'm looking for here," she said, "but I'm pretty sure the fact that there's no noise coming from it is not a good sign. I think it's dead."

Visions from the night before flashed in my head. "You can't stay here like this. Not after what happened."

"This is the last thing I need right now." She scrubbed her hands down her face as we headed back inside.

"It's going to be okay," I assured her. "We'll go get breakfast while we try to get ahold of someone to come look at it. We've got to get you out of here, though, before it gets even hotter."

She smiled and nodded. "Okay."

My stomach flipped as I watched her trudge back to her room in a matching pajama set with a barrage of succulents printed on them. I wasn't happy that Katie's air had gone out or about the stress it was causing her, but I *was* excited for an excuse to spend the day together.

"Are you sure this is okay?" Katie asked later that afternoon as I dropped her duffle bag onto the sofa in the living room of my condo. "I could book a hotel or call Jo—"

I pressed my lips to hers, cutting her off. I'd just kissed

her for the first time hours before, but already I couldn't get enough.

"I'm sure." My fingers found hers, and they intertwined like ivy on a picket fence. "In fact, I think this is going to be fun."

We'd had a late breakfast at Fido and called every HVAC company within a fifty-mile radius only to be told the same thing, which was basically some version of 'take a number.' The heat wave had caused a lot of systems to break down, and the soonest appointment we were able to get was two weeks out, so I'd insisted Katie stay with me until then.

"This is the second time in twenty-four hours you've had to come to my rescue," she said with a laugh as I slid my arms around her. "We're getting off on the wrong foot here."

"I think we're getting off on the exact right foot," I said. "It's okay to lean on people sometimes, and I'd be lying if I said I wasn't glad it was me you were relying on right now."

She wrinkled her nose. "Just so we're clear, I'm no damsel in distress, contrary to what the whole fainting thing might have suggested."

My lips quirked. "Trust me, I know you're like Katie the Top Chef Warrior Princess or whatever, but even warrior princesses require assistance on occasion."

"I suppose you're right."

"I know I'm right." I jutted my chin out in mock indignation. "Even Batman needs Robin."

She broke into a grin. "So, you're admitting you're the Robin in this situation?"

"There was never any doubt," I said, returning her smile as I sat on the couch and pulled her down beside me. "What would you like to do with the rest of the day? You still need to take it easy, so what would be relaxing for you?"

"Oh, I don't know." She flopped against the back of the cushion. "We could get mani/pedis."

I sputtered a laugh. "We can do that."

"I'm kidding." She touched my arm, sending a buzz of electricity dancing under my skin. "Well, mostly."

"Would you believe I've never had a manicure before?" I held my hand out for examination.

"With those cuticles? Yes," she teased.

I pulled my phone out of my pocket and started searching Yelp.

"What are you doing?" she asked with a giggle.

"I'm finding a nail salon, of course."

Her eyes brightened, and the corners of her mouth tugged into a heart-stopping smile. "Seriously?"

My chest tightened, and I knew I would get a manicure every day for the rest of my life if it elicited that sort of reaction.

"With these cuticles? Yes."

ELEVEN

Katie

"Welcome in." The receptionist with purple hair greeted us with a smile from behind the chic marble desk at Onyx Day Spa. "How can I help you?"

"We have three o'clock mani/pedis." My fingers found Dallas' and threaded through them. For the longest time, he'd been so close but just out of reach. It still felt a little—correction, a *lot*—surreal that I could do that now. I could reach out and hold his hand any time I wanted to.

"Perfect," she replied, clicking her long almond-shaped nails across the keyboard. "The couples mani/pedi treatment."

"That's right." Dallas beamed with what could only be described as pride, and my heart twirled.

"You're going to love it." Her purple waves bounced as she stood. "I'll take you back to the nail room so you can relax. Can I get you some champagne or a glass of wine? We also have whiskey and scotch."

"Oooh champagne, please," I said quietly, so as not to disturb the peaceful ambiance. Enya-style music played through hidden speakers as we followed the receptionist down a dimly lit hallway that smelled like lavender and eucalyptus.

"Make that two," Dallas added with a squeeze of my hand.

Once we made it to the end of the corridor, she held open the last door on the right to reveal a cozy space that looked like it came straight off a Pinterest board. The room was lit by vines of twinkle lights and held two pedicure basins with bench-style seating covered in fluffy, oversized white pillows. On the opposite wall were two nail stations, so pristine they almost looked like they'd never been used.

"You two go ahead and make yourselves comfortable. The colors are here on this wall." She gestured just inside the entrance. "I'll be right back with your champagne."

She left us alone, closing the door behind her, and I started scanning through the wall of polish, picking up a glittery shade of green.

"I think you should get this one," I joked as Dallas wrapped his muscular arms around me from behind. "It matches your sparkling personality."

He barked out a laugh. "Glitter isn't really my style." He stepped closer to the shelves, grazing his fingers along the bottles until they landed on a deep emerald, so dark it was almost black, and he picked it up. "Now *this* is more my speed."

I whipped my head around, my eyes wide with surprise. "Are you gonna get polish?"

"Fuck yeah, I am. On my toes, anyway." He grinned. "I want the full experience."

"What's the name of the color?"

"Uh, I don't know. Green?"

I laughed and tipped the bottle upside down in his hand, reading the label. "Go-Getter Green."

"Suppose that's appropriate. I *did* go get her, after all. Finally." He chuckled and tickled my sides. "Now, what color are you getting?"

I pursed my lips and turned my attention back to the rows of polishes in front of me, picking up a simple nude. "I don't know, maybe this one?"

He wrinkled his nose. "That looks like the flesh of a corpse."

"Yeah, it kinda does," I said with a laugh, placing the bottle back on the shelf. "Which one do *you* think I should get?"

His eyes narrowed as he studied the shades, arranged from light to dark, each color family grouped together like a rainbow. I loved how seriously he appeared to be taking his task, picking up each polish, inspecting them with a level of scrutiny that made his forehead crease. Finally, he grabbed a vibrant lilac. A smile stretched across his face as he tilted the bottle to read the name.

"This is it," he said, presenting it to me upside down.

"Love of My Lilac," I read aloud, heat rising to my cheeks as the door opened.

"Your champagne." The receptionist handed us our glasses as two women in black scrubs settled on the small stools in front of each basin. "Can I get you anything else?"

I shook my head. "No, thank you."

"These ladies are going to take good care of you. Enjoy," she said before ducking back out of the room.

"I'm Sonia," one of the women said to me, her partially graying hair tied in a long braid. "Did you have a chance to pick out your color?"

"I'm Katie. And yes, I did." I held the bottle up, and she took it from me.

"I'm going to have you take a seat up here on the bench and get comfortable." Sonia's voice was calm, the cadence relaxed and meditative.

I did as she asked and once my sandals were off, she guided my feet into the warm, sudsy water.

"How's the temperature?"

I sighed as Dallas climbed into the spot next to me. "Perfect."

"Hey y'all, I'm Kyla." The technician at his feet had translucent skin and a platinum-blonde Ariana Grande ponytail, along with a southern drawl that made me think of the molasses I dripped into the Ginger Beer cupcakes at the bakery. "Go on and plop those lil piggies in there, honey."

Dallas kicked off his converse and dunked his feet in the bowl. "I have my color too." He beamed and handed her the polish like a kid showing his mom his latest drawing for the refrigerator.

"That'll look real nice on you, honey," Kyla said.

"What brings you two in today?" Sonia asked as she removed my old polish, a shade of barely-there pink. "Celebrating anything special?"

I opened my mouth to say no, but Dallas reached for my hand and answered before I could.

"We're on our honeymoon." Dallas tossed a smirk in my direction, and I prayed the dim lighting would conceal my flushed cheeks.

Kyla looked up from where she set to work on Dallas' feet. "Newlyweds! Well, aren't y'all cute as a button?" She turned her attention to me. "Come on, sweetheart! Let's get a look at that rock."

I balled my bare hand into a fist. "Oh, uh, I didn't wear it. I didn't want to get anything on it. Polish removers, lotions, that sort of thing."

"Gotta keep it sparkling," Sonia said, accepting my off-the-cuff explanation. "So, what are you two going to do while you're in town?"

"Yeah, *honey*. What did you say you had planned tonight?" I flashed him a mischievous glance. *Two can play at this game.* "Oh, I remember. You wanted to go to Hustler of Hollywood, didn't you?"

"That's right, Love Muffin." Dallas never failed in his ability to think on his feet. "I want to get you that cute little nurse getup you saw in the window."

"Of course." I bit back a grin and took a sip of my champagne, the gears in my mind clicking into place with the perfect comeback. "And that thing you wanted that they talk about in those *Fifty Shades* books. What's it called again? A butt plug?"

Game, set, match.

Dallas nearly choked, and Sonia's eyes widened.

"Y'all should get some of those edible underwear," Kyla said casually, as if she'd just told us what she had for lunch. "They make 'em for men too." She glanced up at Dallas and winked.

He rubbed his thumb along his jawline, partially concealing his face with his hand, and I could tell he was trying to steady his expression.

Sonia was laser-focused on my feet, probably wishing she was anywhere but there, and I couldn't help the satisfied smile that curled the corners of my lips knowing I'd beaten Dallas at his own game.

"Edible underwear, huh?" Dallas echoed.

"Mmmhmm. My boyfriend loves those damn things. Says they taste good, kinda like a fruit roll-up." Kyla lifted her eyes to me and lowered her voice as though that would somehow prevent anyone from hearing whatever was about to come out of her mouth. "But one thing... they can make your... *cookie*... feel a little sticky."

I coughed so hard that a splash of champagne sloshed over the side of the flute.

Dallas squeezed my shoulder. "You okay there, Butter Bean?"

"Yup." I took a big gulp of my drink as Kyla returned her attention to Dallas' toes and Sonia looked like she was silently willing the floor to open up and swallow her.

"Maybe we should do a late dinner, since I'm going to be spoiling my appetite and all," Dallas said with a dramatic pause that had me holding my breath. "Besides, I just got a craving for cookies."

"I still can't believe that *you*, Top Chef Katie, uttered the term 'butt plug' in public," Dallas choked out through fits of laughter as we walked into his condo early that evening. "This is a thing I will never get over."

"And you, *Butter Bean*!" I said with a wag of my finger. "With the cookies!"

"What?" He held his hand to his chest in feigned innocence. "I like cookies."

"Mmmhmm." I swatted his arm as I pushed past him and sauntered into the kitchen, feeling at home, much the way Dallas did at my place. "I bet you do."

I started rummaging through his cabinets and the fridge,

searching for everything I would need: flour, white and brown sugar, baking powder, baking soda, salt, eggs, vanilla, and butter. He didn't have any chocolate chips, but he did have a couple of fancy-looking chocolate bars in the pantry, which were even better.

"What are you doing?" Dallas asked, eyeing me with one arched brow.

"What's it look like I'm doing? I'm making you cookies." I crouched to open one of the lower cabinets to find a baking sheet and located one that looked like it had been used to bake cookies in hell. It was charred with burn marks and ever so slightly warped. I held it out to him. "And getting gift ideas. What did you do to this thing?"

"Hey, I went through a learning curve, okay?" He chuckled as he pulled down a mixing bowl and set out some measuring cups and spoons. "I don't have a stand mixer yet, but I have a hand-held one around here somewhere."

"I don't need one," I said, finding a half-empty jar of cinnamon inside the spice drawer.

"I thought you said we were making cookies?"

"*I* am."

"Then you need a mixer, don't you?"

"Not for this one," I said, rising on my tiptoes to kiss the tip of his nose. "I'm going to show you how to make my Granny's favorite Chocolate Chip Cookies."

He snaked his arms around me. "Dessert before dinner?"

"Look, we have carbs and fat right here." I pointed to the eggs. "And protein. Seems like a balanced meal to me."

"I like the way you think. How can I help?"

I shook my head and ran my fingers along his arms, working my way up the curves of his inked biceps.

"Nope," I said as I set the oven to preheat at three hundred and fifty degrees. "This time *you're* going to watch."

He leaned against the counter next to me and looked on as I combined the flour, baking powder, baking soda, and salt in a bowl, giving it a gentle stir.

"I'm going to roughly chop the chocolate." I unwrapped the candy bars and snapped them in half before laying them on the cutting board. "Chocolate chips are perfectly fine, but with the bars you're going to get a mixture of sizes. And I'm using half dark and half milk chocolate which amps up the depth of flavor."

Out of the corner of my eye, I saw him studying me intently.

"What?" I asked, my body warming beneath his gaze. There was something about his stare that felt almost sensual.

"I like watching you bake." His voice was like my growing pile of chocolate—a mixture of light sweetness and dark desire. "The way your body moves as you chop. The way you sway your hips without even realizing how fucking sexy you are."

I retrieved a sauce pan and placed it on the stove, turning the eye to low before unwrapping a stick of butter and plopping it inside.

"I am *not* sexy," I insisted, but internally, I was jumping up and down, screaming like I was a pre-teen at an NSYNC concert all over again.

"Oh yes, you are. I've spent a long time studying you, Top Chef Katie."

I giggled, grabbing a whisk from the jar of utensils on the counter, gently moving the butter around as it started to spread like beams of light from the sun.

"Like right now." He moved to stand behind me, placing

his hands just below my waist. "Your hips turn these tiny circles that drive me a little bit crazy, and I'm so glad I can finally tell you that. It makes me just want to..." He trailed off and circled his muscular arms around me, making my limbs melt like the butter in the pan.

I leaned my head back against his shoulder, and his lips dragged along my jawline and formed kisses in the crook of my neck. His fingers slid beneath my shirt, grazing the tender skin where my shorts rested on my hips. Warmth radiated down to my core, and I ached with want.

"You're going to make me burn the butter." I teased, giving the pot another good stir before removing it from the heat.

"Well, we can't have that, now can we?" he murmured in my ear, sending a rush of goosebumps down my arms like a wave of dominos. When I moved, he did too, keeping his arms securely around me and his lips hovering over my skin.

"No, we cannot," I said softly as I combined the sugars, eggs, butter, and vanilla into a separate bowl and mixed it well.

His breath tickled my earlobes, causing mine to catch in my throat, and I felt him smile against my cheek.

I inhaled deeply. The scent of sugar and chocolate mingling with Dallas' distinct blend of musk and spice made me dizzy with a happiness I hadn't felt in so long.

"Now, this is the most important part." I slowly poured the dry ingredients in with the wet and stirred until the dough was so firm that it resisted the spatula. Then, I began dropping in the chocolate pieces, folding them in by hand until they were all nestled inside a cocoon of butter and sugar and flour. "Doing it by hand combines it without overmixing."

"I've never wanted to be a dessert more in my life," he whispered against my neck, and I laughed.

"Is that so?" I pinched a piece of dough between my fingers and held it in front of his mouth. "Taste it."

He took the bite, licking every last bit off my skin, and my center throbbed. "God, you taste amazing."

"I think you mean the cookies."

"No, I mean *you*." I wiped my hands on a cup towel, tossing it on the counter, and he turned me so I was facing him. "Your turn." He picked up a piece of dough and passed it over my lips. The sugar melted on my tongue, but before he could take his hand away, I held it in place, sliding my mouth around his fingers, removing every last trace of the dessert.

His eyes closed, and a moan rumbled from deep in his chest.

"Katie…" He said my name in a hoarse whisper. "I… We may need to stop… It's just that I want you, more than I've ever wanted anyone, but I don't want to push you if—"

"I want this," I interrupted him, placing my hands on either side of his cheeks.

"I don't want to rush you into something you're not ready for."

"Dallas, I've wanted to be with you for years now." I tilted his face down to mine. "I'd hardly call this rushing."

His eyes burned into mine. "Are you sure?"

I answered by pressing my lips to his, kissing him long and slow, before pulling away and holding a finger up.

"One sec," I said, grabbing the bowl of dough and shoving it in the fridge before shutting off the oven. "Now, where were we?"

He barreled toward me and scooped me up, tossing me

easily over his shoulder, and I shrieked between peels of laughter.

"Dallas! Put me down!"

"Oh, I'm going to," he said, a suggestive lilt in his voice.

And he did, ever so gently, once he reached his bedroom. He eased me onto the cloud-like comforter and climbed in beside me. The mattress dipped beneath his weight, making me slide even closer to him.

He appraised my face with such concentration that it made my cheeks burn. "What?" I asked.

His tongue flicked out over his lips, and with a subtle shake of his head, he kissed me. Softly, at first, but like a preheating oven, the heat and intensity rose to an unbearable level.

"Do you even realize how long I've wanted to do this," he asked, pulling my tank top over my head, revealing my lacy bralette.

"I think I do," I said, wrenching his shirt off to reveal his tattooed, sinewy chest that tapered to a deep V below his hips.

He lowered himself to kiss me again, and my hands went on an exploring expedition, leisurely tracing every curve, every dip, every line of his muscles. I wanted to feel every last inch of him.

"How do you taste so good?" he asked, planting kisses along the swell of my breasts. I arched my back as he unclasped my bra and tossed the lace to the floor. The longing I felt for him stretched to corners of my body I didn't know existed.

My hands moved to his jeans and I made quick work of the button and zipper, pushing them down until he could kick them off. His hardness strained against the fabric of his boxer-briefs, and the ache at my core flared as I gripped him with my hand.

"Holy fuck," he grunted, and I felt him pulse against my skin.

I wanted to touch him without any barrier between us, so I shoved his underwear down and took him in my hand.

"Katie." He moaned, squeezing his eyes shut. "I don't know how long I can take not knowing what it feels like to be inside you."

"Good," I said, unzipping my shorts and hooking my fingers over the denim. Once I pulled them to my knees, Dallas yanked them the rest of the way down.

He slid his finger between the cotton hipsters that remained on my body, gently caressing my folds, and the ache reached a fever pitch.

"You're so wet," he said with a moan.

"Please, Dallas," I panted, tilting my hips to meet his hand.

With a low growl, he ripped my panties down and discarded them, then reached over to his nightstand and retrieved a condom from the drawer. He tore the wrapper, rolled it on, and lowered himself over me.

His lips collided with mine, and my fingers tangled in his hair. I'd never wanted anyone or anything more than him.

I guided him to my entrance, and he started to ease inside me, but my body tensed. The ache had been replaced by a white-hot searing pain.

He must have felt my muscles clench because he broke our kiss and asked, "Are you okay?"

I nodded. "I guess it's just been a while." I took a deep breath and willed my pelvis to chill the hell out.

"It's okay. We can go slow."

We tried again, getting only a little further before it felt like I was being penetrated with a hot branding iron. I cried out, and Dallas withdrew immediately.

"Katie, what's wrong?" His forehead creased with worry.

"Did I—"

"No," I said quickly, wiping sweat off my brow. "It's not you. It's… I don't know what it is, but it's not you." He placed a kiss on my lips. "We should stop for now. I don't want to hurt you. We can try again another time."

"I *want* to do this," I said, reaching for him, stroking him with my hand. "Please. Let's try again."

"Are you sure?" he asked.

"Yes," I answered, though I wasn't at all. I'd never experienced pain like this during sex before, but as I'd told him, it *had* been a while.

He covered my hand with his, and we tried once again, even slower this time. I steadied my breathing, silently begging my walls to stretch and my body to relax. I'd only wanted this for-freaking-ever.

No pressure or anything.

He pushed inside me a little further this time, and it felt like I was being ripped open at the seams. I shot up, nearly whacking Dallas in the head.

"Oh God, I'm so sorry." I whimpered as he slipped out of me. "I don't know what's wrong with me."

"Hey." His words were soft as he moved behind me and folded me in his arms, pulling the covers over us. "There is *nothing* wrong with you."

"Dallas, we can't even have sex." Tears pricked at the corners of my eyes. "We've waited all this time, and I've ruined it."

"You haven't ruined anything." He nuzzled my neck and

kissed my shoulder. "Having you in my arms like this... You've given me more than I ever could have asked for."

What should have been one of the sweetest moments of my life felt more like a consolation prize. I heard what he was saying, but what I *felt* was that I couldn't please him. Not like I wanted to.

I choked out a sob, burying my face into the pillow, and he immediately turned me to face him.

"Katie, it's okay. Really," he promised. "This is not a big deal."

"What if this doesn't go away soon?" *What if this is my new normal?* It was too hurtful to say out loud, and I was in enough physical pain as it was. Even without him inside me, it felt like I was holding a hot fire poker between my thighs. What if this was yet another new symptom in a laundry list of ailments and I could *never* give him that part of me? I couldn't expect him to just accept that.

He wiped at the dampness on my cheek with the pad of his thumb. "I am positive we can think of *many* ways to please each other."

I sniffed and nodded, unconvinced.

"In fact," he went on, "I can think of something that would be very pleasing to me right this second." He tucked a piece of hair behind my ear.

"What's that?"

"Cookies." A grin tugged at the corners of his mouth. "Of the chocolate chip variety."

I laughed through my tears. "That I can do."

Cookies were hardly a replacement, but they would have to suffice until I could figure out what had gone wrong. Until I could figure out what was wrong with *me*.

TWELVE

Dallas

"Something smells good." Katie yawned as she sauntered over to where I stood in the kitchen the next morning, plating our food. She was wearing my Slacks t-shirt, which was my favorite band tee and a pair of purple panties that skimmed her hips.

"Good morning, sleepyhead. I was about to come get you," I said, pouring her a mug of coffee and kissing her cheek. "I made a hash with chorizo and a side of berries."

"You're going to have me so spoiled I'll never want to leave." She popped a halved strawberry into her pink mouth and stretched her arms over her head, revealing the tiniest sliver of her stomach. My hands were drawn to that little swath of skin like my Roomba vacuum to its charging station in the corner.

"You're already on to my diabolical plan," I said, slipping my arms around her waist. "How are you feeling?"

"A lot better," she answered. "I wanted to go to work, but Ella insisted I take the day off."

"I think that's a good idea. Another day of taking it easy can't hurt."

"Gives me a chance to call and set up that doctor's appointment, I guess," she said with a sigh.

"This one is going to have answers. I can feel it." I pressed a kiss to her lips. "Now, let's eat."

I reached for the plates, but her voice stopped me in my tracks.

"Hey, Dallas... about last night..." She trailed off, eyes cast downward.

"Katie, look at me." I hooked a finger beneath her chin and lifted her gaze to meet mine. "Last night was perfect, okay? *You* are perfect."

The worried lines in her face softened slightly, but she didn't seem convinced.

"Look, Butter Bean," I said with a grin. "I am positive that sex with you is going to blow my mind, but that isn't what I'm here for. I haven't spent nearly four years pining away for you all because I wanted to get laid. I want *you*. And everything that comes along with you." I knew she was worried I'd been disappointed by how our night had gone, but that couldn't have been further from the truth. It took a minute for Katie to get out of her head and relax, but once she had, we'd spent the rest of the night cuddled up on the couch watching movies and eating cookies, and honestly, I'd never been happier.

She opened her mouth as though she were going to say something but changed her mind, kissing me instead. My phone rang from the counter, and I glanced down to see Jo's name flashing across the screen.

I wrinkled my nose. "Why is Jo calling me?"

"Shit." Katie's eyes widened. "I texted her about the A/C

thing yesterday, and I may or may not have also mentioned that we kissed. I told her I'd call her, but I never did. I was a little... preoccupied."

"I held my phone out to her and grinned. "Can't imagine why."

She playfully rolled her eyes and took the phone, swiping across the screen. "Hey, Jo. I'm sorry. I must have left my ringer off." There was a brief pause, punctuated by a sound so shrill that Katie had to pull the phone away from her ear. "I know, I know. Listen, Dallas just made breakfast, so we're about to sit down to eat, but I'll call and fill you in on everything as soon as we're done."

Katie's cheeks turned crimson as she fell silent while Jo said something I couldn't hear.

"Yes," she said. "Everything. Okay. Uh-huh." She pulled the phone away from her ear and covered the mouthpiece with her hand. "She wants to talk to you."

"Tell her I'm not here," I said with a laugh, taking the phone back. "Hi, Jo."

"I heard that," she chided me.

"You were supposed to."

"Ha. Ha. You're a regular comedian," she teased. "I just wanted to say"—she proceeded to let out an ear-piercing screech that rivaled a bird being eaten alive by a cat—"that it's about time!"

I snort-laughed. "I'm glad you approve."

"Alright, that's all. Tell Katie I'll talk to her in a few. Bye," she sang, ending the call.

"Well, I think Jo's happy," I said, picking up the plates and carrying them to the bar as Katie grabbed our coffees.

"Yeah," she said, sitting next to me. "I hope you don't mind that I told her. I swore her to secrecy."

"Of course I don't mind. Everyone is going to lose their minds when they find out."

"Actually, what if we didn't... tell them yet?" she asked tentatively.

My stomach lurched, and my happy bubble was dangerously close to bursting. Was she having second thoughts about us? About *me*?

"It's not that I don't want them to know," she added, as though she'd read my mind. "It's just that I kind of like the idea of this belonging only to us for a while. Everyone is going to make a big deal out of it, and it *is*. A big deal, I mean. But that's why I want to hold on to it a little longer before we hand it over to the whole group. This feels sacred, and I just want to keep it safe."

I took a gulp of my coffee, buying myself a few seconds to think. She had a point. Even though I'd felt this way about Katie for a long time, this part of our relationship was still new. Our friendship made it feel like we'd gotten to skip several steps, but there would still be uncharted waters to navigate. Wouldn't it be better to do that without the added pressure of telling our friends, who would no doubt be ready to give their input? Jo was going to give enough input for everyone anyway.

"I can get behind that," I said. "Besides, it could be kind of hot. Sneaking around. Playing footsie under the table at Sunday dinner."

She kicked my shin, and I recoiled.

"Who the hell taught you to play footsie?" I asked, poking her in the arm.

"Who the hell plays footsie anymore?" She giggled. "Anyway, I do think you should tell Derek. You know, if you want to."

"I do want to." I couldn't think of anyone I wanted to tell more than my cousin. He knew how much Katie meant to me, and he also knew what it meant to care for someone as much as I cared for her. Jo and Derek being the first to know felt right.

Katie speared a bite of hash with her fork and smiled at me, and it felt like I was living in a dream having her next to me. As fun as it would be to tell our friends about our relationship, I knew it would be even more fun to keep her to myself a little while longer.

I COULDN'T HELP BUT SMILE AS I FINISHED LOADING THE dishwasher and cleaning up from breakfast. The sounds of Katie's laughter echoed down the hall as she talked to Jo on the phone in my bedroom. I'd gotten used to the silence that came with living alone now that I wasn't traveling with the band. Back then I couldn't wait for those breaks from our time on the road. As much as I loved touring and the guys, we'd inevitably end up getting on each other's nerves and need our own space.

Even though the band had only called it quits a little more than two months ago, I'd already gotten a taste of what the non-touring life looked like, and it was a little... quiet. Having Katie there had breathed new life into my condo. I'd purchased it back when Jax and Liv first met and the entire band moved to Nashville. Well, everyone except Luca. I'd spared no expense in making sure the place felt like a sanctuary. A place I could charge my batteries. And it was still all those things, but now, it also felt like a home. And that was because of Katie.

My phone rang from my back pocket, and I dried my hands on a dish towel before prying it out. A number I didn't recognize flashed across the screen.

"Hello?" I answered, striding into the living room and flopping on the couch.

"Dallas, it's Brandon," a familiar tenor said on the other end. "From Blackbird."

I swallowed a groan. "Hey, man. What's going on? Is Prose Gold ready to get back in the studio?"

"How'd you know?" he asked as though I hadn't told him to call me when they needed me. "She just got back from the Hamptons and wants to record Thursday. We're gonna get started around eleven a.m. Does that work for you?"

Literally nothing had ever sounded worse. "I'll be there."

"Sweet. Later," he said before ending the call, and I clicked on the tv.

I was not looking forward to this recording session, but even Prose Gold and douchey Brandon couldn't dampen my mood. It was Tuesday, and I had Katie all to myself for the day.

As if on cue, she skipped into the room.

"And how's Jo?" I asked as she curled up beside me, her phone and a small piece of paper clutched in one hand.

"She's good. Excited about us. Worried about me." She held up the piece of paper that I recognized as the information the ER doctor had given her. "She made me promise to call and set up my appointment as soon as we got off the phone."

Katie stared down at the piece of paper and took a deep breath, raising her shoulders to her ears. "I don't know why I'm so nervous."

I placed my hand on her knee and gave it a squeeze.

"Don't be. I'm right here, and if you want me to go with you to your appointment whenever it is, I'll be there too."

"You don't have to do that. I can handle it."

"Are we still doing this?"

"You're sure you wouldn't mind?"

I cocked my head at her and made a 'what do you think' face before threading my fingers through hers.

"Okay." She sank deeper into the cushion, her arms starting to relax. "Thank you."

I stayed by her side as she made the call, explaining what had happened on the Fourth of July and who had referred her.

"Uh huh. That's correct," Katie said into the phone. "Yes, any time really. I'll make it work." There was a brief pause. "This Thursday? At one?" She looked at me for approval and I nodded.

Sorry, Prose Gold.

While Katie ironed out the details and finished giving her information, I slid my phone out of my pocket and fired off a text to Brandon's number:

Hey man. Had something come up for Thursday. You'll have to get someone else for this one. Sorry!

THIRTEEN

Katie

"Hey," McKenzie called when I came through the back door at work Wednesday morning.

"How's it going?" I greeted her as I placed my purse on the hook and tied on my apron.

"We got three big orders yesterday that'll be picked up later this afternoon," she said without looking up at me from where she was expertly covering chocolate cupcakes with buttercream. "I'm finishing the first one and the other two are in the oven now."

I was a little frustrated I hadn't been there to take care of these requests, but when I remembered the day I got to have instead, it was worth it.

"Between the two of us, we should be able to get them iced by noon and"—McKenzie flicked her gaze up at me and did a double take, settling her discerning eyes on mine—"what's with you?"

"What do you mean?" I asked.

"You." She wrinkled her nose and turned her finger in a circle in front of my face. "You look… I don't know. Gooey.

And weird."

"Gooey?"

She nodded. "And weird. Your cheeks are all rosy, like one of those annoyingly perfect girls always taking pictures in front of that angel wing mural down the street."

"That's oddly specific," I said with a laugh as I grabbed the order notebook off the counter and flipped it open.

She returned to piping icing on the cupcakes in front of her. "Did you and Tommy Lee finally do the bango tango or something?"

I inhaled sharply, choking on my own spit.

She gasped, the frosting now forgotten. "Oh my God, you did." She quickly grabbed me a bottle of water from the fridge, which I chugged before swiping the back of my hand over my mouth.

"I gotta say, I was beginning to think you didn't have it in you." She smirked, crossing her arms over her chest. "But it's about damn time. Anytime he's in here, you two are always making googly eyes at each other and—"

"We did *not* do the *bango tango*," I insisted, but heat rose all the way up to my hairline, spelling out my feelings for Dallas in bright red lipstick.

"Is that why your face looks like a ripe tomato?"

"I don't know what you're talking about." I cleared my throat. Geez. Was I really that transparent? "But, um, actually, I do need to talk to you about something."

"To be clear, it's not about banging Tommy Lee?"

I ignored the question and instead gave her the *Reader's Digest* version of what happened on the Fourth of July, minus the fireworks with Dallas and me.

"Wow, Katie," McKenzie said once I'd finished. "I'm sorry. I had a feeling something was up when Ella asked me to fill in, but I didn't want to pry. Do you think it's related to some of the other stuff you've had going on?"

"Maybe? I really don't know."

"I wonder if you could have fibromyalgia." She raked her teeth over her bottom lip. "My mom has that, and your symptoms are similar. Unexplained pain, fatigue. Hers goes through periods where it's worse than others too. Have you seen a specialist?"

"The ER doctor referred me to a rheumatologist, but the appointment is tomorrow afternoon," I explained. "I know you had to fill in for me yesterday, and I'm really sorry about that but—"

"Katie," she interrupted me. "Have you considered taking some time off? Running around this hot kitchen can't be good for you, especially after you had freaking heatstroke."

"I know, but I think I'm good. At least for now."

"Okay, but if you change your mind, I'm happy to help."

"Thank you. I'm really sorr—"

"Stop apologizing. Go to your appointment tomorrow." She swatted at my arm. "Don't worry about this. I've got it covered."

"I know you do. But I'll get as much done as I can myself before I leave. I don't want you having to save me all the time."

She shrugged. "I'm happy to do it. I mean, this place is kind of my life, and you're my friend, so of course I want to help."

The shock I felt at that admission must have registered all over my face.

McKenzie laughed. "Don't look so surprised."

"I'm not," I lied. I liked McKenzie a lot, but I never would have thought she considered me a friend.

"I know I'm not exactly the warm and fuzzy type, but that doesn't mean I don't, you know... care or whatever." She averted her gaze and returned her attention to the cupcakes on the island.

My heart swelled. Were we having a moment? I stepped closer to her, a smile growing on my face.

McKenzie turned toward me, sensing my presence.

"It's not a big deal," she said, her cheeks turning pink. "We don't have to hug or anything."

"But can we?"

"Fine." She rolled her eyes, pretending to be put out, but she hooked one arm around my shoulders and gave me a squeeze. "But now that we're all Facebook official or whatever, you have to promise you'll stop apologizing for everything."

I laughed. "Deal."

"I'M SURPRISED YOUR PREVIOUS PHYSICIANS HAVEN'T TESTED for Lupus or Lyme Disease or even Epstein-Barr." Dr. Childers scanned her laptop screen over her tortoiseshell glasses Thursday afternoon. "How long have you been experiencing these symptoms?"

The exam room felt less imposing than the others I'd been in. Even better, there wasn't a food pyramid or BMI chart in sight. If it wasn't for the standard exam table, it would've been easy to forget I was in a medical office. The walls were decorated with soothing colors and abstract paintings. Even the chairs were a soft chenille, and the lobby where Dallas was waiting for me looked like someone's cozy living room. After meeting Dr. Childers, it made sense.

Everything about her felt warm, from her kind voice to the way her brown eyes glowed against her tawny skin. She wore a mustard-colored dress with a lightweight cardigan instead of a lab coat.

I rolled my lips inward. "Um... a while." The truth was, I couldn't remember. It had started out slowly at first. Headaches. Blurred vision even though a visit to the optometrist told me my eyesight was fine. Then the pain and the pins and needles and the vertigo crept in, but it had been easy to write them off as stress or overworking myself.

"I know you've been through a lot of lab work, but I'd really like to run a more comprehensive panel today if that's okay with you. And I think you should set up an appointment with your gynecologist to check for endometriosis. That could certainly cause the pelvic pain you described."

"Of course. Anything that gets me closer to an answer." I paused for a moment, considering whether I should bring up what McKenzie had told me about her mother. "A friend of mine mentioned fibromyalgia. Is that a possibility? Is that something we could test for?"

"It's definitely a possibility," she said, "but it's not something you can really test for. The test is ultimately the ruling out of everything else."

"Oh." That didn't exactly fill me with confidence.

"Katie, I know how frustrating this is." Dr. Childers snapped her laptop shut and gave me a smile. "My mom was diagnosed with Lupus when she was in her fifties, but it took her years to get that diagnosis."

"Years?" Tears formed in the corners of my eyes. For me. For women like Dr. Childers' mom. Why was it so hard to find someone willing to listen? To dig a little deeper? To not make snap judgements rooted in untrue stereotypes? And why weren't there better tests? Ones that provided answers instead of more questions."

She nodded. "What she went through is what made me decide to pursue a path in rheumatology. I'll never be able to give my mom back the years she lost to being in pain, shuffled in and out of doctors' offices. But I can hopefully help women like you take your lives back."

Fear squeezed my throat with its gnarled fingers. "What if... what if this is all in my head?"

"Do you really think that?"

"Sometimes."

"What you're feeling is real, but the cards are stacked against women in our healthcare system. Always have been," she said with a resigned sigh. "When we look back as far as the nineteenth century, what do we see? Women being diagnosed with hysteria for deigning to complain, for simply wanting to feel better. We still see that now. A lot of medical professionals are quick to see a woman in pain and assume it's anxiety or depression manifesting itself into physical symptoms and not the other way around."

Her words were a bright light at the end of a dark tunnel. However, I'd felt the promise of answers before only to have it squashed like a spider who'd dared to trespass over the threshold. But this time felt different. Dr. Childers didn't just make me feel hopeful—she made me feel heard.

"You've taken a big step by being here today," she said. "You're not giving up, and that in and of itself is worth celebrating. The road to diagnosis can be a long one. We have to take the wins where we can get them."

"I appreciate that."

"Now, here's what I'm proposing we do from here." She pulled a prescription pad from the pocket of her cardigan.

"I'm going to draw some labs and run the tests we discussed, but I also want to put you on some steroids. We'll start with a higher dose and taper it down over the course of a month. I think we're likely dealing with at least some level of inflammation, so the steroids should help you get some relief while we work to get to the bottom of this. I'll call you as soon as those results come back, but regardless I want to see you again in a month." She ripped the paper off and handed it to me. "Do you have any questions for me?"

"I've taken steroids before for sinus infections, but nothing this long-term. Are there any side effects?"

"Increased hunger, a rise in blood sugar, but they're generally pretty well-tolerated. If you start feeling any worse, don't hesitate to call or send me a message through the portal." She rose to her feet. "Sit tight, and the nurse will be back in shortly."

"Thank you, Dr. Childers."

"And Katie, it's okay to rely on those around you for help as you navigate this. In fact, it's necessary," she added. "Do you have people you feel like you can talk to? People you can trust to hold space for you?"

"Actually, I do," I said. "Have someone, I mean."

My mind flashed to Dallas out in the lobby, and my chest surged with gratitude. I couldn't imagine going through this without him now. Just knowing he was out there waiting for me made me feel stronger somehow, like this wasn't something I had to fight alone. Not only did I have Dallas, but I had Jo and some really great friends who cared about me.

She reached into the pocket of her sweater again, scrawling something across the prescription pad before tearing off the page. "This is the name of a colleague of mine who runs a support group for people who deal with invisible illness. They meet once a week in the basement of the old Presbyterian Church off West End Avenue."

"Oh," I said, clutching the piece of paper in my hands. "Thank you."

Was I sick enough for that? What if the answers I finally got showed something simple and not chronic?

"A solid emotional support system is vital for everyone, but especially when you're on the road to a diagnosis. It can be lonely and frustrating at times, but having someone to talk to who understands and can validate your feelings on the tough days can be really helpful."

I nodded, tucking the page in my pocket. "Okay." I had a great support system in place, so I doubted I'd need it, but I didn't want to seem ungrateful.

She reached down and squeezed my shoulder. "We're going to figure this out, okay?"

And for the first time, I believed it was true.

"As awful as what happened on the Fourth of July was, it might end up being one of the best things that could have happened," Dallas said later that evening at his place over dinner. We'd made a simple meal of pan-fried salmon and roasted vegetables. "Because that's what ultimately led you to Dr. Childers, and she really seems to know her stuff."

I swallowed a bite of my fish. "I feel like I hit the jackpot with her. Who knows how long it would have taken me to find someone like her without that trip to the emergency room? Dr. Childers was telling me how long it took her mom to get a diagnosis, and it was *years*." It could still take years, but at least I'd found a provider who listened to me. That seemed like at least half the battle.

"I feel good about this. I'm confident she's going to find the answers you've been looking for."

"Me too," I said, spearing a green bean with my fork. "What I'm not confident about is our ability to keep our secret under wraps at the concert Saturday night."

He flashed me a mischievous grin. "Afraid you won't be able to keep your hands off me?"

"It's definitely not just me I'm worried about." I laughed and took a sip of my wine.

Jax and Liv were one of the headliners for a new weekend-long music festival that opened Friday night at Ascend Amphitheater. They were playing alongside artists like Dermot Kennedy, The Lumineers, Billie Eilish, and Dallas' favorite band, The Slacks, and a few of us were going to support them.

He placed his muscular forearms on the table, and my heart started to race. "I had to keep my hands to myself for years. It won't be easy, but I think I can manage."

"Is that so?" I asked, an idea bubbling just below the surface. "Then what do you say we make it interesting?"

"How so?"

"We can't touch each other at all the entire time we're there, even when our friends are out of sight," I said. "First one to break loses."

He waggled his brows at me. "So, what do I get when I win?"

"*If* you win," I corrected him. "What do you want?"

He folded his arms across his broad chest and considered the question a moment before answering.

Finally, he flicked his tongue over his lips. "You. On this dining table. Wearing only edible underwear."

I sputtered out a laugh and covered my mouth with my hand. "You can't be serious."

"Top Chef Katie," he said, his voice a low rumble I could feel at my core. "Are you blushing?"

"Nope," I lied, clearing my throat.

My heart hammered inside my chest as the visual he'd painted came alive inside my head. Me, laying exposed on the very table we were dining on, with the exception of a strawberry-flavored thong, and Dallas, with his head buried between my thighs, devouring me like I was the most coveted confection on a dessert buffet.

But then I thought about our failed attempt at having sex the other night and the pain I'd felt. What if this turned into a repeat of that and, once again, I left him dissatisfied?

"And I don't want you to be worried," he added quickly. "This is all about making you feel good. If you don't feel good, we stop. Simple as that."

"The only thing I'm worried about is what I get if *I* win." I squared my shoulders and put on an expression that was far more confident than I felt.

"What do you want?"

"I want the same thing." I held his gaze and threaded my fingers together below my chin. "Except it will be you featured on the dessert table."

"You're on."

I grabbed my napkin from my lap and dropped it on the table. "And you, mister, are going down."

He leaned forward, a devilish glint in his eyes as he scanned my body. "You better believe I am."

FOURTEEN

Dallas

"Where's Katie?" Ella asked, peering past me as though she thought I was somehow hiding her. We were standing backstage at Ascend Amphitheater watching the opening act while Liv and Jax were getting ready. "I thought she'd be here by now."

"Uh, I don't know. Haven't heard from her," I lied. I'd talked to her in my bedroom that morning before she'd left for work. She'd invited McKenzie to come to the concert and said she was going to get a ride with her. Nobody except Jo knew Katie was staying with me or about the problem with her AC. I hadn't even had a chance to tell Derek yet.

"Where are Cash and Grace?" I asked. "I thought for sure they'd be here."

Her mouth curved downward. "LA. *Again.*"

I placed my hand on her arm. "I'm sorry."

"We've just got to push through for a few more months. We're actually… We're looking for a place there."

"Wow, really?" I already knew, of course, because Katie had told me, but Ella and Cash hadn't shared that information with everyone yet, so I pretended this was the first I'd heard of it. "What about your place here? I know how much you love it."

"I do," she said with a wistful smile. "*We* do. It's already paid off, so no matter what, we'll keep it. It would allow us to visit more often, maybe even split our time between here and LA. But my plan is to give it to Grace one day when she's ready for a place of her own—which may be sooner than later given how serious things are with her and Sam."

I studied her face. Ella's usual spunk and wit had been replaced by a seriousness that was out of character for her.

"You okay, El?" I asked, following her gaze to where she'd spotted Liv and Jax, who were chatting with a stage manager. They noticed us and waved in our direction.

She shrugged. "It's just... everything's changing. It's not necessarily a bad thing. I guess I'm feeling the growing pains, you know?"

"Yeah. I get that." *Do I ever.* Being backstage, surrounded by the energy of the artists and the crew, hearing the raucous cheers from the crowd was a sobering reminder of how different my life was now. Was this what athletes felt like when they retired? How did they do it? How did they go from running plays on the field to being just another fan in the stands?

"Sorry we're late." I heard Katie before I saw her. "Traffic was insane."

I turned toward the sound of her voice, and I had to clamp my mouth shut to keep it from falling open. She had on a short, tight, pale-blue sundress covered in little roses, and the neckline dipped deep between the valley of her breasts. So deep that I wondered if she had anything on underneath.

"Damn girl," Ella said, echoing my own thoughts. "You look gorgeous. That dress!"

Katie giggled. "Why, thank you." She did a twirl, which revealed that the dress was completely backless.

I bit back a grin. "You look nice, Top Chef Katie."

"Sorry, I didn't get the dress-up memo." McKenzie gestured unapologetically down at her plain T-shirt and denim cutoffs. "And even if I had, I don't own a dress so I wouldn't have done it anyway."

"Well, you look great," Ella said. "And I'm glad you were finally able to make it out with us."

"Thanks for inviting me." McKenzie glanced around and pulled her arms in around herself. "Wow. This is... overwhelming."

"Okay, I need a drink," Ella said. "Anyone want anything?"

"I'm good," Katie answered.

I couldn't take my eyes off her. "Me too."

"I'll come with you," McKenzie said quickly. "Anything to get out of this craziness."

"We'll be back," Ella called over her shoulder as she and McKenzie disappeared into the crowd.

Once they were out of earshot, I crossed my arms and grinned at her. "I know what you're doing."

She tilted her head up at me, her long lashes fluttering. "You do?"

"Uh-huh. And it's not gonna work."

She gave me the sweetest smile, the kind that would get her anything she ever wanted from me, then raised herself up on her toes so that I could feel her breath against my ear.

"Well, that's too bad," she whispered. "It would have been fun to see you lose."

My throat went dry, and I bit down on my lip to keep myself from losing the bet and kissing her then and there.

"I'm going to go say hi to Liv." She flashed me a flirtatious grin and sauntered away.

I turned to watch as she went, admiring the sway of her hips and the way the dress hugged the curve of her ass. It was going to be a really long night.

"Excuse me," someone said from beside me. I turned to find a woman with shiny black hair and a nose ring. "Dallas Stone?"

"That's me."

She held out her hand, and I took it. "Lisa Johnson. I was a big Midnight in Dallas fan. Still am. I was bummed to hear about the split."

"Thanks. I appreciate that."

"What brings you out tonight?"

I nodded toward where Katie was standing with Jax and Liv. "I'm here to support those two."

"Wow, so you guys are all actually still on good terms?"

"Yeah, we're like family."

"I wish I could say the same for my guys," she muttered. "I'm the manager of The Slacks."

"Oh, no way," I said. "I'm a huge fan. Not gonna lie, they were also a big selling point for coming tonight. *Shades of Blue* is a killer album."

"Really?" Her eyes brightened, then she looked around as though she was making sure nobody was close enough to hear what she was about to say. "Look, this is all very hush-hush right now, but Patrick is leaving the band. He and Deacon are basically one show away from murdering each other."

"That's tough. I'm sorry to hear that." I'd never actually

met them, but I knew Patrick was the drummer, and Deacon was the lead singer.

"The rest of the guys get along great, but Patrick... Well, frankly, he's a massive dick."

I scrunched up my face. "That would certainly make for a hostile working environment."

"You have no idea," she said with a laugh. "That being said, they're looking for a new drummer, and when we were talking about our pie-in-the-sky picks for Patrick's replacement, your name came up."

My eyes widened. "What? Really?"

"We all just figured you probably had something else lined up already, but selfishly, I hope you don't because I think you'd be perfect for The Slacks."

"I've been doing a few sessions here and there," I admitted. "But I haven't really thought about starting a new project." That wasn't entirely true. The thought had definitely crossed my mind, but the idea of anything *but* Midnight in Dallas still felt strange.

"Well..." She looked at me hopefully. "Would you consider it? Because I'd love to set up a meeting with you and the guys. I mean, not Patrick, for obvious reasons."

I rubbed my thumb along my jaw. *What could it hurt? We might not even hit it off. But what if we did? I'd always thought the band would be my whole story, but maybe they were just the first half.*

"Yeah, why not," I said. "Let's set it up." I gave her my email, and she promised to be in touch early the following week before thanking me and striding off into the crowd.

Katie, who had been deep in conversation with Liv, locked eyes with me from across the room, her lips curling up ever so slightly.

Before I could go to her, a streak of red flashed before me and nearly tackled me into a hug.

"Hey, Dal." Jo chirped as Derek bumped my fist with his.

"Traffic was bananas. Did we miss anything?"

Katie caught my eye again, and I rubbed my hands together. "Actually, I think the show is just getting started."

WHILE JAX AND LIV WERE DEALING WITH SOME SORT OF hiccup in the lineup, we stood at the side of the stage and watched The Slacks perform. They put on a great show, but even they couldn't top the one happening right in front of me. Katie's hips were shaking to the beat, and she gathered her honey waves in her hands, piling them on top of her head, which gave me a perfect view of her sexy back.

I wanted to lick the salt right off her skin.

Derek nudged me with his elbow. "Dude. Are you okay?"

"Huh?" I blinked, willing my eyes to look away from Katie.

"I've been talking to you, and you're off on another planet," he said with a chuckle.

"Sorry," I mumbled. "What were you saying?"

"I said these guys are really good. I see why you like them."

"They're, uh, they're looking for a drummer," I said. "Their manager told me tonight. They're keeping the whole thing under wraps for now, but um... They want to talk to me."

He gave me a light shove in the chest. "Are you serious? That's amazing."

"We'll see." I shrugged, my gaze drifting back to Katie

who glanced at me over her shoulder, and *fuck,* I wanted to kiss that shoulder. "It's just a meeting."

Jo whispered something in Katie's ear, and she grinned before sharing whatever the secret was with Ella and McKenzie. I wanted to know what had her smiling like that, but more importantly, I wanted to be the *reason* she smiled like that.

Derek leaned into me again. "Seriously, man, you haven't taken your eyes off Katie all night. What's going on?"

I took a few steps back and gestured for him to follow me. "Katie and I... We've started seeing each other."

"I knew something was up." Derek laughed and shook his head. "Jo has been all 'I know something you don't know' with me the last few days."

"Why doesn't that surprise me?"

I filled him in on everything, including our decision to keep it on the down-low, and he clapped me on the shoulder. "Well, it's about time."

Jo turned and when she saw us talking, bounded over. "Did you tell him?"

"I did," I said, and she let out a dog whistle of a squeal that was luckily covered up by a guitar solo.

"I'm so excited," she squeaked.

"Really?" I feigned surprise. "I couldn't tell."

"Oh hush." Jo swatted my arm. "Okay, my feet are killing me. I think I need to find a place to sit for the rest of the show."

"Come on. Let's go find a spot." Derek slipped his arm around her shoulders and guided her through the throng of people.

Katie flashed me a coy grin and continued to dance as I took Jo's place beside her. My eyes were glued to her, afraid to miss a single second of this show she was putting on for me.

I stepped closer and leaned into her ear, careful not to touch her and lose on a technicality. Even though I was bound to lose anyway. Her cleavage shimmered in the glow of the stage lights that reached us, and I silently thanked the brilliant soul that invented sundresses.

"You're killing me," I whispered. "You know that right?"

She twisted her hair off her neck with one hand and fanned herself with the other. "You didn't really expect me to make it easy on you, did you?"

"Hey Dal," Liv said as she and Jax approached on my other side. "We need your help."

I reluctantly shifted my gaze away from Katie. "What's up?"

Jax pinched the bridge of his nose. "Our drummer is still stuck on I-40. We can do the set as just us, but this show was supposed to be a full band thing."

"And you're already here, *and* you're familiar with the material." Liv gave me her best sad puppy dog face. "Will you play our set with us? Please?"

I sucked in a breath. I didn't exactly love the idea of playing back-up on stage. With the band, I'd been an equal member and not just a hired gun, but there was no way I was going to leave them in the lurch. I could set aside my pride to help out my friends.

"Of course," I said.

Liv let out a sigh. "Thank you, thank you, thank you."

"We're on in five," Jax said, slapping me on the back. "I owe you one, brother. I'm going to go call John and tell him we got it covered."

"And I need to find a bathroom." Liv was bouncing with nervous energy as she disappeared behind Jax.

"Is everything okay?" Katie asked, wrinkling her brow. "They looked stressed."

"Yeah, their drummer isn't going to make it, so they asked me to fill in."

"Oh?"

I gave her a wanton smile. "Looks like it's your turn to get a show."

FIFTEEN

Katie

I WAS GOING to lose this bet. Watching Dallas play drums was as sexy as watching him cook, but in an entirely different way. Sweat dripped down his ripped arms making it look like they'd been slathered in oil, and *oh my God,* I wanted to do that. I wanted to rub oil into his skin, and I wanted to kiss every dip and curve of his biceps.

Instead of pulling his hair back in its signature bun, he'd opted to leave it down, which drove me even more crazy than I already was. He was on fire, soaking up the energy of the crowd like a sponge and then wringing it out, raining magic all over the stage. Seeing him that way was like foreplay. It made me imagine all the ways I could make him sweat like that. Us, in the shower together. Me, pressing him into the tile, kissing down the length of his smooth chest until I reached his—

The sound of a throat clearing pried me out of my fantasy land.

"You're looking at Tommy Lee like he's a medium rare

steak, and you're a lion at feeding time," McKenzie said, nudging my arm.

"I am not." I wrapped my arms around myself as though that would somehow conceal my feelings.

She chuckled. "Yeah okay. Whatever you say. Anyway, you might want to put your eyeballs back inside your head before Ella returns from the bathroom."

I bit back a grin. "My eyeballs are in my head, thank you very much."

"I know. That's your story, and you're sticking to it," she said with a laugh. "But that definitely won't hold up in the court of Ella with evidence this strong, so I suggest you pull yourself together."

I blew a rogue hair out of my face and steadied my shoulders as Dallas finished with a flourish.

"If I thought my bladder was tiny before, it's now the size of a kidney bean," Ella said, returning to stand between McKenzie and me. "Oh shoot. I missed the last song."

Jax and Liv thanked the audience as Dallas tossed his drumsticks into the crowd, and they started off stage together.

Time slowed as Dallas walked toward me, little shimmering diamonds falling to the ground with each molecule of sweat that dripped off him. The cheers of the crowd faded to the back of my mind until the only thing I could hear was the sound of my own heart thudding in my ears.

He lifted the hem of his T-shirt and wiped his face, giving me a perfect view of his abs. When he let the fabric fall, his eyes locked with mine, and his lips curled into a seductive grin.

"That was great, you guys," Ella said. "It was good to see you playing again, Dal."

"Yeah?" Dallas asked, not taking his eyes off mine. "You liked that, huh?"

"You were on fire," she continued, her eyes shifting over to me. "Are you okay, Katie? You look woozy. Are you woozy?" McKenzie raised her brows at me as if to say *I-told-you-so.*

I swallowed the lump of longing in my throat, feeling the burn of Dallas' gaze.

"Yes," I choked out. "I am, actually."

"*Oh no,*" McKenzie said with exaggerated concern. "Do you need me to take you home? We can leave. I'll even pull the car aroun—"

"I can take her," Dallas interjected. "I mean, no sense in you missing the rest of the show. Billie Eilish is playing next." He stifled a yawn that I was pretty sure was fake. "I'm beat. I'm probably going to hit the hay early, anyway."

"I'm sure you'll be hitting *something,*" McKenzie said under her breath, and all eyes fell on her.

"Sorry, McKenzie." Liv popped out her ear monitor. "What did you say?"

"Oh, uh, I said I'm sure you're all exhausted." McKenzie played it cool and turned to Dallas. "Well, if you really don't mind giving Katie a ride, I'd like to stay for the rest of the show. I just love crowds." No one else but me seemed to pick up on the sarcasm in her voice.

"Of course I don't mind." Dallas eyed McKenzie as though he was trying to read her mind.

"I hope you feel better," Liv said, giving me a hug.

"Me too." McKenzie gave me a one-armed embrace and whispered in my ear. "I'm sure you'll be feeling better *very* soon."

I pinned her with a pointed glance as we pulled apart.

"Thanks again for filling in." Jax patted Dallas on the back. "We owe you one."

"Tell Jo I'll text her later," I said to Ella, giving her a parting squeeze.

"I will. Get some rest," she called after me.

"Are you ready?" Dallas asked. The tension between us was as thick as a curtain, and I couldn't wait to peel it back inch by glorious inch.

My breath hitched in my chest. "Ready."

I led the way, and he followed close behind as we weaved through the crowd. We rounded the corner, and the exit came into view at the end of the long corridor that seemed to stretch for miles. I couldn't wait till we got back to his place to put my hands on him. I couldn't even wait until we got outside.

There was a stack of equipment against the wall, and I ducked behind it, grabbing Dallas' shirt.

Heat flashed in his eyes as he placed both hands on the wall beside me, a sly smile on his face. "Well, Top Chef Katie, you just touched me. I think this means you lose."

I snaked my arms around his neck. "Shut up and kiss me."

"Fuck," Dallas said as we walked through the door of his condo. "We forgot to stop at Hustler for the edible underwear."

I hadn't forgotten, but the ride back to Dallas' place had been torture enough without having to make any pitstops, so I'd kept my mouth shut. The anxiety I'd felt about attempting to get intimate again had been overshadowed by my desire for him.

"We can just order some on Amazon Prime," I joked, poking him in the arm as we kicked off our shoes in the foyer. He chuckled. "I feel like that's not gonna be a same-day delivery item."

"Oh *darn*. Guess we're out of luck."

He threaded his fingers through mine and led me to the kitchen. "If I didn't know any better, I'd think you were trying to get out of this."

"Me, trying to get out of wearing a perverted fruit snack?" I pressed my palm to my chest in feigned innocence. "Never."

"Oh good," Dallas said, playing along. "So, you're not, then?"

"Of course not."

"Then you won't mind if we improvise."

I narrowed my eyes at him as he opened the fridge. "Improvise?"

He pulled out a can of whipped cream, a mischievous glint in his eyes.

I cackled. "You cannot be serious."

He reached back in the fridge and withdrew a small jar. "I have maraschino cherries."

"A whipped cream bikini," I said, folding my arms over my chest. "Really?"

"Fine." He playfully rolled his eyes as he started to put the items back.

"Listen, there's only one way I'm doing this," I said in the sassiest voice I could muster.

He arched his brow. "Oh really."

"There has to be chocolate sauce or it's no deal."

He flung open the fridge and pulled out a bottle of chocolate syrup. "I have Hershey's."

"What? No Godiva? I can't possibly be expected to

perform with anything less than Ghirardelli." I pursed my lips in mock indignation and started to turn away from him.

"Good thing I'll be the one doing the performing," he said, catching me by the arm. "I want you to just sit back and enjoy it."

I slid my hands beneath his shirt and up his chest, loving the way the ripples of his muscles felt against my skin. "Hershey's it is, then."

"You do realize I was just messing with you, right?" he asked, gently catching my wrists and tracing slow circles on them with his thumbs. "I know we made a bet, but we really don't have to do this if you don't want to. Trust me, being with you is more than enough."

"I mean, if you don't *want* to cover my body in whipped cream and—"

"Oh, I do," he said. "I really, *really* do."

I stood on my toes and kissed him, long and slow. "Then I suggest you do it. Before I chicken out."

"Yes ma'am." He grinned and swung open the fridge, gathering the ingredients we'd need for our sexy sundae. He then followed me to the dining room, where he lined up the goods like an artist preparing paints to work on their latest masterpiece.

I turned, facing him with a boldness that felt both strange and comfortable, like slipping on a silk gown after a hot bath. Even though turning my body into a dessert bar was entirely out of my wheelhouse, I felt safe experimenting with Dallas.

He gently backed me against the table, his hips flush with mine, and I could feel how much he wanted this—how much he wanted *me*.

"So," he said, sliding his hand around the back of my neck and his lips along my jaw.

"So." My stomach fluttered as he tilted my head to the side and kissed the sensitive skin below my ear. I picked up the bottle of whipped cream and popped the top off with my thumb. "Do I have to put this on myself or—"

He cut me off by cupping his hands under my butt and lifting me onto the end of the table.

"Sounds like someone can't wait to be the dessert after all," he whispered as I wrapped my legs around his waist, causing my dress to pool around my hips.

"More like I can't wait for you to lick it off me," I said, biting my lip.

"Then I guess we shouldn't waste any more time."

He hooked his fingers around the lace of the cheekies I'd carefully selected just for this occasion and eased them down, tossing the fabric over his shoulder. I covered his hands with mine and guided them back over my thighs.

"I have to say, I'm really glad you lost," he murmured, gripping the hem of my dress and pulling it over my head. His gaze didn't leave my body as he dropped it to the floor. The dress I'd worn hadn't allowed for a bra, so there was nothing left concealed. There was something sexy and invigorating about being completely exposed in front of him, like all the doors that had been closed between us had been torn off their hinges.

"Me too," I said softly, and I meant it. Watching him devour me with his eyes as though I was some intoxicating, delicious creature was a feeling I could never get enough of.

He leaned in so his lips grazed my ear, sending goosebumps down my arms. "I'm starved."

He reached for the bottle of whipped cream, but I grabbed his hand. "Not so fast. You're still wearing too many clothes."

"Am I?" He smirked, and I leaned back and admired his

toned body as he ripped his shirt over his head, causing the muscles in his shoulders to flex. "How's that?"

"Good." My gaze dropped to where the v of his chest dipped into the top of his jeans. "But I think you can do better."

He unfastened his pants and shoved them down along with his boxers, kicking them aside. I reached for him, but he took both of my hands in his and clicked his tongue.

"Ladies first." He laid me back on the table, and I shifted slightly, planting my feet on the edge.

He palmed my breasts, massaging until the buds of my nipples turned into soft peaks. "I want to know what makes you feel good."

"This is definitely at the top of the list." If he didn't have his hands on me, I was certain I'd be floating. But his touch kept me tethered to the moment—no worries, no insecurities. Just me and him. His forearms flexed as he moved, reminding me of how sexy he'd looked on stage, but nothing could ever compare to this.

I moaned as he picked up the whipped cream and shook the can before swirling it over my breasts until they were completely covered. Once he was satisfied with his handiwork, he placed another dollop just above the soft mound of flesh at my center, careful not to get any in my most sensitive spots. I was almost shocked that the cold cream didn't melt on contact against my flushed skin.

"Now, for the toppings," he said, swapping out the whipped cream with the chocolate syrup, and I giggled as he drizzled it over the patches of white. "And last but not least, the cherry on top."

He took his time plucking the cherries from the jar,

placing one at the center of each sundae that now decorated my body.

"Perfect." He capped the jar and slid it down the table. "Now I'm going to enjoy every last bite."

He hovered over me, taking in whipped cream by the mouthful, lighting up every single nerve ending in my body. When he reached the cherries in the middle of my breasts, he tugged on my nipple gently with his teeth, sending a rush of heat to my core.

"Fuck, you taste good." He cupped the outside of my breasts, creating a sweet pond in the valley of my chest for him to bury his face in. When he brought his eyes back to mine, he had a whipped cream mustache.

I laughed. "You have a little something on your face."

He grinned. "I'm just getting started."

I wriggled beneath him as he devoured the bikini top and kissed his way down my stomach. My breath caught in my throat as the warmth of his mouth trailed along my hips, and I bucked against him, greedy for his touch. I wanted to feel him everywhere.

Once all that remained of the whipped cream was a sticky trail of sugar, he knelt before me, slid me down the table, and hooked my legs over his shoulders.

"Dallas…" I gasped as his lips grazed along my skin, teasing my inner thigh. Desire burned through me like a candle that had been lit, turning my limbs into a melted, velvety pool.

"Yes?" he whispered against my folds, before sliding his tongue between them.

My answer was swallowed up by a contented sigh as he licked and sucked ever so gently, causing tension to build at my center. But this wasn't the kind of tension I'd experienced from the first time we'd tried to have sex. That was the kind that felt like cement being poured into my limbs, shutting my body down no matter how much I wanted to keep going. This was different. This was like water building behind a dam. With every touch, his pace quickened, pulling me deeper and deeper below the aching surface.

"I've wanted you for so long, Katie." He kissed my tender flesh again with an urgency that told me it was true, causing me to dig my heels into his back, my toes curled. With one last lick, the dam burst, flooding me with pleasure. My legs quivered as he pressed his palm against me, aftershocks sparking through me.

"Oh my God," I said, once I was able to catch my breath.

He slipped his hands behind me and helped me sit up, crushing his lips to mine.

"You're fucking delicious," he murmured when we finally broke apart. "Do you know that?"

I wrapped my legs tight around him, bringing our hips together so that I could feel him pulsing against my thigh.

"Now I get to find out what flavor you are." I reached between us and stroked him, slowly at first, before picking up the pace.

"Fuck," he groaned, his forehead against mine. "I'm not going to last long."

I placed a kiss on his lips and scooted off the table, dropping to my knees in front of him. Looking up at him was like staring up at a statue of a Greek God or something equally as perfect. I took him in my mouth, moving my lips along his tip as I used my hands to work his shaft.

"Shit," he cried out, gripping the edge of the table with one hand and fisting my hair with the other.

I sucked and licked as he bucked against me, moving faster and faster.

"I'm gonna come," he choked out. When I didn't stop, he asked, "Are you sure?"

I locked eyes with him and held his gaze, letting him know I was giving him the greenlight. I wanted him. All of him.

In a matter of seconds, he exploded in my mouth—salty, sweet, and smooth. His moans of ecstasy were a total turn on, and in that moment, I no longer doubted if I could satisfy him. I knew I could and I would, over and over again.

He trembled slightly as I released him and wiped my mouth with the back of my hand.

"Come here," he said, helping me to my feet. He ran his thumb along my bottom lip, his eyes boring into mine.

"A penny for your thoughts?" I asked, snaking my arms around his neck.

"It's just... you're everything." He shook his head and smiled. "Everything I've ever wanted."

"You're everything I've wanted too."

I pressed my body to his. Sweat, remnants of whipped cream, and chocolate syrup combined to form a sticky, sweet adhesive, practically gluing us together. So much so that when I pulled back to look at him, we made a soft ripping sound, like a piece of tape being pried off a hard surface.

"And a shower," I amended. "A shower would be a close second."

He chuckled, then kissed the tip of my nose. "Let's do it."

SIXTEEN

Dallas

"You've got to be kidding me," Katie said into the phone, massaging her temple as she paced around the kitchen. "You said it was going to be two weeks over *four weeks* ago."

There was a pause as she listened to the person at the HVAC company, then huffed out an aggravated breath. I caught her by the shoulders mid-step and kneaded her knotted muscles.

The August heat had dropped on the South like an unwanted visitor, making July look mild by comparison. We were already halfway through the month, and Katie's air conditioner still wasn't fixed—and it didn't look like that would be changing anytime soon.

"Yeah. Yep. I understand." Her voice was snippy, like scissors cutting through string. "Fine. Thank you." She howled in frustration as she slid her phone onto the counter.

"Went that well, huh?" I teased, trying to lighten her mood.

"He said it was going to be at least *another* two weeks. There's some kind of shortage, and they're having a hard time getting the parts they need." She turned and wrapped her arms around me, burying her face in my chest. "Are you sure you're okay with me still staying here?"

"Of course I am." I decided not to tell her that I'd secretly hoped for this so she'd stay longer. "I love having you here."

"I love being here," she said, rising on her toes to kiss me. "I also love your French press." She moved around me to grab a mug from the cabinet. "You want some?"

I glanced at the clock on the microwave. "I'm gonna have to take mine to go. I've got to get to rehearsal."

"It sounds like things are going well with these guys." She pulled down a stainless steel tumbler and poured us both some coffee before handing me my cup. "This could be huge."

She was right. From the first meeting with The Slacks and their manager Lisa, something had clicked into place. Nothing would ever be the same as Midnight in Dallas, but I'd really hit it off with the guys. We'd been doing some test rehearsals and jam sessions for the last couple weeks to get a feel for each other, and though they were doing the same thing with one other drummer, I was their frontrunner according to Lisa.

"It could be." If things continued to go well, I could be writing music, recording, and playing shows again a lot sooner than I'd anticipated. When I'd found out Midnight in Dallas was splitting up four months ago, I thought that was all I wanted. But as I watched Katie move around the kitchen barefoot with her hands wrapped around her mug, it was hard to imagine going back out on the road.

"I better finish getting ready for work. I'll probably be a little late tonight. McKenzie and I are doing a big wedding order since I won't be there Friday afternoon."

"Your appointment's at one, right?"

"Yep," she answered, taking a sip of her coffee. "And if

they end up needing you for another rehearsal Friday, don't sweat it. I can go alone this ti—"

I cupped her face in my hands and kissed her. "I'm going with you."

She smiled up at me. "Thank you."

"How are you feeling about the appointment?"

"Considering the bloodwork didn't give us any new hints? Not great." She blew out a breath. "But I still believe if anyone can figure out what's going on with me, it's Dr. Childers."

"Me too. I mean, the steroids helped you feel better for a little while."

"They did. Up until the last week or so. Now the pain and tingling in my hands is back, and that makes these long days at work extra long." She shrugged. "Anyway, enough about me. You're going to be late if you don't get going."

I kissed her again. "I'll see you tonight."

"Have fun," she called over her shoulder as she started out of the kitchen.

I watched her saunter down the hall, and my chest tightened. Our living arrangement was only meant to be temporary. I knew that, but I also knew the idea of Katie going back to a place we didn't share and me going back on tour—missing moments, mornings like this—made my heart ache.

"Fuck yeah!" Deacon shouted as we finished the song 'Wild.' It was never released as a single, but with its rousing beat and soul-piercing lyrics it had become a crowd favorite.

Lisa rose to her feet, whooping her approval as the last notes faded out.

"I'm just gonna go ahead and say it." Knox placed his Fender in its holder, sweat glistening on his Black skin. "We've never sounded better."

"That was a killer solo, man." I pointed my drumsticks at him. "Fucking badass."

"This just *feels* good, you know?" Bennett propped one foot on his amp, shaking his shaggy brown hair out of his eyes. "You have great energy, Dallas. It's like you've been playing with us forever." He was the bass player, and his kind, calm presence reminded me a lot of Derek.

Lisa clapped her hands together. "I couldn't agree more."

"That was fire, guys. Pure fucking fire." Deacon punctuated the words with his hands.

Mack, the rhythm guitarist, placed his instrument in its case and grabbed two bottles of beer out of the cooler that sat at the front of the room, handing me one.

"Thanks," I said, twisting off the top.

"So," Mack began in his southern drawl, "what do we have to do to get you to play The Ryman with us next month?"

My eyes widened. "Whoa, seriously?"

"Hell yeah, brother." Deacon showed his excitement with his entire body, much the way he did on stage. With his raw, gravelly tenor and animated movements, he was what lead singer dreams were made of. He did and felt everything in a big way. "We need you! We have to let everyone know The Slacks aren't going anywhere. In fact, we're going to be better than ever."

Lisa held out her hands as though she could stop the Deacon train before it derailed and ran me over. "What he means to say is that you'd be billed as our special guest.

You'd get a feel for what it would be like to actually be a member of the group and see how the fans react."

"They're gonna fucking love it!" Deacon said as his phone rang. He pulled it out of his pocket and answered the call, bouncing away like a rubber ball out of one of those old machines at the grocery store.

Knox smiled and shook his head. "He can be a little intense sometimes, but it's because he cares."

"I like that." It was clear how much Deacon loved the band from the way he interacted with everyone during rehearsal, giving his all as though we were playing to a sold-out crowd. He was quick to compliment and slow to criticize. I knew he and their previous drummer hadn't gotten along, but it was hard to imagine why. He was so damn likable.

"Don't feel like you have to give us an answer right now," Knox said. "Think about it."

"I definitely will." I wanted to talk to Katie about it, but I could already anticipate what she'd say. She'd want me to go for it, and to be honest, I wanted to as well. It was a local show and as their guest, I didn't have anything to lose. It was the perfect opportunity for a test run to see if this would be a good fit, not just for us, but for the fans. I wasn't exactly excited about the idea of getting back out on the road yet, but luckily, that wasn't something I'd have to do until next year. Maybe by then I'd have that itch again. Maybe I'd feel differently.

I stood and grabbed my phone off the floor to check the time. It was a little after six. "Well, friends, this was fun, but I need to head out. My girl's had a long day, so I'm making her dinner."

"That's cute." Lisa tilted her head. "If working with

Patrick hadn't made me dead inside, that would probably make me feel all warm and fuzzy."

Bennett clapped me on the back. "Great rehearsal."

"See ya later, man." Mack gave me a salute.

"I'll walk you out," Knox said, packing up his gear.

"Thanks, Dallas," Deacon called from across the room before returning to his phone call.

"So, how long have you been with your girl?" Knox asked as we pushed out the door and into the muggy evening air.

"Katie. It's pretty new actually," I admitted. "We've only been dating for a month and a half, but we were friends for about four years before that."

He chuckled. "Oh wow, so you really had to dig your way out of the friend zone."

"How did you know?" I asked with a laugh.

"Because that was me and my wife too," he answered, shifting his case to his other hand. "Except I'd been in the friend zone for about ten years."

"Oh shit. That's brutal."

"Tell me about it. But it all worked out the way it was supposed to. We'll be married six years next month."

"Congrats, man. That's awesome." I ran my hand along the back of my neck. "I... uh... what's it like?"

"What?" he asked. "Marriage?"

"Yeah... no, not exactly." I blew out a breath. "Being away from each other while you're on the road."

"Ah. That. Well, if I'm being honest, it's not been easy. Our first couple years were rough, but we found our rhythm." He glanced at me as we walked toward our cars. "You're worried about leaving Katie."

"I guess I just don't really have anything to compare it to. I haven't had any serious relationships *because* of being on the road. Jax got with Liv, and they started their own thing, so they weren't away from each other all that much. Derek left the band and works with his girlfriend. Our manager, Cash, has been away for work a lot lately, and his fiancée is miserable without him."

"It's not easy, and it's not for everyone." He shrugged. "I can't tell you how many anniversaries and birthdays I've missed being on the road. I think what I long for the most, though, are the everyday things. Deciding what to order for dinner or which show to watch together before bed. Taking our dog to the park."

"But I bet when you get home it's like you never left."

"Not quite. I'm on the road a lot, so Kira kinda has her routines," he explained. "When I go home, I just do my best to fit into them where I can. Sometimes that means sitting alone at the house while she has her weekly dinners with her sister, and I've definitely watched way more of her Netflix dating shows than I care to admit." He smiled, but it didn't quite reach his eyes.

"Do you ever wish it wasn't like that?" I asked as we neared my car. "That you got to be with her every night?"

"All the time." His gaze fell to his feet. "I know how that probably sounds. I know how lucky I am. People spend their lives dreaming about being extraordinary, doing something that makes them famous, and all I want is to pretend to argue with my wife about which takeout we're going to get when we both know damn well I'm always going to let her choose."

My chest constricted. It was hard to imagine not having dinner with Katie every night, fussing over who was going to cook for whom. Or pretending to be annoyed when she picked yet another romantic comedy to watch, though I secretly loved them for the sole reason that they always made her teary-eyed. Of course, she tried to pretend that they didn't. If I went out on the road would things feel different when I came back? Would she have her own life that I'd be left trying to fit into when I was home?

"Speaking of," Knox said when his phone pinged from his pocket. He plucked it out and glanced at the screen. "Looks like we're having sushi tonight. I better get going. Wouldn't want to miss whatever dating disaster show Nick and Vanessa Lachey have cooked up." He laughed and started toward his truck that was a couple spaces down from me. "Good rehearsal today, man. I'll see ya."

"See ya," I echoed before climbing into my car. I checked my phone before pulling out of the lot to find a text from Katie waiting on me.

Katie: Crazy day! I'm ready to curl up on the couch with you and Richard Gere and Julia Roberts.

I smiled to myself and tapped out my reply.

Dallas: I can't wait.

SEVENTEEN

Katie

"So, the steroids did help?" Dr. Childers asked me in her office Friday afternoon as her coral-tipped fingers clicked across the keyboard of her laptop.

"They did," I answered. "At least until I got to the lower end of the dosage."

She pursed her lips and nodded slowly, tapping a nail against the edge of her computer. Finally, she snapped it shut and turned toward me.

"I think we may be onto something here," she said. "The bloodwork we ran when you were here last didn't give us anything new, but I did run your ANA again on the off chance your previous results were a fluke."

"And?"

"As I suspected, it was still positive. Now, sometimes that can be a marker for Lupus, but your symptoms aren't really consistent with that," she explained. "I was looking over your chart, comparing the notes from your previous doctors and your emergency room visit, and I think it would be worth scheduling you with a neurologist and getting some imaging done."

"Oh." I wrinkled my brow. "Well, I had some X-rays done not too long ago."

"Yes, but I think we need something quite different." She leaned forward, resting her forearms on her knees. "Katie, have you ever had an MRI?"

My pulse thudded in my ears, and panic clawed at the inside of my stomach. Thanks to all the medical dramas I'd consumed over the years, when I heard words like neurologists and MRIs, I thought of things like cancer. Did she think I had cancer? A brain tumor?

"I've never needed one," I said. "Do you think I need one? That sounds... serious."

"MRIs are just another useful diagnostic tool." She gave me a reassuring smile. "And neurologists treat a variety of conditions, including nerve-related issues. As your doctor, I would be remiss if I didn't explore every possible avenue."

"Okay." My throat felt dry. I thought of Dallas out in the waiting room and wished I'd asked him to come back with me. I'd have given anything at that moment to be able to reach over and take his hand.

"My brother-in-law's name is Dr. Madison, and he's a neurologist at Vanderbilt. He tends to book out pretty far in advance, but if you're okay with it, I'd like to discuss your case with him and see if we can catch a cancellation."

I gulped. "Of course."

"Perfect." She rose to her feet. "I'll be in touch as soon as I speak with him. By the way, were you able to get in with your gynecologist?"

"Oh, yeah." The visit had been so unhelpful I'd almost forgotten about it.

"How did that go?"

"Aside from how excruciating the exam was? Fine," I said with a shrug. "She said she didn't see any obvious causes for the pain and that some women are just more sensitive... you know... down there."

"So, she had no suggestions for you. No possible solutions?"

"Nope." She sighed heavily and pulled out her prescription pad. "Tell you what, I'm going to give you the name of a pelvic floor physical therapist. Set up an appointment with her."

I blinked. "I'm sorry. What?"

"Pelvic floor physical therapy." She gave me an easy smile. "I promise, it's not as strange as it sounds. It's a specialized form of PT that uses exercises to help strengthen your core, but it can also help relax those pelvic muscles."

"Exercises? Like kegels?"

"Yes, but it's so, so much more than that. Honestly, many women could benefit from it at some point in their lives, be that for painful sex, bladder control, or the unfortunate toll that gravity takes on our bodies as we age," she said with a chuckle. "It may help with some of the discomfort you're experiencing in that area."

"Thank you, Dr. Childers," I said, taking the paper with the information scrawled across it.

"And you still have the info for that support group I gave you, right?" she asked.

I nodded.

"It might be worth checking out one of their meetings," she said. "I know how overwhelming and confusing this process can be, and it can be really helpful to talk to people who've been where you are."

"Yeah," I said. "Maybe I'll do that."

But at that moment, the only person I wanted to talk to was waiting for me in the lobby. Dr. Childers assured me again that we were going to get answers before leading me out of the room and toward the check-out counter. I thrusted my credit card at the receptionist before she could even tell me what I owed, drumming my fingers along the Formica desk. After what felt like an eternity, I scrawled my signature onto the receipt and pushed through the door that separated me from Dallas.

He looked up over an issue of *Good Housekeeping* and smiled when his eyes met mine. I laughed to myself as he tossed the magazine on the chair beside him, and my muscles relaxed with every step that brought us closer to each other.

"Hey, Butter Bean." He curled his arm around my shoulders, and we fell into step beside each other as we started toward the exit. "Everything okay?"

I leaned into him, gazing up into his eyes that felt like home. "It's much better now."

"ON A SCALE OF ONE TO TEN, HOW WRONG WOULD IT BE FOR me to turn that sign over to 'closed' before the bachelorette party across the street can make it over here?" McKenzie peered out the glass door, a broom clutched in her hand.

"That depends," I said flatly, leaning against the front counter. "Is ten the worst?"

"Yes," she answered, whipping her head back at me. "Hurry. They're crossing the street."

I yawned. "Negative nine. Flip that sign."

"Thank God." She clicked the lock, turned the sign, and

sprinted from the door as though it was seconds away from exploding.

Ella was out because the baby had an ear infection, Sydney had to leave at noon, and Jacob was visiting his sister in Seattle, so we'd had a skeleton crew all day. It was barely after three, but we were completely knackered.

A gaggle of women wearing sashes and hot-pink cowboy boots approached with their hands cupped around their eyes and attempted to peer in.

"Hurry before they turn into zombies and start doing TikTok dances to Shania Twain songs." McKenzie hit the lights and grabbed my arm, dragging me through the back.

"We're terrible," I said with a laugh.

"We're almost out of everything anyway." She waved me off as she stepped over to the sink and started doing the dishes. "Really, we did them a favor. How devastating would it have been for them to come all the way over here in their hot-pink boots to find out we were out of Strawberry Fields? Their entire trip *and* their Instagram aesthetic would have been ruined."

"You're so nice to look out for them," I said, as my phone rang from my back pocket.

"Ooooh is that your boyfriend?" McKenzie teased, and I nearly dropped it as I glanced down at the screen.

"Hello?" I answered.

"What time do you finish at the bakery today?" Luca's tone was urgent, panicked.

"We're actually closing up a little early. Is everything okay?"

"I need your help with something. Can you meet me?"

"Um, sure. When?"

"As soon as you can. I'm about fifteen minutes away."

I covered the phone with my hand. "Hey, McKenzie. Mind if I duck out?"

"Of course not." She eyed me curiously. "We've almost done everything anyway."

"I'll see you in fifteen minutes," I said into the phone.

"Frothy Monkey across the street from the bakery."

"Meet me on the patio."

"What? Why? It's a million degrees out."

"I'll see you soon," he said before ending the call.

"What was that about?" McKenzie asked. "Everything okay?"

I shrugged. "I don't really know. My friend Luca just said he needed my help."

"Well then, you better get out of here. I hope everything's okay."

"Me too." I gathered my stuff and started for the door. "Thanks again," I called over my shoulder.

A few minutes later, I was waiting inside the coffee shop, watching for Luca with an iced coffee in hand when I saw him approach. But he wasn't alone.

I sucked down the last of my drink and tossed the cup in the trash on my way out the door and onto the patio.

"What on earth?" I asked once I was in front of him, covering my mouth with my hands. "Who is this?"

Tucked under his arm like a fluffy football was a tiny dog the color of a toasted marshmallow with a pink flower attached to her collar. She had on what looked like a diaper with pigs printed on it.

"This"—he held the dog out for my inspection as she wagged her poofy tail—"is Emilia, according to the tag on this very pink collar."

"You got a dog?" I asked, giving her a gentle pat on the head. She was so cute she almost didn't look real.

"Not exactly," he said with a huff. "I had, uh, relations with her owner on Tuesday night, and she left her at my apartment. I didn't even know she'd brought a damn dog with her. She must have been in her purse or something. I found her waddling around my living room Wednesday morning. And let me just tell you, she's not wearing the diaper for fashion purposes. I took it off of her, and she immediately pissed on my rug."

"Did you call the owner?" I cocked my head to the side. "Wait, do you not remember her name?"

He rolled his eyes. "I remember. Well, actually I didn't, but it's on the dog tag. I tried to reach her for three fucking days, but she didn't answer till this morning when she let me know she doesn't want the dog."

"What? She just left her?" I didn't know how anyone could desert an animal, let alone one this adorable. She looked like one of those designer pups some rich influencer would probably pay a ridiculous amount of money for.

"Yep. She said she doesn't want her anymore."

I gasped and pressed my palm to my chest. "How could someone do that?"

"She said the dog is old and mostly deaf, and she can't take care of her anymore." He pinched the bridge of his nose with his free hand. "Katie, I don't know what to do. I thought about Derek and Jo, but they're going to have their hands full when they have the baby. I could take her to a shelter but—"

"You most certainly will not." I reached for the pup and took her in my arms, nuzzling her cotton-soft fur. She responded with a gentle lick on my nose, her big ears standing straight up. "I'll take her."

I said it without thinking about the fact that I wasn't even staying in my own house at the moment. But Dallas would be on board if he knew it would make me happy. And it would.

"Are you sure?" His eyes were wide with hope. "I'm not really a dog person, but I know you have a lot going on with your health and—"

"I'm sure. Honestly, this could be good. Gives me something else to focus on." I kissed the top of her head, and she settled into my arms as though she'd always belonged there. "What have you been doing with her these last few days?"

"As far as dogs go, I guess she's pretty easy. She mostly just lays around and goes out to piss a thousand times a day."

"She's as sweet as she can be."

"She's a prissy little shit too." He scruffed the back of his mop of dark hair with his hand. "I put a pillow on the floor for her to lie on, but apparently that wasn't good enough because all she did was huff and fuss and do this little prancey thing until I put her in bed with me."

My heart melted, imagining the elderly pooch snuggled up to an ornery Luca.

"I've got some food for her in the car," he said, motioning for me to follow him out to the lot. "The guy at the pet store said it was the best."

When we got to his car, he popped the trunk and pulled out a small bag of kibble and a large tote bag. He held the bag open so I could see its contents.

"There's a leash in there and a bag of treats they talked me into. And some food and water bowls." He retrieved a tiny stuffed lamb chop. "And I got her this and a ball in case she wanted to, you know, play or something." He clicked the trunk closed. "Come on. I'll carry these over to your car. You both need to get out of this heat."

I couldn't suppress the smile that spread across my face.

"What?"

"Nothing," I said as nonchalantly as I could manage as we crossed the pavement toward my Bug.

"What was that look for?"

I beamed up at him. "What look?"

"The one you're giving me literally right now."

I laughed as I hit the key fob to unlock my car. "Nothing. You're just sweet. You've taken such good care of her. It's cute."

He grimaced as he lifted the trunk, placing the items inside. "I am *not* sweet."

"You've always been kind to me."

"You're easy to be kind to." He pushed the trunk closed and moved to the driver's side door, holding it open for me. "Now get in and turn the AC on. It's hot out here."

"Fine." I chuckled but did as he said. Once inside I held Emilia up, took her paw in my hand and made her wave. "Say bye to Uncle Luca."

"Oh God." He rolled his eyes, but a hint of a smile tugged at the corner of his mouth. He rubbed the top of her head. "Goodbye, Princess Piss-a-lot."

"Thanks, Luca," I sang.

"Buckle up," he said, raising his hand in a wave as he closed my door and started back toward his car.

Emilia settled on my lap, and I gently scratched the length of her back.

"Well, girl, what do you say we get out of here? There's someone I'd like you to meet."

EIGHTEEN

Dallas

I WAS SPRAWLED across the sofa watching some baking contest on Netflix when I heard Katie come in.

"Hey," I called. "You're home early."

"Yeah, we ran out of everything so we decided to close up." Her voice was on the move from the foyer, likely to the kitchen. "Crazy day."

On screen, one of the contestants was presenting their lopsided cake to a panel of judges, and I clicked my tongue.

"Oh, come on," I said to the tv, tossing the remote on the couch. "I was rooting for you. We were all rooting for you." I waited a moment, thinking Katie would appear in the living room at any second, but she never did. "Katie? Where'd you go?"

"Uh, I have something I need to show you," her voice chattered from the next room. "And tell you. To show *and* tell you. It's kind of a surprise. Actually, it's definitely a surprise."

"A surprise, eh?" I rose to my feet. "I'm intrigued. Does this have anything to do with those edible underwear we never got? Because I could use a snack—"

"Um, no," she said loudly, cutting me off. Nervous laughter floated through the air.

"So, where is this surprise?"

"In here," she answered. "In the kitchen."

"I see," I said, moving slowly from my spot. "Is it edible?"

"No, but it's definitely sweet."

I rubbed my thumb along my jaw. "Give me another hint."

"It's soft."

I pictured Katie in something lacy with a feathery robe over it. *That* would be pretty damn sweet.

I chuckled. "My mind is in the gutter here, Butter Bean."

"It's wearing a diaper," she added quickly.

"Did you kidnap Ella's baby?" I asked, before rounding the corner into the kitchen to find Katie standing there with a tiny, furry creature that resembled a baby Ewok in her arms. "What is this? You found a real-life teddy bear."

"She looks like one, doesn't she?" A smile stretched across Katie's face. "This is Emilia."

"Can I hold her?" I asked, already reaching for the little fluff ball.

"Of course," she said, relinquishing the pup to me. She couldn't have weighed more than six pounds, and she fit right in the curve of my arm.

"Look at you," I said in a syrupy voice I barely recognized as my own. The dog peered up at me through cloudy eyes and gave me a lick on the chin and a shake of her tail before settling into my arms. "Where did you come from, little lady?"

Katie launched into an animated story of how an elderly Emilia came into her possession after one of Luca's one night stands.

"I can't believe someone would do that," I said, holding the pooch closer to my chest.

"I know you weren't expecting another houseguest, but I promise it's only temporary until I can go back home."

"It better not be temporary," I said, kissing the top of the dog's head. "You can't bring something this cute in here and then take it away."

Katie's eyes lit up. "This is okay? Are you sure?"

Even if it wasn't, the look of sheer joy on her face would have made me do it anyway. I would adopt a million Emilias if it made her happy.

I grinned. "I love her already, and if you take her away, I *will* cry."

She held her intertwined hands to her chest, her eyes wide. "So, you... want to adopt her with me?"

"I do. I mean, if that's okay with you." My inflection rose as though I were asking a question, and in a way I was. It wasn't like I was asking her to share a plate of spaghetti with me. This was a dog—a real, living being. I knew what the implications of adopting a dog together were. It was a commitment, both to the pup and to each other. And I wanted her to know I was all in.

Her eyes shined. "I would really like that."

"Did you hear that, Emilia?" I cooed. "You got yourself a new mom *and* a dad today."

Katie wrapped her arms around me, sandwiching the pup between us. "Now is probably a good time for me to tell you that she can't really hear so well."

"That's okay." I kissed her forehead as Emilia stirred, giving each of us a lick. "I think she knows."

"Katie, hurry. You've got to come look at her," I said later that evening, stroking the end of Emilia's ear. She was curled in a ball on the bed between my head and Katie's pillow, snoring softly.

The buzz of her electric toothbrush stopped, and I heard her spit before she rushed out of the bathroom.

"Is she okay?" Katie asked. "Is something wrong?"

"No, no. She's perfect." I reached for her hand and pulled her onto the bed. "Look how cute she is when she sleeps. What do you think she's dreaming about?"

She giggled as she climbed under the covers and propped her head on her hand. "Probably about a time when she was able to sleep without two people staring at her. Or when she could control her bladder. Poor little thing."

"Who knew you could Amazon Prime puppy diapers?" I chuckled.

"What will Jeff Bezos think of next?"

We were completely smitten with our new dog. We'd quickly discovered she had to go out at least every couple of hours unless she was sleeping. She'd popped a squat right in the middle of the kitchen with no warning while we were cooking dinner, soiling the one diaper she'd come with. We were in a frenzy trying to find something that would cover her until we could wash and dry the one we had and order more. Katie had somehow managed to throw together a crudely fashioned pair of undies for her using a cut up maxi pad and one of my old bandanas.

I traced my fingers along the length of Katie's arm, leaving behind a trail of gooseflesh.

"This is incredible," I said, releasing a contented sigh.

"Watching Emilia sleep?" she asked. "I have to agree."

"No. I mean, yes. But not just that." I brushed my thumb across her cheek. "*This.* You and me."

"Yeah, it *is* pretty incredible." She covered my hand with hers and turned so she could kiss the inside of my palm. "Speaking of incredible things, have you decided what to do about The Slacks show at the Ryman?"

I blew out a breath and laced my fingers through hers. "Not exactly."

"Are you having doubts about potentially joining the band?"

"Kind of," I admitted. "Don't get me wrong—the guys are great. We get along, and I think we work well together. But…"

"But what?"

"The Ryman is one thing, right? I do the gig, and then I come home to you." I kissed the top of Emilia's head. "To both of you. You might even be able to come watch me play."

"Of course I will. I wouldn't miss it for anything."

"But what happens when the band goes out on the road?" I asked. "When I'm back to living on a bus and in hotels, being gone more than I'm home. The Slacks are huge, but they haven't quite reached the status of Midnight in Dallas. I'd be gone even more. They have their own small tour coming up, plus they're opening for Ed Sheeran next year. I'd be out of the country for at least six months."

She studied my face. "You love touring, though."

"I did love it. But that was before… this." I gestured between the two of us. "That was before I had you to come home to. And Emilia."

"But you'll always have us to come home to."

"You know what I mean."

"I do," she said gently. "It would be an adjustment, but it's nothing we can't handle. Just look at how long we waited for each other. We are the World Champions of waiting."

"That's just it, though," I admitted. "I don't want to wait. Having you here these last few weeks has given me a taste of what our life could be like, and it's perfect. It's everything I could ever want."

Her gaze dropped to the mattress. "I don't want you to give up something you love just because you're worried about how it will affect us. I'm not going anywhere."

"*You* are what I love." The words dove from my mouth before I could stop them, splashing between us like someone shouting 'cannonball' as they plunged into a lake.

I held my breath as I watched her eyes widen, then fill with tears.

"Dallas," she whispered.

I shifted my gaze toward the ceiling and scrubbed my hand down my face, wishing I could scoop up the words and put them back in my mouth. What I'd said was true, but what if it'd been too much too fast for her?

"I'm sorry. I—"

"I am?" she asked softly, cutting me off.

"Yes." I turned toward her and cupped her cheek as a faint smile played on her lips. "Katie, I've always loved you. It just took me a long fucking time to get up the nerve to do something about it."

"I love you too," she said finally, her emotion-filled voice music to my ears.

"Really?"

She nodded. "Really."

I rose up onto my elbows and kissed her tenderly, Emilia still nestled between us.

I broke our kiss and tucked a wild strand of her hair behind her ear. "I really want to make out with you right now, but it feels weird with her here. Like having a baby in the bed or something."

She laughed and gazed down at our snoozing pooch. "You're right. It's kinda weird."

"What do you say we change locations?"

She waggled her brows at me. "How about you come get in the shower with me?"

"Didn't you already take a shower this morning?"

"Yes, but one can never have too many showers." She flashed me a salacious grin that could convince me to spend the rest of my life in the confines of my black-tiled bathroom.

"Is it me you love or my water pressure?" I teased, as she gingerly rolled out of bed and slipped her T-shirt over her head.

"Can I only pick one?" she asked, shimmying out of her cotton shorts.

I crossed my arms over my chest in mock indignation. "Yes."

"Hmmm…" She propped one hand on her hip and tapped a finger to her chin.

"You really have to think about it, huh?"

"Well, you have great water pressure. It's a tough call."

"That's it." I launched myself from the bed. She squealed as I chased her into the bathroom. Once I caught her, I pressed her back against the wall and tickled her sides. "Just for that, I'm going to use this amazing water pressure and my fancy shower head to torture you."

I slid my hand down her chest and caressed her inner thigh, causing a soft moan to escape her beautiful mouth.

"Oh no. Not the shower head." She pressed her palm to

her chest in feigned concern, and a grin quirked on her lips. "What can I say? I guess I'm just a glutton for punishment."

NINETEEN

Katie

I WAS DREAMING I was at a rave. The bass was thumping through my limbs, but the sound was muffled, as though I were on the roof above the party. I'd never been to a rave before, but I imagined people moving to the beat, their arms flailing around like one of those windsocks outside of a car dealership. But instead of dancing, I was frozen in place. Because this wasn't *actually* a dream. I was very much awake.

I was lying motionless on a table in a room cold enough to be a morgue as the MRI machine clanged around me at Vanderbilt Hospital. The technician had given me a pair of headphones to drown out some of the noise and a washcloth to lay over my eyes in case I felt claustrophobic. Even with my eyelids pinched shut and the scratchy cotton over my face, I still sensed the proximity of the machine. The warm condensation of my own breath that formed against the cage clamped snuggly over my head made my nose itch, but I couldn't move, so instead, I tried to distract myself.

I thought about the fact that my HVAC *still* wasn't fixed,

but that only made me more frustrated. Then I thought back to my most recent appointment with the pelvic floor physical therapist. I'd only been a couple of times, and I liked her well enough. The idea of essentially working out *down there* was still strange to me, but if it helped me to get closer to Dallas—to have more than just oral sex—it was worth it. We'd been too scared to try again since that first time, but I didn't know how long I could wait.

My mind floated to the lobby where he was waiting for me, and I started counting the seconds until I would be out there with him. We'd leave, get coffee, and head back home to Emilia, and all would be right with the world again.

An extra loud bang from the MRI startled me into losing count somewhere in the upper two-hundreds. So I shifted gears, mentally running through everything I had to look forward to over the next couple of days. It was the first Friday of September, and I was thankful for the busy weekend ahead that would hopefully keep me from stressing about what the results of this test would reveal. I'd gotten Saturday off so Dallas and I could take Emilia to the Dog Days festival at Centennial Park, and then Sunday was our first family dinner in several weeks. I had two days full of puppy snuggles and time with my favorite people. All of that was waiting for me on the other side of *this*.

Dr. Childers had gotten me an appointment with her brother-in-law earlier in the week, and I was grateful. If it hadn't been for her I would have been waiting *months*, not days, to get closer to an answer. The neurologist, Dr. Madison, looked like a mad scientist with his wiry hair and thick glasses, but he'd seemed nice enough at our first meeting. It had gone much like the appointments I'd had before but with the added scheduling of the MRI. I'd asked him what he thought we could be dealing with, but he'd said he didn't like to speculate. At first that had made me more nervous, but Dallas pointed out it was better that way. No sense in getting us worried unless we needed to be.

After what felt like hours the clamoring of the machine stopped, and the table I was on slid out of the tube, pulling me from my thoughts.

"Alright, Ms. Kelley." The technician's voice was loud enough that I could hear her over the noise-canceling headphones as she lifted the cage. "We're all done."

I pulled the washcloth off my face and squinted, my eyes adjusting to the fluorescent lighting of the stark-white room.

"You doing okay?" she asked.

"I'm just glad it's over." I sat up, shivered, and rolled my neck from side to side. "When will I get the results?"

"Your doctor should be in touch with you early next week," she said as I swung my legs over and hoisted myself off the table before she could lower it. "With our portal system sometimes you'll receive the report before the doctor does, but I tell patients you're better off not looking at it. Without context, things can sound a lot scarier than they are, and you don't want to spend your weekend going down the Google rabbit hole over something that's probably nothing."

I laughed. "Yeah, I've been down that road before."

"Very hazardous," she said. "Enter at your own risk."

"I won't," I promised, though I wondered if I'd have that same conviction when the notification I had test results waiting for me popped up on my phone.

"Good. Do you remember how to get back to the locker room so you can change?"

I nodded. One of the most humiliating parts of this whole ordeal had been my walk of shame from that very locker room to the testing area wearing nothing but my undies and a gown as flimsy as a potato sack, so I'd paid close attention on our way just in case I needed to make a quick escape.

"Then you're free to go," she said, handing me the key to the cubby that held my things. "Have a good weekend."

"You too," I called over my shoulder, already halfway out of the room, clutching the gown closed around me. The cold tile pierced through the paper-thin socks they'd given me to wear as I rounded the corner and swung open the door to the locker room.

I shoved the tiny key into my locker and grabbed my clothes, shoes, and purse out and skipped to one of the stalls. Once I was dressed I dug my phone out of my purse to see if I had missed any messages.

There was only one. A smile spread across my lips when I opened the text to find a selfie of Dallas holding an iced coffee.

I giggled as I read the accompanying text.

Dallas: Did you know that UberEats delivers to hospital waiting rooms? Love you a latte. See you soon!

"Katie, really." Dallas squeezed my hand over the center console of his car. "You know I don't care where we are as long as we're together. And this one cares even less." He gently scruffed the top of Emilia's head where she was sitting in my lap.

Tears pricked at the corners of my eyes, but I blinked them back. "I know, but I was looking forward to this. It's like the Fourth of July all over again. Being excited about something only to have my body come along and ruin it."

Luckily, it wasn't as severe as the previous debacle, but I was so worn out and weak that simply walking around was a struggle. Not even thirty minutes into the festival, I was toast. I tried to push through, not just for Dallas or Emilia but for me. My legs grew heavier with every step as though I were trudging through thick mud. All it took was for Dallas to catch me swaying ever-so-slightly on my feet, and I'd bought us a one-way ticket back to the car.

"The day is *not* ruined," he insisted. "We can still have fun."

"If you consider naps fun, then yes, we can have a blast," I said through a yawn.

"I do. In fact, I can think of a lot of fun things we can do from the comfort of the bed."

He waggled his brows at me, and I covered Emilia's ears.

"Not in front of the baby," I teased.

He smirked. "Get your mind out of the gutter, Butter Bean. I was referring to watching more *Hell's Kitchen*."

"Ah, you know I love to fall asleep to the ambient sounds of Gordon Ramsay calling someone an idiot sandwich."

"As you should. The man is a worldwide treasure."

I relaxed a bit as we fell into an easy conversation about which season three contestant we were rooting for during the short drive home. As we pulled into the parking garage, my phone pinged from my lap.

My stomach lurched when I saw it was a notification from my Vanderbilt portal:

You have one test result ready to view.

"The MRI report is in." My fingertips prickled with temptation. It would be so easy to swipe across the screen and see what it says. I could just—

"Don't do it," Dallas said. "Remember what the technician told you."

"Yeah, yeah." I hit the button on the side of my phone, making the screen go black. "I know."

We parked and got out to go inside. I shoved my phone inside my back pocket, then tucked Emilia in the sling I wore across my chest.

"So, about tomorrow." Dallas threaded his fingers through mine, swinging our hands lazily. "Are you ready to tell them about the MRI stuff?"

I shook my head. "Not yet. I've told Jo, of course, but I don't want to tell everyone else until we know something more concrete."

"Fair enough," he said. "Are you ready to tell them about us?"

I pretended to think about it, but there was no thought needed. I felt safe in the bubble Dallas and I had built, and I was ready to share that with everyone else. Jo and Derek already knew, of course, and McKenzie had figured it out too, but she'd proven herself to be a vault. She'd kept my secret safe from Ella and Liv, and she'd even swooped in to change the subject earlier in the week when Ella mentioned the idea of me participating in some speed-dating event she'd heard about on the radio.

"I'm sure someone will inevitably ask if I'm bringing a date to Ella and Cash's wedding next weekend."

"And?" he pressed. "You are, right?"

"I don't know."

"What?" His forehead creased, and his eyes widened. "What do you mean? I thought we'd go together."

I flashed him a coy smile. "*Well*, you haven't asked me yet."

"Oh." His entire body sagged with relief. "I guess I haven't."

Dallas stopped in his tracks, and I bounced backward against his resistance.

"Katie." He tugged me toward him and grabbed my other hand, Emilia nestled between us. "Will you be my date to the wedding?"

I beamed up at him, the notification and my phone forgotten in my pocket. "I thought you'd never ask."

TWENTY

Dallas

"Oh, and I think this goes without saying, but please don't bring 'Brandi with an i' to our wedding next weekend." Ella pinned Luca with a steely glare over the dinner table at Jax and Liv's house Sunday evening. The dishes had already been cleared, but we lingered around the table. "Or anyone else whose name you do not know."

Luca straightened in his chair and crossed his arms. "I'll have you know I'm going stag. This wild buck can't be tamed."

Ella mimed sticking her finger down her throat and gagged.

"What about you, Katie?" Liv asked. "Are you bringing a date?"

Katie's cheeks flushed, and she chewed her bottom lip. "Well… it's… *new*."

Jo and Derek exchanged a knowing glance.

"Who is it?" Liv squealed. "How did you meet?"

Everyone except Jo and Derek looked at Katie, but I could

feel her eyes on me, even though I was trying not to look at anyone.

"Katie, girl, don't do this to me," Antoni pleaded. "You know my heart can't handle suspense."

"It's true," Nate said. "He'll only watch shows that have all the episodes available."

"That's absolutely right. I binge my tv shows the way God intended." Antoni returned his focus to Katie. "Now, spill!"

I raised my eyes to meet Katie's, and Ella immediately noticed and covered her mouth with her hands.

"Oh my God!" she shrieked.

"What?" Liv cocked her head to one side, her forehead wrinkled in confusion.

"Am I missing something?" Luca asked.

Everyone looked from me to Katie then back to Katie, but her eyes remained on me.

"Why are you looking at Dal—" Antoni gasped, cutting himself off. "*Shut up.*"

"Am I just an idiot or what?" Luca threw his hands up. "What's going on? Who's Katie's date to the wedding?"

"Me." I cleared my throat and smiled, not taking my eyes off Katie. "She's going with me."

Antoni slapped his hand on the table. "Well, hot damn!"

"Finally." Cash raised a fist in the air.

"Oh my God," Liv said, fanning her eyes. "I'm gonna cry." She jumped to her feet and embraced us both, and the next thing I knew, the entire room was buzzing with congratulations. Grace and Sam led Liv and Jax's kids, Jonathan and Chloe, in a round of applause, though they definitely didn't know what on earth they were clapping about.

Our friends celebrating our relationship was the last piece

of a puzzle being clicked into place. My heart swelled with every hug and supportive word.

"And we knew the whole time," Derek bragged, squeezing Jo's hand.

"Congrats, man." Luca clapped me on the back and gave me a genuine smile. "It's about damn time."

Katie caught my eye from across the table, and drumsticks banged on my heart, building to a crescendo. We were finally together, and now, everyone knew.

Jax leaned back in his chair, eyes crinkled in a grin. "Look at us. Who would have thought one meet and greet would lead to all of this?" He gestured around the table. "One chance meeting brought so much into our lives."

"These are the kinds of stories we report on all the time," Jo said, resting her hands on her growing belly. "But they never cease to amaze me."

Every face surrounding me was lit with joy and shining eyes.

"We've got a lot to be grateful for," Cash said.

"Yes, we do." Antoni snapped his fingers. "We have a wedding next weekend, a baby on the way, and Dallas finally got his head out of his ass. It's a blessed day."

I wadded my napkin and tossed it at his head.

"And Dallas has that gig with The Slacks on Friday," Derek said. "We're gonna see him back on the Grammy stage soon. I can feel it."

"That's incredible, Dal," Cash said.

"Wait." Luca snapped to attention. "You joined another band?"

"Nothing's official yet," I explained. "This is just a test run."

"But you're considering it?" he asked.

"Yeah, I am." I wasn't sure why, but I got the distinct feeling he was shocked by my news. "Why? Is that a bad thing?"

"No. Of course not." Luca cleared his throat and smiled, but it didn't reach his eyes. "Good for you."

His words fell like quarters in a wishing fountain, hard and flat.

"We actually have some news too." Cash reached out and squeezed Ella's shoulder.

My stomach tightened when I noticed the tearful glance Ella gave Cash.

Katie's face fell, anticipating what I knew she'd feared for some time.

"We're moving to California. Cash, Grace, Sam, and I." Ella forced a smile through glossy eyes, and Liv pulled her best friend into a hug, clearly already aware of the news.

"What?" Luca asked. "When?"

"After the first of the year," Grace answered.

"Work just has us in LA so often," Cash added. "And I feel like I'm missing a lot with Bettina."

Ella nodded in agreement. "It wasn't an easy choice, but we want to be together, and right now that means needing to be in Cali. We're keeping the house, and we'll come back a lot. Y'all know we won't be able to stay away."

"Oh wow," Derek said, scrubbing his hand down his face. "What does that mean for the bakery?"

"We're still figuring that out," Liv answered, and I wished I could reach across the table and take Katie in my arms. Her cheeks were pink, and her lips were folded in like she was trying to stop herself from crying.

"Well shit." Antoni pressed a hand to his mouth and

exchanged a worried glance with Nate. "That makes what I'm about to tell y'all a lot more difficult."

My concern was mirrored by the faces around me as Nate covered Antoni's hand with his own.

Antoni shifted in his seat. "Nate's granny hasn't been doing well, and his mama's gonna need some assistance."

"My dad does what he can, but his health isn't all that great," Nate explained. "Mom needs help getting Granny to her doctors' appointments and keeping up with things at the house."

"You're moving?" Liv's lip quivered. "To Nebraska?"

Antoni nodded, silent tears spilling over onto his cheeks.

"When?" I asked.

"The first of October," Nate answered, pulling Antoni into him and kissing his temple.

Katie covered her mouth with her hands, and my arms ached to hold her.

"Fuck." Jax sniffed, rubbing Liv's back.

"I didn't mean to rain on your gratitude parade." Antoni smiled, dabbing beneath his eyes with his ring fingers.

"Let's do another Sunday dinner before everyone leaves," I said. "We've got to have one more."

"We're gone on our honeymoon for a week after the wedding," Cash said, panic flashing in his eyes.

"We're out of town for work the next week, but what about the one after that?" Jo asked with a hopeful smile.

Grace frowned. "Cash and I are in LA that week."

"So... this is our last dinner together?" Luca's voice cracked slightly.

"No," Ella said quickly. "Of course not. Just for... a while."

The room was silent except for the sounds of sniffles as

the reality of what this meant settled over us like a coat of ash. The flames of excitement from moments before had been extinguished, replaced by a bittersweet sadness so thick in the air I thought I might choke.

Everyone was being pulled in different directions. Possibly even me. I swallowed the lump that formed in my throat. If I ended up back on the road, we might never be in the same place at the same time again.

Luca scrubbed his hand down his face and scooted his chair back. "I've got to get going."

"Luca," Katie said, holding out her hand as though she could stop him. "Wait. Don't leave."

"I'll see you guys next weekend." Luca didn't look at anyone as he left the room, and seconds later we heard the front door shut behind him.

It echoed throughout the house like the crack of a book snapping shut. It was the last line of a chapter, the period at the end of a sentence. And a new chapter was starting, whether we liked it or not.

"Did you see Luca's face?" Katie asked later that night as we lay in bed with Emilia nestled between us. "I'm worried about him."

"I know," I said, stroking her shoulder. "I am too." Katie and I had both tried calling him, but we'd been sent to voicemail.

Her chin trembled. "Everything's changing."

"Hey." I swiped a tear from her cheek with my thumb. "Not everything. You and me—*this*— isn't changing."

As soon as the words left my mouth I wondered how true

they were. I didn't doubt how solid our relationship was, but if I did end up joining The Slacks things *would* be different.

Katie nodded, but a shadow passed over her puffy red eyes. Though she didn't say as much, I suspected the same thought had crossed her mind. That even we weren't safe from the winds of change.

Moments like these would be replaced by games of phone tag and late-night FaceTimes wedged inside a bunk while I was carted from one city to the next. But more than that, who would take care of Katie if I was on the road? Who would go to doctor visits with her or cook for her after she had a tough day? Everyone was going their separate ways, moving away and moving on. If I joined the band, I'd be no different.

"What if I get some crazy diagnosis and it changes things too?" She drew her arms in, snuggling deeper beneath the covers and let out a soft sigh. "You hear about it all the time. Someone gets sick and people kind of pull away. They don't know how to act around them so they just… disappear."

"Katie, I know everything feels scary and unknown right now. Because it is," I said. "But one thing I know for sure is that we're still going to be a family. Everyone loves you, and no amount of distance is going to change that. I know that if the shit hits the fan, they're going to rally for you. *I'm* going to rally for you."

If I was on the road and she needed me, I'd come home, contracts and commitments be damned. *If only it was that simple.*

She smiled at me through tear-stained lashes. "Promise?"

I couldn't guarantee a lot of things—who would move away or where we'd be months or even years from now or what our lives would look like—but one thing would remain true. I would always love her.

"I promise." My hand found hers, and I placed a gentle kiss along the tops of her fingers.

Her shoulders seemed to relax a little, and we laid in comfortable silence for a moment before she spoke again.

"Do you think the MRI is going to show anything?" she asked. "Do you think it's something bad?"

I swallowed hard, and my chest stiffened. The truth was I didn't know, and I was scared. But the last thing she needed was to hear my worries when she was already dealing with so much. I needed to be her rock, to care for her the best way I could, and that meant shoving my own fears aside.

"I hope not," I answered finally. "But whatever happens, it's you and me, okay? I'm always going to be here for you."

She lifted herself up, careful not to disturb Emilia, and moved to lay beside me, resting her head on my chest. I tightened my arms around her and kissed her forehead.

I didn't know what tomorrow held, but right now all that mattered was holding her.

TWENTY-ONE

Katie

"It's probably nothing. I mean not *nothing,* nothing," I rattled off, wringing my hands. "But then again, if it *is* nothing, why bring me in here, you know?"

When Dr. Madison's nurse called Monday morning and asked if I could come in sometime that week to go over the test results, I was filled with a mix of emotions. Surely if it was something life-threatening she'd have requested I come in right away. But if it wasn't anything to worry about, would they really have me come all the way to the office only to tell me the report was all clear?

"Breathe, Butter Bean." Dallas placed his hand on the small of my back as we stepped onto the elevator Wednesday afternoon. "This might just be their protocol."

"Right." I took a deep breath in through my nose as the doors groaned closed.

I tapped my foot and rolled my lips inward, unable to stop myself from fidgeting. Dallas wrapped his arms around me as we ascended to the tenth floor, and for the first time all day my limbs let go a little.

"Will you go back with me?" I whispered, even though we were the only two people on the elevator.

"Of course I will."

We weren't in the lobby long when a nurse with a messy blonde bun called my name. She led us to an exam room, took my vitals, and let us know the doctor would be in soon before closing the door behind her.

Dallas squeezed my bouncing knee from where he sat beside me. "It's gonna be okay."

I nodded and looped my arm through his, thankful I wasn't alone, both figuratively and literally. Jo had called that morning, trying to ease my nerves, and McKenzie kept me distracted at work with a game she'd made up on the spot called Bachelorette Party Bingo.

I was at the bakery when I'd gotten the call about the appointment, and I'd kind of freaked out. McKenzie talked me down and kept me calm until I could get ahold of Dallas after his rehearsal with The Slacks.

A knock on the door snapped me to attention.

"Ms Kelley," the doctor said, entering the room. "Good to see you again." He turned to Dallas. "I don't believe we've met. Dr. Madison."

"This is Dallas," I said, and he extended his hand to the doctor.

"I'm Katie's boyfriend."

"I'm going to call you Mr. Kelley then." Dr. Madison gave us a jolly grin, quite taken with his own joke, as he took a seat across from us.

Dallas squeezed my hand. "Happy to be."

"That's what we like to hear." He clicked around on the computer for a moment until the large monitor above him sprang to life with some kind of black and white scan.

In the top right corner, I saw my name and held my breath. "I called you in here so we can go over the results of your MRI." Dr. Madison focused on me with his droopy eyes.

"Yes," I said. "And I'm really hoping you're gonna tell me it was nothing." Even as the words left my mouth, I knew it wasn't nothing. The way I'd been feeling was not nothing, and the solemn, stony expression on Dr. Madison's face told me it was most definitely *something*.

"I wish I could tell you that." His shoulders dropped, and he gave me a rueful smile. "I really do."

"Oh." A chill washed over me, and I pressed my fingers to my mouth. Dallas tightened his grip on me, but I couldn't bring myself to look at him.

I didn't ask what he found because I didn't want to know. All I wanted to do was hang onto these last few seconds of the in-between. The last remaining moment of *before*. Before Dr. Madison and his empathetic basset hound eyes sent my world spiraling off its axis.

Dr. Madison laced his fingers together, holding my fate in his hands. I wished he would just hold it there a little longer. Or maybe forever. He could let me walk out of here and live in ignorance.

"Katie, you have Multiple Sclerosis. Your MRI showed that you have lesions on your brain and…"

Dr. Madison's lips were moving, so I knew he was still speaking, but his voice faded until it sounded like I was listening to him from inside the deep end of a swimming pool.

Before had slipped right through my fingers, and all I could do was watch helplessly as it floated away.

FEAR, SADNESS, ANGER, AND RELIEF LINKED ARMS INSIDE ME, enveloping me in a group hug. Terms like 'brain and spinal lesions' and 'infusions' echoed inside my head.

Dallas had sprung into action, being my words when I couldn't find any. He'd asked questions, taken notes on his phone, and by the time we made it to the car, he was already talking about treatment plans. But mentally I was still in the exam room, the words Dr. Madison said and their possible implications stacking up inside me like bricks.

What if I got worse? What if it got to a point that I couldn't work? At least not to the extent that I did now. How would I survive? Would I qualify for disability? What if I got to a point that I needed help? What if I didn't *want* help? What if…

My heart hammered inside my chest, steady like the wipers that scraped across the windshield.

What if Dallas realized he hadn't signed up for this?

"Hey," Dallas said softly, squeezing my knee from the driver's seat. "You haven't said anything since we left the doctor's office."

"I'm giving you an out." The words sprang from my mouth before I could chicken out or change my mind.

"What?" he asked. "What are you talking about?"

"An out," I repeated. "I'm giving you one. If this is too much to handle. If *I* am—"

"Stop," he interrupted me, his voice low and soothing. "You're freaking out. Understandably so. But I told you last night, and I'll say it again—"

"But that was *before*," I blurted out. "Before when whatever was wrong with me was still just a possibility. I wouldn't blame you if you didn't have MS on your girlfriend bingo card, and it's okay if you need to walk away. You shouldn't have to try to fix me."

He fell silent, his eyes focused on the road ahead, and I wondered if he was considering what a future without me would look like. Easier, probably. A lot less stressful.

A couple seconds later, he pulled off into a Starbucks parking lot and stopped in a spot facing the highway.

"What are you doing?" I asked as he cut the engine, but he stared at the busy, rainy street ahead.

My chest constricted, preparing for the worst. "Dallas?"

"I don't want to 'fix' you." He turned toward me, his eyes full of emotion. "Listen, I know you've just had a lot thrown at you, but I need you to hear me when I say this. I am all in on this thing with you, Katie. There's nothing that's going to change that. I promised you I'd always be here for you, and I meant that."

My bottom lip trembled. "But what if things progress? You heard what Dr. Madison said. It could get worse. I don't want you to feel like you're stuck with me."

"I don't know how to get this through your head, but I love you," he said with a soft chuckle. "There is nowhere I'd rather be than with you. I can't be stuck if I never want to leave. In fact, if anyone in this situation is stuck, it's you. With me. We share a fur child together. You can't get rid of me that easily. I'd do anything for you."

Tears spilled over onto my cheeks. "Even drink an iced coffee?"

He let out an exaggerated sigh that gave way to a broad smile. "I gotta draw the line there, Butter Bean."

"You *said* anything."

"But coffee is not meant to be cold."

"*Anything.*"

"Fiiiiiine."

I took his face in my hands and pressed a kiss to his lips.

"I love you."

"Love you too." He wiped away the dampness on my cheeks with his thumbs. "Even if you drink coffee milkshakes."

I smiled, but a small nagging feeling lingered in the pit of my stomach. Maybe this wasn't too much for him right now, but what if one day it was?

"Okay, coffee and then what?" he asked. "*Hell's Kitchen* marathon and a nap?"

"Actually, I need to get back to the bakery to finish Ella's cake."

His forehead creased. "Don't you think you should rest? Take some time to process everything?"

I shook my head. The last thing I wanted to do was think about this any longer than I had to.

"I've got to get that thing finished," I said. "It's my gift to Ella and Cash, and it's got to be perfect."

"Then how about I come with you and be your assistant?"

"No, that's okay. It'll be good for me to be able to go to work and get in my zone."

He opened his mouth as though he might protest but changed his mind.

"I'll call McKenzie if I need help," I added.

Dallas studied my face for a moment. "Promise?"

"Promise." It was a little white lie, but this was something I needed to do on my own.

TWENTY-TWO

Dallas

"You guys sounded great," Lisa said when I walked off the Ryman stage with The Slacks Friday afternoon at soundcheck.

"Great?" Deacon pumped a ring-covered fist in the air before gripping my shoulders. "We sounded fucking amazing. Thanks to this guy right here keeping our shit tight. Magic, bro. That's what you are. Fucking magic." He let out a wolfish howl.

Guilt washed over me. I hadn't exactly given the performance my all. Drumming had come as easy as breathing to me from the second I'd picked up my first pair of sticks. It was so effortless that only those closest to me would notice if something was off because technically my performance would be perfect. But my heart wasn't in it. It was nowhere in this room because it was with Katie. After getting her diagnosis she'd thrown herself back into work like nothing was different, even though everything had changed.

"Uh-oh. Did one of the roadies give you espresso again?" Mack teased Deacon with a pointed look, but he didn't seem to notice as he skipped away and started chatting up a pretty blonde.

Bennett scooped his curls out of his eyes. "Nah, he's just high on life. I haven't seen him this happy since he found out Harry Styles called him one of the most underrated vocalists of our time."

Lisa slapped his arm. "Not so loud. It took him six weeks to stop talking about that. If he starts up again we'll never hear the end of it." She shook her head and steered Bennett toward the backstage area with Mack on their heels.

Knox sidled up beside me and nudged me with his elbow. "You good, man?"

"Yeah," I lied. "Just, uh, a little nervous about getting back out there."

He narrowed his dark eyes on me. "Bullshit."

"What?"

"I said that's some bullshit." He chuckled and gave me a warm smile. "I mean that as respectfully as possible, of course. You're one of those magnificent freaks of nature who doesn't *get* nervous. You own any stage you're on, and today was no exception. But no, there's something else."

I ran my hand along the back of my neck, wiping away the beads of sweat that had formed.

"Deacon's not pressuring you over this, is he? Because I'll talk to him."

"No, no, he's been great," I said. "You all have."

"I'm sensing a 'but' coming."

I puffed air through my lips. "No... I mean, yes, but no."

"Follow me," he said, clapping me on the back.

And I did. I trailed behind him as he led me through the auditorium, all the way through the front of the house where we wove through the pews and up the stairs until we reached the highest point of the venue.

"Best seat in the house in my opinion," he said, sliding into the top row of the balcony, dead center, and patting the worn wood beside him.

"Would you believe I've never been up here?" I asked.

"It's beautiful, isn't it?"

I marveled at the way the late afternoon sun poured through the stained glass windows, casting colorful beams of light along the walls of the Mother Church. We were the only people out front except for someone sweeping near the first row. A single spotlight shone on the vacant stage, making the floor that had held up so many legends shimmer.

"This is where I like to sit when I need to gain a little... perspective," he said after a moment.

"At the Ryman?"

He gave a hearty laugh. "At any venue. Don't get me wrong, this one is definitely my favorite. But I think the last row center holds a certain power."

"Why's that?"

He held out his hand and gestured around the room. "Because you can see the whole picture from here, and I've always found comfort in that."

"How so?"

He scrunched up his face in thought. "Because it reminds me there's more to life than "—he nodded toward the stage—"*that*. I love being on stage and getting to do what I do for a living, but this is where I feel most like myself. Where I'm just Knox, a guy who loves his wife and dog and music and playing stupid video games that are probably rotting my brain." He paused for a moment. "As musicians, as artists... We spend our lives creating experiences for other people.

They come to our concerts, listen to our albums, and watch our videos to feel something and then they move on to the next thing. To them, we are a moment in time."

I tilted my head to look at him, but his gaze remained focused on the stage.

"Don't get me wrong, man. It's an amazing gig and one I'm grateful to have," he said, finally turning toward me. "But you know what happens when you're busy creating moments for other people? You stop creating them for yourself. Your entire life becomes about making other people feel something."

"Why are you telling me this?" I asked.

He shrugged. "Like I said, this is where I come when I need to gain some perspective."

His words settled over me like a misty rain, gentle enough not to soak you but steady enough to let you know it was there.

I'd always thought being on stage was what I wanted. Back when Derek and the rest of the guys first posed the idea of breaking up the band I'd kind of lost my shit because I was so blinded by what *I* wanted that I didn't stop to consider what *they* wanted.

Over the course of the last couple months, Katie and I had created so many beautiful fucking moments together. For the first time, I had a life that didn't revolve around music, and in doing so I found parts of me I didn't know existed. Quieter parts. Ones where I was happy just being in someone else's orbit instead of feeling the need to be the center of the damn universe.

The silence was pierced by the sound of Knox's phone chirping. He pulled it from the pocket of jeans and smiled down at the screen.

"I've got to get going," he said, rising to his feet. "My wife just got here. We're gonna grab an early dinner before the show."

"Have fun. And thanks, man." I extended my hand to clasp his. "For showing me the view."

"See you tonight," he called over his shoulder as he started toward the exit.

I relaxed into my seat, resting my arm over the back of the pew, enjoying the stillness. But as I took in the whole picture, there was only one person I wanted front and center: Katie. More than that, I wanted her right by my side, to love her and take care of her as long as she would let me.

When I considered my identity, who I was at my core, I'd always thought of myself as a musician first. Everything else was secondary until her. I had no idea what the future held for me, only that being in a touring band was no longer part of it.

"Are you sure you're feeling up to this?" I asked Katie as we strolled inside the Ryman that evening.

"Yes," she insisted.

I raised my brow. "And you'd—"

"Yes, I would tell you if I wasn't," Katie finished for me, already anticipating what I was going to say.

I was probably asking too much, but ever since her appointment with Dr. Madison we'd both been kind of walking on eggshells. It was like her diagnosis was an uptight houseguest we were afraid of disturbing. Her first infusion wasn't until early the following week, and though it sounded scary the way the doctor had explained it made it seem fairly simple. All she had to do was sit back and relax while the medication with a name I couldn't begin to pronounce was dripped into her veins through a catheter. Dr. Madison felt confident she'd feel a noticeable difference even after one treatment. We just had to get through the weekend.

"I'm sorry," I said, wrapping my arm around her shoulders. "I know you've had a busy week. You've worked a lot of late nights so you could finish the cake and we've got the wedding tomorrow. It's a lot."

"Yes, but I'm fine, Dallas," she said. "Nothing's changed. Not really."

Hadn't it though? The proverbial monster under the bed was no longer creeping around in the dark, casting shadows along the walls. It was out in the open now, ready to attack.

"Okay." I kissed the top of her head.

"Look who it is." Deacon beamed when we made it to the backstage area. "The man of the hour. And is this your beautiful moon goddess?" He stepped forward and took Katie's hand in his, kissing the top of it as he knelt in an exaggerated bow. "Enchanté, mademoiselle."

Her eyes widened. "Oh, um, hi. Hello." She shot me a quizzical glance and then whispered, "Am I supposed to curtsy or something?"

"You must be Katie," Knox said with a chuckle, jumping in to save her from Deacon's overdramatic ass. "I'm Knox. That's Deacon. You'll have to excuse him. He watched *Ratatouille* last night, and now he thinks he's French. Except that's the only French phrase he knows."

Katie laughed and her face relaxed, immediately put at ease by Knox's warm presence.

"The one with the toothpick hanging out of his mouth like a common hillbilly is Mack, and the one with the shaggy-dog hair is Bennett." Knox pointed out each of the guys, and they waved. "And this is our manager, Lisa."

"Hi," Lisa greeted, bounding forward to throw her arms around Katie. "I'm a hugger. Dallas has told us so much about you that I feel like I know you already."

"Same here," Katie said with a smile. "It's nice to meet y'all."

"Your friends are still coming tonight, right?" Lisa peered around us as though we might be hiding a couple of stowaways.

"Yeah, they'll be here soon," Katie answered. "Jo texted and said she and Derek met McKenzie at Will Call and should be in shortly. They're going to meet me at our seats. Thanks again for doing that, by the way."

"Don't mention it," Lisa said with a wave of her hand. "I'm so glad you guys could be our guests tonight. Speaking of, we should get you out there before the show starts."

Katie's eyes sparkled when she grinned. "I can't wait."

I pulled her into me and whispered in her ear. "Are you good?"

She stepped up on her tiptoes and kissed me. "For the millionth time, yes."

"Come with me," Lisa said, already steering Katie from the room. "I'll show you to your seat, and we'll make sure your friends get in okay."

"Break a leg." Katie tossed a smile at me from over her shoulder before disappearing around the corner.

"Alright, Slacks. Let's fucking do this," Deacon bellowed, emitting a guttural yell.

"You ready, brother?" Knox asked, squeezing my shoulder.

"It's showtime." I sucked in a breath and blew it out.

It was time for the final curtain call, and I was ready.

I'D FOUND KATIE FROM MY SPOT ATOP THE DRUM RISER during the opening beats of the show, and my eyes returned to her like some sort of homing device throughout the entire hour and a half we played.

We performed for a sold-out crowd, and I gave them everything I had and then some. It was exactly what a final performance should be. Of course, nobody but me knew it would be my last. There would be no pomp and circumstance, no big celebration. I would walk out of the Mother Church that night, hand in hand with the woman I loved, and that was more than enough.

I counted off our last song, the last I would ever play on a stage. The audience roared, and I locked eyes with Katie, who was dancing and cheering for us. It was a hell of a way to go out, in my favorite venue of all time, with Katie front-row center. I loved the high of being on stage, but I didn't love it near as much as I loved being with her. I didn't know what this meant for me or what I would be doing. Maybe I'd produce or keep playing sessions, even though the idea of working on another song with Prose Gold made my brain hurt. But I'd do it with a smile on my face if it meant going home to Katie every day.

I didn't need to have it all figured out. For now, I just wanted to enjoy the moment. I wanted to feel every second of it.

After the last notes rang out and we took our bows, I walked off the stage to a standing ovation with my head held high. I felt good. For the first time since the band split up, I had a sense of direction.

Deacon nearly toppled me over once we got into the dressing room.

"That was fucking brilliant," he yelled. "Did you see that standing O?"

Mack wiped sweat from his forehead with a towel as Lisa handed Bennett a bottle of water.

"What do you say, Dallas?" Deacon asked, gripping me by the shoulders. "Can we make it official?"

My eyes flickered over to Knox, who raised his brows in a silent question.

I swiped my beanie from the counter. "I'm sorry, fellas. I think my journey ends here."

"What?" Deacon's mouth fell open. "Do you need more time to think about it? I wasn't trying to be pushy. You know me, I tend to get a little over excited."

Bennett pushed sweaty strings of hair out of his eyes. "Yeah, you don't have to decide now. Take your time."

"I promise this has nothing to do with you guys," I said, shoving my hands in my pockets.

"Did someone else offer you more money?" Deacon asked. "Because we'll double it. Triple it even."

"That's not it. Trust me, if I was going to be in another band, it would be The Slacks," I promised. "No question."

Deacon's mouth was drawn in a frown. "What is it then?"

"Tour life isn't for me anymore," I answered, and Knox gave me an encouraging nod. "My world is here."

"I get it," Mack drawled, extending his hand to me. "But I hate to see you go."

"We all do," Bennett said.

"I'm gonna miss you, bro." Deacon threw his arms

around me and clapped my back in an almost aggressive embrace. "You are magic, man." He took my face in his hands and gave me a loud kiss on the cheek. "Never forget that."

"We can always see if Patrick will come back," Mack said, a mischievous twinkle in his eye.

"Fuck that guy," Lisa and Deacon said together.

Lisa groaned. "I'll learn to play the drums myself before that ever happens."

"Sorry, Lisa." I leaned down and gave her a hug. "I appreciate everything."

"Come on." Knox patted me on the back. "I'll walk you out."

I said my goodbyes and headed into the hallway with Knox.

"So, what's next for the amazing Dallas Stone?" he asked once we'd managed to get away from the bustle of the backstage area.

"I don't actually know," I admitted with a shrug. "Just gonna enjoy the view for now."

He nodded. "Good man."

"What about you? Will you get some time off soon?"

"It's funny you should ask. I actually got some news today. It's gotta stay between us, though. I haven't told those guys yet."

"Of course, man."

"Kira's pregnant." A broad smile stretched across his mouth. "We're having a baby."

"Dude." I gave him a congratulatory hug. "Congratulations. That's amazing."

"Thanks," he said leaning against the wall. "So, you might not be the only one who needs a change of pace."

"Wow, you really did need to gain some perspective, huh?" I teased.

He chuckled. "I did, and I'll be honest, up until we were on that stage tonight I didn't know what I was going to do. But when I looked out into the crowd, I saw a guy about our age with the cutest little girl on his shoulders, and she was clapping her hands and having the time of her life. That's when I knew. I can live without all of this, but that guy... he had the best seat in the house. And I want that."

"That's beautiful, man. I'm happy for you."

"Deacon is going to lose his shit," he said with a laugh. "At least until he finds out he's going to be the godfather. Then I think he'll forgive me."

"Do you think they'll replace you and keep going?"

He shook his head. "Deacon has always been destined to be a solo act, and I think this might give him the push he needs to finally go out on his own. I hope so, anyway."

"Me too," I said, holding my hand out to him. "Knox, it's been a pleasure."

"Keep in touch, alright? Take care of that moon goddess of yours." He smirked as I turned away.

"You too," I called over my shoulder as I started down the hall, pulling my hat over my hair. "And your moon... *baby*."

The last thing I heard was the echo of his laughter as I left the backstage area and stepped out into the front of the venue, becoming just another face in the crowd.

When I locked eyes with Katie from across the room, my chest tightened, filled to the brim with love and admiration for her. With her by my side I'd always have the best seat in the house.

TWENTY-THREE

Katie

"How are you feeling?" Jo asked, leaning over the table, keeping her voice low.

"I'm good." Even though I didn't feel great physically, it had still been a perfect day.

Ella and Cash's wedding was beautiful, but it was hard to believe it would be the last time we'd all be together for a while. I'd told Jo and by proxy Derek as well as McKenzie, but I wanted to wait to tell everyone else until after the wedding.

"I can't wait for everyone to see the cake," McKenzie said. "You knocked it out of the park. You hit that fucker into another zip code."

"Thanks." My heart swelled. I'd worked a lot of late nights making the five-tier confection. It had taken me twice as long as usual to pipe on the lace detailing because my hands wouldn't stop cramping, and I'd nearly forgotten the topper that morning, but everything had come together in the end.

"She's about to toss the bouquet," Antoni said, rushing

over to where I was sitting with Dallas, Derek, Jo, and McKenzie at Santa's Pub. "Don't y'all want to catch it?"

They'd rented out the doublewide trailer that housed the dive bar for the reception because it was one of the places they'd been on their first date. We were seated in the gorgeous tented space out in the parking lot just after sunset.

"No, thanks." McKenzie scrunched her nose. "Isn't that bad luck or something?"

"The old wives tale is that you'd be next in line to get hitched," Antoni explained.

"Like I said." McKenzie took a gulp of her punch and shuddered. "Bad luck."

Antoni grinned and held out his hand to her. "I don't believe I know you yet, but I like you already."

"I think I'm sitting this one out too," I said, and Dallas held a hand to his chest, pretending to be offended. "What? My feet hurt."

"Oh, what the heck." Jo hoisted herself off her chair. "I'll go."

She waddled toward the center of the space where they'd created a small dance floor. Ella was facing us, stunning in her strapless, low-cut sweetheart gown.

A small gaggle of women, including Grace and Jo, gathered behind her, as did the majority of the partygoers, so they'd have a great view of the mad dash to be the next one at the altar.

"Alright, everyone," the DJ announced in a cheesy car-salesman voice. "It's time to toss the bouquet. Who will be the lucky lady to catch it?"

"I can think of about a *million* other things I'd rather catch," McKenzie muttered under her breath, and I choked on a laugh. "Including, but not limited to the flu, a punch to the nose, or my death."

"Are y'all ready?" Ella asked, a broad smile on her face as the girls cheered.

The photographer knelt on the floor just ahead of us to capture the big moment.

Almost in slow motion, Ella lifted her right arm to toss the cluster of pink peonies in her hand. The force of her toss caused her dress to slip ever so slightly, allowing one pert boob to pop out for millisecond before dipping back into the silk fabric like the moon behind the clouds.

Antoni gasped, and McKenzie clutched my arm.

"Was that..." Dallas trailed off.

"A wardrobe malfunction?" Derek finished, blinking slowly.

"A *malfunction*?" Antoni cackled. "Honey, her whole ass titty jumped right out of there and said 'peek-a-boo.'"

"Did... that... just happen?" I asked through spurts of laughter.

Ella, who was blissfully unaware of what had just transpired, turned to see Grace emerge victorious from the group, holding the bouquet up like an Olympic torch.

"And did the photographer catch it?" Dallas nudged me and pointed to the young man who must have heard because he turned around wide-eyed, clearly stunned by the peep show he'd had a front row seat to.

We erupted into a cacophony of snorts and giggles so loud we managed to catch the attention of Jo, who wrinkled her brow.

"What's so funny?" she asked as she returned to her seat.

We responded in a chorus of guffaws, unable to squeeze out so much as a single word.

Jo laughed awkwardly. "I don't get it."

Tears streamed down my face, and my shoulders shook as I attempted to straighten up so I could tell her, but before I could, Luca appeared at our side.

He rubbed his thumb and forefinger along his jaw. "Am I seeing things, or did Ella's headlight just pop out of her dress?"

"Headlight?" Jo shook her head, still confused.

"You know," Luca said, patting the spot over his heart. "Her tit."

Jo gasped, throwing her hands over her mouth. "No!"

"Yes," we cried, dissolving once again.

"Oh my God," Jo whispered. "We have to tell her."

"That sounds like a great way to ruin her entire day," McKenzie said, crossing her arms over the front of her cute black jumpsuit. "There's nothing she can do about it now, anyway."

"Exactly." Luca smirked. "No sense in getting her titties in a twist."

McKenzie sputtered out a laugh as Luca shrugged and walked away.

I couldn't help but notice her eyes linger on him as he disappeared through the crowd.

"Hey," McKenzie said, leaning into me. "Who was that?"

"That was Luca."

"Oh." She looked taken aback. "*That's* Luca? Really?"

"Yeah," I said. "Why?"

"No reason." She shrugged. "I'm just surprised, I guess."

"Why?"

"I... I don't know." Her cheeks pinked. "After all the stories I've heard about him, I just expected him to look more like an asshole."

I laugh. "And what does an asshole look like?"

"Not like an underwear model for Calvin Klein."

"I'm sorry. I should have introduced you. I just figured you knew who he was because of the whole band thing." She pulled a face. "No offense to your boy Tommy Lee or anything, but Midnight in Tuscaloosa—or whatever they were called—wasn't really my style. I mean, I know who Jax is now because he married Liv and that Derek dude because he knocked up Jo."

I stifled a laugh, but before I could say anything else, Liv approached.

"Are y'all ready to bring out the cake?" she asked.

McKenzie rose to her feet and extended her hand to me. "C'mon. It's your time to shine."

"THAT CAKE IS A WORK OF ART, KATIE," LIV SAID. WE WERE standing off to the side while everyone made a beeline for the dessert table as Cash and Ella finished the ceremonial cutting of the cake. McKenzie was still handing out pieces, and I laughed when she swatted away Dallas' hand for attempting to take two.

"Ella deserved the perfect cake for her special day."

"It's stunning." Liv sighed, a far off look in her eyes. "I still can't believe they're moving."

I followed her line of sight to where Cash and Ella stood with little Bettina sandwiched between them as Grace fed her a bite of buttercream.

I curled an arm around her. "I know."

She sniffed. "For as long as I can remember, it's always

been me and Ella. Ella and me. I guess I kind of took for granted that it would always be that way."

"Ella living in a new zip code won't change that," I said as she dabbed at her eyes. "And you know we'll always have each other."

"I know." She leaned her head against mine. "I don't tell you enough how much I love you, Katie. How thankful I am to have you in my life. Finding out that Ella's moving and then Antoni... It's been kind of a reality check for me. A reminder that sometimes I get so caught up at home and work that I forget to give the people I care about their flowers, you know? That I don't tell people how much they mean to me until they're about to leave."

My heart squeezed. "Well, if it makes you feel any better, I don't have plans to go anywhere."

She took a deep breath and turned toward me. "I've been thinking about the future of the bakery."

"Oh?" I gulped.

"I'm not there anymore, and now that Ella will be leaving I think it's time to make some changes."

My eyes stung as I prepared myself for the worst.

She'd thank me for the years I'd spent working there, but tell me that with Ella leaving it would be too painful to keep the business open. That she'd hope I would understand. That she'd give me the best job reference and do anything to help keep me afloat till then and—

"I'd like to give the bakery to you."

And she would give me the—

"Wait. *What?*"

"Shit. I'm sorry." She touched my arm, the only thing that let me know this was actually happening and wasn't some crazy dream. "I hadn't intended to spring it on you like this. I just got all emotional, and it felt right in the moment."

"I just..." I trailed off, shaking my head. "I thought you were going to tell me you were closing the place. I never imagined..." I never imagined she was going to suggest giving me a whole damn bakery.

"I don't want to close it," she promised. "That place holds some of the best years of my life. Of *our* lives. It means the world to me, but I can't give it the love it deserves, and Katie, nobody loves that bakery more than you."

"But you can't just *give* me a business. Liv, this place was your baby. I know you're sad about Ella leaving, and I am too, but you should think about this—"

"I have," she said, cutting me off. "After things with my music career took off and after Ella found out she was pregnant, we knew we'd want to make a change in the not-too-distant future. We planned to bring you in as part owner one day, but her moving kind of changed things, and now we want to give it to you."

"That's... wow... That's so amazingly generous and kind, but you can't just *give* it away," I insisted. "It's worth a fortune."

"I don't want the money." She placed her hands on my shoulders. "What I want is to keep Livvie Cakes in the family with someone who loves it. Someone who deserves it. I could sell it, but it's always been your dream to have your own place. Of course, you can change the name. You can change anything you want because it would be yours, but you don't have to make any decisions right now. Take your time."

"You're really serious." I studied her shimmering eyes. Liv had no idea about my MS diagnosis, and I wanted to wait until after the wedding to tell everyone. The focus of the weekend needed to be on Ella and Cash and on all of us being together one more time before Antoni moved.

She nodded. "I am."

My chest swirled with emotions. How could I accept a gift like that? I was still trying to figure out what having MS meant for me. What if I took over the business only to get worse and be forced to let it go? That would break my heart, and I'd be letting Liv down.

Before I made any decisions, I wanted to talk to Dallas. This wasn't just my future anymore. It was *ours*.

"Say you'll think about it?" Liv steepled her hands in front of her as though she were praying. "That's all I ask. And if it's too much, I promise I'll understand."

"Okay," I said finally. "I'll think about it."

"Good."

She beamed, and I threw my arms around her.

I longed to say yes. Liv was handing me my dream on a silver platter, but there was so much more to consider now. She was right—I loved the bakery, but because I loved it I needed to consider if I was the right person to take it over. What if it just wasn't the right time?

"Thank you, Liv," I whispered, and she squeezed me tighter.

My heart exploded with gratitude knowing I had people in my life whose belief in me was so strong they'd give me something that meant so much to them.

"Ew, are you guys crying?" McKenzie's voice pried me from my thoughts. "I leave you two alone for like five seconds and I come back to *this*."

I looked up to find her smiling at us, and I laughed through my tears.

"Alright, bring it in," I said, holding an arm out to her.

"Group hug."

"Y'all are so weird." She rolled her eyes but joined in anyway.

Ella noticed us enveloped together and screeched happily, and she, Grace, and little Bettina came barreling toward us, pausing only long enough to grab Jo's hand and drag her along.

The next thing I knew, I was cocooned within the safety of some of my favorite people on the planet. I didn't know what my answer would be or what the future held. I didn't know if I would be brave enough to try or what would happen if I failed. But it didn't really matter.

All that mattered was that if I fell, I'd always have a soft place to land.

TWENTY-FOUR

Dallas

I PUSHED inside the trailer where Antoni and Nate were on stage singing an off-key rendition of "Islands in the Stream." Everyone was gathered around them, swaying with their drinks in the air. I was attempting to squeeze through the crowd to get to the bar when I noticed Luca in the back corner, spinning a bottle of water on the table where he sat alone.

"Hey," I said, pulling out the chair across from him after snagging a beer. "What are you doing over here by yourself?"

He shrugged, his dull eyes staring past me.

I leaned forward, resting my elbows on the scratched wood as I studied him. I'd known Luca my entire adult life. We butted heads more often than not, but he was still like a brother to me. And something was wrong. It had been building for a while, but it didn't really click with me until he'd left dinner on Sunday. Maybe because I'd been in my own head for so long that I couldn't see it.

I cleared my throat. "Is everything okay? We tried to call you after dinner the other night, but you never answered. Ella and Cash said you were screening their calls too."

"I know." He ran his hand along the back of his neck. "I'm sorry. I should have taken the call. I just... couldn't."

"Why not?"

He sat quietly for a moment and picked at the label on his water bottle, peeling away the flimsy plastic.

"Luca, what is it?" I asked.

Finally, he lifted his eyes to meet mine. "It's *everything*. Everybody's fucking moving on and changing. Everybody but me."

"What? I don't understand. I haven't changed."

"You have. And even though you get on my last goddamn nerve most of the time I guess I was sort of counting on you staying the same. Because if you did, then it would make it okay that I have no fucking clue what I'm doing with my life."

"I don't know what I'm doing either," I admitted, scratching behind my ear.

"Bullshit. You've got Katie. You're joining The Slacks."

"I'm not. Joining them, I mean."

"What? I thought—"

"I haven't told anyone yet. Not even Katie. I couldn't do it. I didn't *want* to do it."

"But music is your life. It's everything to you."

"It was. You're right. But ever since Katie... I can't explain it. My priorities, everything I thought I knew about myself has kind of shifted."

"You can't give up your career, though. Katie wouldn't want that."

"See, that's just it. I don't feel like I'm giving up anything. I'm gaining something so much greater. I have a life now. One that belongs to me and not thousands of other people. I can have dinner with Katie every night and pretend to fight about what we're going to watch on Netflix. I can sleep in my own bed instead of a bunk that's two sizes too small."

"But... like... what are you gonna *do*?" He scrunched up his face. "Become a Real Housewife of Nashville? That doesn't sound like you."

I chuckled and took a swig of my beer. "I have no idea. I guess I can keep doing sessions while I figure it out, or I could try my hand at producing. Or maybe I'll be like Derek and find something I love that has nothing to do with music. I don't have to have it all planned out yet. And neither do you. It's okay to not know."

He opened his mouth to say something, but before he could get a word out, McKenzie appeared at the table.

"Hey, Katie's been looking for you," she said. "She said she needs to talk to you and that if I spotted you inside while I was finding the bathroom I should send you out to her."

"Oh, is she okay?" I asked, my mind immediately going to the worst-case scenario. Between her work schedule, the concert, and the wedding, I'd been worried this weekend would be too much on her.

"Go find out for yourself." McKenzie rolled her eyes and lifted her chin. "I'm not your secretary, Tommy Lee."

Luca nearly choked on a sip of water.

"Anyway, I told you," McKenzie said with a shrug. "My work here is done. Now, go forth and find Pammy."

"Yeah, okay, I got it," I said, rising to my feet. "I'm going."

"Tommy Lee?" Luca smirked as she walked away. "How come I never thought of that?"

I held up a finger. "Don't even think about it."

When I found Katie, she was sitting at a table outside, staring at the dance floor with a dazed look on her face.

"Hey," I said, placing a hand on her shoulder. She was so zoned out she jumped at my touch. "Are you feeling okay? Do we need to get you home?"

She turned, grabbed my arm, and tugged me down into the chair beside her. "I have to talk to you."

"Are you okay?" I asked again. "Do you want me to pull the car around?"

"What?" She shook her head furiously. "No, no. I'm fine. I mean, I'm not fine. I'm kind of freaking out."

I fixed my eyes on her. "What's going on?"

She sucked in a breath and blew it out. "Liv talked to me today. About the future of the bakery."

"Fuck," I muttered. *"Today?"*

My heart sank. I couldn't believe Liv would tell her the bakery was closing at Ella and Cash's wedding, of all days. It was already an emotionally charged day with it being our last time all together for a while. Why would she—

"She wants to give it to me," Katie said, her eyes wide.

My mouth dropped open. "She *what*?"

"It's crazy, right? I still can't believe it myself." She rubbed a finger along her brow. "She said that with Ella moving, they want to make some changes, and nobody loves that place more than me. She made me promise to think about it."

I blinked, at a loss for words.

"Crazy. It's crazy, isn't it? I can't take on a whole business. Not right now," she said, speaking quickly. "It's not like she's asking me to take care of her cat, which to be fair would be a huge ask because that cat is psychotic. But this is a business. That other people, including me, depend on for their livelihood. I couldn't. I can't. It's... out of the question, right? It's not possible."

I stared at her, my mouth slack, my thoughts scattering like confetti being tossed in the air.

When I didn't say anything, Katie tilted her head and looked at me as though she were peeking in a window to see if anyone was home.

"Dallas?"

"Why isn't it?" I finally asked.

"Why isn't it what?"

"Possible. Why is that so crazy? Liv's right. You do love it more than anyone, and you've always wanted to have your own place."

"But..." she trailed off, her gaze falling to her hands in her lap. "What if my health gets worse? What if I take it over and it fails? I can't be the person responsible for running Livvie Cakes into the ground. What if—"

"But what if you don't get worse?" I countered. "What if you make that place even better? Katie, this is a once in a lifetime opportunity. This is your dream."

"Yes. A dream. And sometimes dreams are just that. *Dreams.* Once upon a time I dreamed of being the sixth member of the Spice Girls. Sometimes these things don't happen because they're not supposed to."

I couldn't help but grin. "The world wasn't ready for Chef Spice."

"I'm serious," she said, stifling a laugh.

"So am I. The only thing that would be crazy is if you didn't at least seriously consider this."

"What if I can't do it?" Her voice was small as she

wrapped her arms around herself. "This is a huge undertaking. There are just too many unknowns right now with my health, and I don't know if I should take something like this on alone."

"Who said anything about doing it alone?"

"Dallas, are you listening?" she asked, placing her palms over her temples. "Liv would be stepping out completely. Ella is *moving*."

"Yeah, but you have me."

"You're going to be back on the road before long. No offense, but what good are you going to be hundreds of miles away?"

"I'm not going anywhere."

"But... What do you mean?"

"I'm not joining The Slacks."

"No. Nope, nope, nope." She crossed her arms over her chest. "I'm not letting you turn down the band for me. It's not happening."

I shrugged. "It's already done. I told them last night after the show."

"But why? I don't understand."

I covered her hands with my own. "Katie, when the band first split up, I was lost. My entire sense of purpose, my sense of self was shot to hell."

"You'll find it again," she said. "I know you will."

"That's just it. I *did* find it, but it had nothing to do with music and everything to do with you." I squeezed her fingers. "For so long, I thought music was it for me. So much of my identity was wrapped up in it that when it was gone, I didn't know what to do with myself. But then I started spending more time with you and everything clicked into place. I love being able to see you every day, go to the grocery store, and curl up with you and Emilia every night."

"But you have so many fans who adore you. I saw it last night at the show. People loved seeing you back on stage. Are you sure this is what you want?"

"I don't need to be adored by thousands of screaming fans. I only want to be loved by you. And I want you to be happy. This is your dream, and I want to do anything I can to make sure you get it."

"What about *your* dreams?"

"You're not hearing me. Life with you—a simple, quiet, beautiful life with you—*is* my dream. I can pick up some sessions here and there while we get the business running and still be home in time for dinner. So, what if we did this thing together? I know my experience is limited, but I'd have the best boss on the planet showing me the ropes." I leaned in as though I were telling her a secret. "And I don't know if you know this about me or not, but I'm actually pretty good in the kitchen."

"In fact, I do know that about you." Her lips curled into a smile. "I love the idea of you staying here, but are you sure? You'd really want to do this with me?"

"I really want to do this. Plus, the idea of you being my boss might have just unlocked some sexual fantasies I didn't know I had."

She giggled and cocked her head to one side. "Well, I guess I have a lot to consider then."

I leaned in and pressed a kiss to her lips. "Yes, you do."

TWENTY-FIVE

Katie

"I'M NEVER LEAVING THIS SPOT," I said as we sat on Dallas' couch and he rubbed circles into the balls of my feet. Emilia was enjoying a midnight snack in the kitchen since we'd stumbled in late and destroyed her slumber.

The wedding was beautiful, and I'd soaked up every second being with my friends. I'd even let Antoni drag me on stage to sing karaoke to an old Fergie song. By the time the night ended my cheeks hurt from laughing, and I was beat. It was that cozy, satisfied kind of tired I remembered feeling as a kid on those summer days Granny took me and Jo to the pool.

My entire body was sore, but it was worth every second.

Dallas worked his way up my calves, and I let out a contented sigh.

I didn't know what the future held for my MS. When I'd gotten my diagnosis just days before, I'd been terrified. It felt like an intruder, an unwanted guest. Like some imposing force I had to battle for rights to my own body.

But what if life didn't have to be that way? What if my MS and I could learn how to coexist?

I thought about what Dallas said earlier that night when I told him about Liv's offer. I'd been so focused on all the ways it couldn't work that I didn't stop to think about all the ways it *could*. In the car on the way home, I wondered: if Liv had made this offer before I got diagnosed with MS, would I have accepted?

And I knew the answer was a resounding yes. So, what had changed? The mask had been pulled off the Boogie Man, and now that I knew what I was dealing with, maybe we didn't have to be enemies.

Liv believed I could take over the bakery. She wouldn't have offered it to me if she didn't know I was capable. No, she didn't know about my diagnosis, but Dallas did. And he believed in me too. The question was, could *I* believe in myself?

"What do you think of Katie Cakes? Or Katie's Kitchen?" I lolled my head against the back of the sofa, my voice slow and dreamy. He stopped mid-massage, and I pouted. "Hey, I was enjoying that."

"Does this mean you want to do it?" He sat up straight with my feet still in his lap.

My cheeks flushed, and a smile spread across my mouth. "It would be really freaking cool, wouldn't it?"

"Is that a yes?"

"It's not a no." I wanted this. With Dallas by my side, what could go wrong? We made a great team.

"But is it a yes?"

I raised up and leaned forward, my legs still stretched in front of me beneath the creamy blush satin of my dress.

I bit back a grin. "It does have a nice ring to it, doesn't it?"

"Does this mean…" He trailed off and raised an eyebrow at me. "Are you saying yes?"

I covered my cheeks with my hands and squealed. "Yes."

"Are you serious?" He jumped up, tossing my feet aside. "Really? We're doing this?"

"We're doing this."

He pulled me to my feet and folded me in his arms. "Can I be your first employee?"

"That depends." I flashed him a coy smile. "Will you accept payment in the form of sexual favors?"

"As it happens that is the only form of payment I will accept." He kissed the tip of my nose. "Makes doing my taxes a breeze. Can you believe the IRS doesn't recognize blow jobs as a legitimate form of payment?"

"You're hired," I teased.

"Yes." He pumped his fist. "What's my first assignment?"

"Hmmm," I murmured, rubbing my hands over his pecs. He'd undone the top three buttons of his shirt, giving me a nice view of his tatted chest. "Perhaps a full body massage?"

"A *full* full body massage?" he asked, his tongue flicking over his lips. He traced the swell of my breasts with his fingertips.

I nodded as he dipped his thumb inside my dress and caressed my nipple. "Yes."

His eyes darkened. "Well, in that case." He threw me over his shoulder, and I giggled as he carried me toward the bedroom. "You enjoy your snack, Emilia," he called over his shoulder. "Mom and Dad have some important business to take care of."

Once we made it to the bedroom, he set me on my feet, and our laughter subsided as he tucked a loose piece of hair behind my ear.

"Have I told you today how beautiful you are?" he asked.

"Only about fifty times," I teased. "But what's one more?"

"You're the most beautiful woman in any room, Katie Kelley."

My breath caught in my throat as he placed tender kisses along my jawline, and my fingers fumbled with the remaining buttons on his shirt.

I pushed the sleeves over his biceps, sending it falling to the floor. "I think you're pretty beautiful too."

My hands moved over the tattoos on his chest of their own accord. I loved studying them, each one a constellation in my own personal sky.

He reached behind me and slowly unzipped my dress, his fingers sending chills cascading down my spine as he slipped the straps over my shoulders. The satin collected in a pool at my feet.

He drank me in, and I'd never felt safer or more loved.

"How did I get so lucky?" he murmured, unfastening my strapless bra and tossing it aside.

I wondered the same thing. I'd loved him for so long, but that love had deepened into something so much more. Sure, he knew how to make my heart race, but what I loved most was the way he made me laugh, the way he made me feel like I could do anything, *be* anything I wanted.

"We both did." I undid his belt and the button of his pants, gingerly sliding them down his muscular legs. He stepped out of them and picked me up, placing his hands beneath my bottom as I wrapped my legs around his waist.

I sighed when he laid me down gently on top of the comforter and began sweeping kisses along the valley of my breasts, all the way down my belly.

He hooked his fingers over the lace of my thong and slipped it down my thighs.

"You're perfect," he whispered, returning his lips to mine.

Our tongues moved in time together, perfect dancing partners to a song only we knew. As the heat of our kiss grew, so did the fire deep at my core.

I tugged down his boxer briefs, the only thing left separating us, and I took him in my hand, working my way up and down his length.

He moaned, pushing himself against my palm.

"Dallas, I want to try something," I said, my voice trembling slightly. "I want to feel you inside me."

He studied my face. "Are you sure? I don't want you to be uncomfortable, and if this is about me, you know I'm more than satisfied with what we do."

"This is about me," I promised. "I want this. I want *you*. I don't know if it'll work, but I really want to try."

"Okay," he said and kissed my forehead. "We'll just take it slow like your physical therapist said. We have all the time in the world. Now, roll over. I have a massage to give."

He grabbed the bottle of lotion I kept on the nightstand, pumping some into his hands. He warmed it against his skin, then took his time, kneading my muscles until they relaxed against his touch, melting like butter.

"How does this feel?" he asked, working his way from my shoulders down my back.

"So good." My eyes fluttered closed for a moment as he rubbed along my lower back, unwinding me like a ball of yarn.

He stretched his strong hands down my legs, making me feel like I'd somehow grown three inches taller. When he finished, he gently shifted me onto my back and began tracing circles into the bottoms of my feet and then up my ankles.

"Can you do this every night?" I asked, a satisfied smile spreading over my face.

"If it makes your face light up like that, I'll do it every morning too."

I sighed as he moved up my calves and then my thighs, his fingertips grazing over my most sensitive spot before trailing up my stomach. I writhed beneath him, craving more, wanting to feel him everywhere.

"Your skin is so soft," he murmured as his hands covered my breasts. He massaged them until the buds at their center perked.

He was straddling me, and I lifted my hips to meet him, running my hand along his hardness.

"I'm ready," I said, but it came out more like a whimper.

I continued to stroke him as he reached over to the nightstand and pulled out a condom and a bottle of lube that my physical therapist had recommended. He tore the wrapper with his teeth, and I took it, rolling it over his length.

"You promise you'll let me know if it hurts?" he asked as he applied some lube to the tip of the condom.

I nodded as he lowered himself over me, hovering just outside my entrance.

My body clenched in anticipation.

"Breathe," he reminded me, kissing my temple.

And I did. I inhaled deeply before guiding him inside me. My walls tightened around him, but he waited patiently as I breathed through it until my body relaxed enough to grant him entry.

"You feel better than I imagined," he whispered, kissing me tenderly.

"So do you." Nothing could have prepared me for how good it would feel to connect with him like this, to feel so close to him.

I tightened my legs around him, pulling him deeper inside

me as I curled my fingers in his hair. Everything about this moment felt so good, so right. I willed my mind to record every beautiful sensation so I could remember it all.

He kissed me as he moved in and out of me slowly, stirring me from the inside, making my muscles turn to liquid. Each thrust caused the blaze at my center to grow, and every kiss fanned the flames. He moved one hand down to my clit, rubbing gentle, rhythmic circles into my soft flesh, taking me higher and higher.

"Oh God." I moaned, wriggling beneath him as the tension built to a point of no return.

"Let go for me, Katie. I want to let go with you," he said in my ear, his words sending me falling over the edge with him diving in after me. My eyes closed so tight I saw bursts of color and light shoot across the backs of my lids.

We cried out, our bodies humming a tune all their own as I buried my face in his neck.

"Wow." His breaths came in shallow bursts as he sagged against me and kissed my shoulder.

I took his face in my hands and stared into his warm brown eyes. I'd always thought the term 'making love' sounded strange—like something a character on a soap opera would say. But at that moment I understood. It was the only way to describe what Dallas and I had done, the way we'd given ourselves to each other so completely.

"I love you, Dallas."

He rested his forehead against mine, and time stood blissfully still. "I love you too."

There was a shift in the days after the wedding beginning after my first infusion. For a moment, things were looking up. Dr. Madison had started me on some daily medication to help control my symptoms, and I continued to do pelvic floor physical therapy every couple weeks. By the beginning of October, I was feeling a bit better. Physically, anyway.

It was early on a Friday morning in the middle of the month. We'd woken to the sound of Dallas' phone chirping.

He grabbed it from the nightstand and squinted as he read the text. "It's Brandon from Blackbird. He wants me to go in for a session."

"Good, you should go," I urged, careful not to disturb Emilia who was sleeping soundly next to me.

"Nah. It's not until tonight." He tapped out a reply and returned the phone to its spot facedown. "If I go, who will be here to make you dinner?"

"Um, me?" He'd had offers for numerous sessions over the past few weeks, and he'd turned down every single one, giving excuse after excuse.

He chuckled and kissed me on the nose. "No way. Not after you've worked all day."

"Don't you think people will eventually stop calling you for gigs if you never accept them?"

"I'm fine with that," Dallas said through a yawn. "I've got different priorities now."

And that priority is me. Only me.

I took a breath and gave him a tight-lipped smile. My HVAC unit was *finally* being fixed next week after being delayed numerous times due to backordered parts. I hoped being back on my own turf would help Dallas chill out a little.

I loved his condo, but I missed my house. More importantly, I missed being able to do things on my own.

"Dallas, you know I can take care of myself, right?" I asked. "Besides, I'm feeling a lot better."

"And I'm going to make sure you stay that way." He stretched and rolled out of bed. "How about an omelet for breakfast with a side of fresh berries?"

I stifled a groan. "Sounds good."

"Coming right up," he said with a smile as he backed out of the room.

I pulled the covers over my head and mentally ran through my day. My time was consumed by coming up with new menu items and recipe testing, and I enjoyed every second of it. Katie's Kitchen was officially happening. I loved Dallas, but I was looking forward to being at work more and more. There, I was the master of my domain.

I'd been busy making preparations to take over the bakery after the first of the year with McKenzie by my side and Dallas up my—

"You want some turkey bacon?" Dallas called from the kitchen.

"Sure," I hollered back, returning to my thoughts.

Jo and Derek were coming in to try the apple dumplings I was working on, adapted from Granny's recipe. All my friends were excited, dying to be my first taste testers, and when I'd told the rest of them about my diagnosis they'd been beyond supportive. They checked in regularly and offered to pitch in any way they could. But with Dallas there, no one needed to. His entire life now revolved around making sure I was sleeping enough and not overdoing it. Unfortunately, we had very different ideas of what 'overdoing it' meant.

A few minutes later, Dallas returned to the bedroom with my breakfast.

"You don't have to do that," I said, sitting up. "Let me come in the dining room."

"Nonsense." He pinned me between the legs of the tray my plate was stacked on. "You stay here. Coffee or orange juice?"

"Coffee, please."

He nodded and disappeared from the room again.

I hung my head and sighed. It was hard to believe there'd been a time when breakfast in bed or having dinner cooked for me had been romantic. Now, it was a reminder of how my MS diagnosis had changed everything.

Autumn moved in softly, like a whispered secret. Treatment had left me with some relief, but as the cool winds of November came, my MS symptoms began to get worse. With my next infusion scheduled for March, I was left in a holding pattern. The milder days were nice, but the cold nights made it feel like my bones would snap under the lightest pressure. It didn't help matters that Dallas hovered over me as though I might shatter if he took his eyes off me for one second.

"Maybe you should turn in early," Dallas suggested as I sipped my tea where I was curled up on my couch. We'd been splitting our time between both our places and tonight we were at mine. "You've had a long day."

I loved how much Dallas cared and the way he worried about me. Really, I did. But sometimes it was too much. There were days I wanted to decompress by cooking alone in

Granny's kitchen or staying up a little too late to binge one of my favorite shows. But he was always there, scrutinizing my every move. It was exhausting having to spend every second doing something to take care of myself. Sometimes, I wanted to just *be*.

"And miss watching another episode of *Gilmore Girls*? Never." He chuckled and patted Emilia's head where she sat snuggled between us. "You know it's literally on demand. Netflix will be right here waiting for you."

"It's barely eight p.m." I pouted. "I know I keep grandma hours, but that's pushing it even for me."

"I know, I know," he said. "I just want to make sure you're getting enough rest."

"I am," I insisted. "And I'll get plenty of sleep after we see Luke kiss Lorelai."

"First of all, spoiler alert."

"It's not a spoiler if it's been out since 2004."

"Second of all, haven't you watched this show all the way through multiple times?"

"That's beside the point."

"Is it?"

I grabbed the remote from the coffee table. "Buckle up. I've got at least two episodes in me."

He peered at me through slits. "How about one and then bed? You've got an early day tomorrow."

"*Two*," I said again, scrolling through my Netflix queue. "This is not up for negotiation."

"One and then I'll give you another of those full body massages."

He waggled his eyebrows, and I bit back a grin. "Deal."

TWENTY-SIX

Dallas

"Are you sure you're okay?" I'd asked the question at least half a dozen times after Katie lost her balance and stumbled off the step stool in the kitchen while trying to reach an extra large dutch oven.

"I told you I'm good," she insisted. "I looked up too fast and got dizzy."

"You should have waited for me. I would have gotten it for you."

She waved me off. "You were in the shower. It's not a big deal. I'm fine."

I studied her face, searching for any signs she may be feeling worse than she was telling me.

"Are you sure you're not getting vertigo again?" I asked. "Maybe we should call Dr. Madison and get you an appointment just in case."

She lifted the lid off the dish and poured in a little oil. "It's not vertigo, okay? Trust me. I would know. This was nothing like that. I promise I'm fine."

Worry lined my face. As the weather had gotten cooler,

Katie's symptoms started creeping back in. The doctor had told us that was a possibility, that even with her daily meds and infusions scheduled every six months she could still have some trouble, especially around more extreme weather. As the nightly lows dipped into the forties, I'd noticed she was having more pain than usual. I knew this could have just signaled a minor flare, but what if it was something more serious? What if her illness was progressing?

"It's been a couple months since you went in. Maybe it wouldn't hurt to—"

"Dallas." She gripped me by the shoulders. "I'm fine. I've got too much to do right now anyway with Thanksgiving coming up. Work is nuts, and I can't get away."

"Can't or won't?" I asked.

"Both," she said, and I folded my arms across my chest. "You're making that face again."

"What face?" I asked.

"The one you make when you think I'm some damsel in distress. Like I can't take care of myself."

"That's not it." I sighed and pulled her into my arms. "I just worry about you."

"I know." She rested her chin on my chest. "And I appreciate that, but really, I'm okay. I just want to make this soup to take to Ella's since her entire household has the flu."

"I know you're the Top Chef and all, but I could just DoorDash them some soup from Panera or something."

She looked at me as though I'd suggested sending them a McDonald's Happy Meal to split.

"How about I make the soup, then?" I suggested, grabbing an onion off the counter. "Under your watchful eye, of course."

"I can do it," she insisted, reaching for the vegetable in my hand, but I pulled it away.

"I could really use the practice. And with me helping you in the kitchen at the restaurant soon, I'll need as much hands-on experience as I can get," I said, trying to reason with her. I could make potato soup in my sleep, but I knew if I made it about work she'd give in and let me do the heavy lifting.

She pursed her lips, and I could see my plan was working.

"My instincts are good because I learned from the best," I said with a wink. "But I need to work on speed if I'm going to be in the trenches with you and McKenzie. You won't be able to do everything."

"Well, I guess that's true."

It wasn't a total lie. I did need all the practice I could get, but Katie also needed to work on accepting help. Running a business was a lot of work even without a chronic illness. She needed to get more comfortable with delegating. Sure, I was being a little sneaky with how I was showing her that, but she was stubborn. It was the only way she'd ever willingly take a step back.

"Fine," she relented. "You can make the soup."

I grinned, tossing the onion in the air and catching it. "Where do I start?"

I CHECKED THE CLOCK ON THE WALL IN THE KITCHEN. KATIE would be getting in around seven, leaving me about ten minutes to put the rest of the boxes in the attic. It was the day before Thanksgiving, and she and McKenzie had been swamped at the bakery with holiday dessert orders. She'd been working crazy hours on top of not feeling well, so I wanted to do something to surprise her.

She'd mentioned the weekend before how she'd always decorated for Christmas early, putting up her hodgepodge collection of cozy decor while drinking hot cocoa. But between work and how she'd been feeling lately, she hadn't had the time or energy yet. We'd planned to do it together tonight, but I knew she'd come home exhausted, so I did it for her instead. I'd even gone out and bought her a real tree because the artificial one I'd found in the attic looked a little worse for the wear. While I was out, I'd picked up a few new decorations and a little red sweater for Emilia.

I admired my handiwork before carefully placing her Granny's star on top of the tree and putting the empty storage containers back in the attic. As I came downstairs, the oven timer dinged, alerting me the sugar cookies I'd made were done. After getting those out of the oven, I lifted the lid on the crockpot and stirred the hot chocolate. Between the cookies, the cocoa, and the scent of the pies I'd made for us to take to Liv's house for Thanksgiving, Katie's house smelled like a holiday wonderland.

The sound of a car door slamming outside let me know Katie had just gotten home, so I quickly ladled some cocoa into one of her Granny's Santa mugs and met her at the door.

"Something smells good," she said as she came in. "Did you light a candle?"

"Not exactly." I grinned and handed her the cup. "I made hot chocolate. I found your Granny's recipe."

She inhaled deeply, closing her eyes. "Smells like home."

"I have a surprise for you," I said, taking her hand, but her eyes landed on the stove behind me.

"Did you... make cookies?" she asked. "And pie?"

"I did, but that's not the surprise. Close your eyes."

"What are you up to?"

"Close 'em." Once her eyelids were squeezed shut I guided her into the living room that was illuminated only by the twinkle lights on the tree, the garland over the mantle, and the extra strands of lights I'd hung over the windows. "Okay. Open them."

She did, and her mouth fell open as she looked around the room. "Oh. Oh my."

"Do you like it?" I asked as she dropped my hand and stepped closer to the tree, running a finger along its branches. "The tree in the attic looked kind of sad, so I went and got a live one instead."

She nodded. "Yes... I see that."

"Shit. You're not allergic, are you?" I kicked myself for not thinking to ask.

"No." When she turned toward me, her eyes were glossy. "It's just... that sad tree? That was my Granny's. I've never not put it up."

My chest tightened. "Oh." In my excitement to surprise her, I hadn't considered the possibility that maybe the Charlie Brown tree was in the attic for a reason. "I'm sorry. I didn't mean to... I can take this one down and put the other one up."

"You don't have to do that. It's... a lovely tree. It is. This was all very... thoughtful of you."

Her slumped shoulders and down-cast eyes said otherwise. She glanced around the room, the somber expression on her face growing until tears spilled onto her cheeks.

"Katie," I said, reaching for her. "What is it?"

"I'm sorry." She dabbed at her eyes and shook her head. "It's just that... it all looks different, and I guess I didn't realize how attached I was to doing things the way my Granny did, like using her ugly old tree."

I pressed my palm to my forehead. "I'm sorry. I just didn't think." Of course this stuff was meaningful to her. It was the way she was able to keep her Granny with her during the holidays. "I'll take it down and—"

"No, no. Don't. You went through all of that trouble. Maybe I'm being overly sentimental, but..." She trailed off, her gaze rising to where the faded gold star rested atop the tree. "There's nothing left for me to do. The decorations are up, the pies are baked. You even made Granny's cocoa."

"Well, yeah," I said gently. "I wanted you to be able to come home and relax. We can put on a Christmas movie, and you can rest instead of having to decorate and bake."

"That makes sense. And I *am* pretty tired." She smiled, but it didn't reach her eyes.

"Are you sure?" I asked, feeling chastened and a little embarrassed. "I really don't mind taking it down and putting your Granny's tree—"

"I'm positive. Really." She cut me off and gave me a quick kiss on the cheek before placing her mug on the coffee table. "I'm going to change. Let's just forget about it, okay? You want to pick a Christmas movie for us to watch?"

"Sure." I tried to sound enthusiastic, but my excitement had waned. "And I thought maybe we could order in Chinese for dinner?"

"Sounds good," she called over her shoulder as she left the room.

A fist clenched around my heart as I wondered if *anything* I'd done that day had actually been good at all.

TWENTY-SEVEN

Katie

"I HATE THE HOLIDAYS." A guy named Caesar who looked to be in his mid-twenties with thin lips and a mop of curly black hair had been telling the group about his struggles with celiac disease. "I don't know how to make my family understand I can't just go to fucking Chili's like they can."

A woman next to him nodded in agreement. "My mom still takes it as a personal offense that I can't eat the desserts she makes at Christmas. Diabetes isn't like the tattoo I got on my ankle spring break my freshman year in college. I didn't get it to piss her off."

The circle of twelve people, including me, laughed politely. It was early morning on the first Tuesday of December, and the old Presbyterian church where the invisible illness support group met was drafty and smelled a little like mildew, but they had a really nice refreshment table set up. There was coffee with lots of dairy-free creamer options, as well as some gluten-free vegan donuts, granola, and an assortment of muffins. There was also a box that contained wheat and dairy, but it was very clearly marked and placed at the other end of the table.

"Seriously," Caesar said. "Last year, I went with them to some place back home in Columbus that my brother swore was gluten-free, and I ended up with the flare-up from hell. Blew up like Violet when she ate that gum at Willy Wonka's. Never again. I pick and *vet* the restaurant, or I don't go."

"And that is perfectly okay." The leader of the group, a nurse practitioner named Sarah, sat beside me and folded her hands in her lap. "Having those boundaries in place keeps you safe, both mentally and physically." She turned toward me with a warm smile. "Before we get too much further into our discussion I want us to all give a warm welcome to Katie. This is her first time with us."

"Hey Katie," Caesar said with a wave. "What are you in for?"

The lady next to him jabbed him in the side. "It's not prison."

"It sure feels like it sometimes," he mumbled under his breath.

"Would you like to introduce yourself?" Sarah asked.

"Um, sure." I sucked in a breath. "I'm Katie, and over the summer I was diagnosed with Multiple Sclerosis. I had my first infusion back in September and it helped, but I don't know. Extreme heat and cold seem to make my symptoms flare up."

"They do," the woman next to me said. She looked to be a few years older than me with short, pastel-pink hair. "I'm Margot, by the way. I've got MS too. The weather is a bitch. Sometimes I think I'd like to move to California or somewhere where it's a little more mild, but I love actual seasons, even if they don't love me."

Sarah chuckled before turning her attention back to me. "How can we best support you today, Katie? Is there anything on your mind you'd like to share?"

I glanced around the room full of strangers, and suddenly I wondered why I'd come. I already had a good support system. Dallas was always there for me. He did everything for me. But that was kind of the problem. He literally did *everything* for me. Even when I didn't want him to.

"You don't have to," Sarah said gently. "It's okay if you just want to observe."

Eleven expectant faces stared back at me, and I cleared my throat.

"I feel guilty even complaining," I began. "This is probably going to sound like a stupid question, but have any of you ever had a partner or friend be... well, a little *too* supportive?"

"What do you mean?" Sarah asked.

"I'm having kind of an issue with my boyfriend," I explained. "Not an issue. That makes it sound more serious than it is. It's just that he's always there, which is great, except he won't stop doing stuff for me. He treats me like I might break in half at any given moment—like I can't do *anything* for myself. It started out harmless enough. He would try to get me to go to bed a little early or make me dinner so I didn't have to cook. Which I know sounds great, right? But I *love* to cook. I'm a professional baker, and sometimes I just want to zone out and make some elaborate meal because it's fun for me. Yeah, it can be a lot of work, but it's a stress reliever for me too. I know that probably sounds ungrateful."

"Trust me," Margot said. "Not at all."

I gave her a faint smile, thankful to have my feelings validated.

"And then there was the whole thing about my Christmas decorations," I continued. "He put them all up without me and even went out and got new stuff because he said my Granny's old artificial tree was sad. It was a nice gesture. I know his heart was in the right place, but when I came home and saw my house decorated with a giant tree that wasn't even mine..."

"How did that make you feel?" Sarah asked when I didn't finish my sentence.

"Angry," I admitted. "Hurt. Like I'm just a bystander in my own life instead of an active participant."

"I went through something like that with my wife after my first bad flare-up," Margot said. "If I so much as stubbed a toe she was ready to call the doctor. We had our first big fight that year."

My heart dropped. That was the last thing I wanted. "What happened?"

She leaned forward on her elbows. "I'm a runner. Always have been. 5Ks, tough mudders, I love all that stuff. I'm not quite as fast as I used to be, of course, but I'm not half bad. I decided that year I wanted to train for the Boston Marathon. It had always been a dream of mine. When I tell you Nora was *livid*—she even went so far as to torch my Nikes on the grill to keep me from running. I couldn't take a walk around the block without her reading me the riot act. She wanted to make me tea and have me try whatever new holistic treatment plan she'd found on the internet that week. And she got on this kick where she ran me a bath every night. I *hate* baths." She shuddered. "I don't want to sit in a pot of swamp tits soup. Gross."

I choked on a laugh. "So, what did you do? How did you handle it?"

"I told her she was being a jackass." Margot shrugged. "A well-intentioned jackass, but a jackass nonetheless. I simply wasn't willing to live half a life in order to make her comfortable. Being chronically ill is hard enough. We don't need the added emotional labor of helping others cope with our diagnosis. That's on them."

"That's correct," Sarah said. "We are not responsible for anyone's feelings but our own. With that said, it's important to encourage those in a caretaker type role to have identities outside of this and to prioritize their own physical and mental health. And it's just as important for us to establish boundaries."

"Yeah." Caesar made a fist and held it out. "Tell that man of yours to get out of your kitchen."

"Tell him to come to my house," Margot teased. "Nora's a shit cook, and so am I."

She launched into a story about the time they'd attempted to make Christmas dinner for their kids that ended in a call to the fire department, but my mind drifted.

How could I tell Dallas to back off without hurting him or seeming ungrateful? I knew his concern and overprotectiveness was coming from a place of love, but I'd pushed my own feelings aside for so long I was starting to lose myself. It was tough not to get bitter on the hard days—to not get frustrated about the cards I'd been dealt. And if I allowed Dallas to continue doing so much that I became obsolete in my own life, the woman he'd fallen in love with was going to fade away.

THE NEXT MORNING, I ENTERED THE BACK DOOR OF THE bakery to a symphony of clanging metal and a string of expletives. My hands rose instinctively to cover my ears as I stepped inside to find McKenzie, red-faced and wild-eyed, pacing around the room. She hadn't even heard me come in.

"Hi," I said, and she did a double take, finally registering my presence. "Is everything okay?"

She pressed her lips together and steadied herself. "I just... I wish you would have given me a heads up that you were rearranging the kitchen last night. I mean, it's gonna be your place, of course. You can put things anywhere you want, but I would have come in a little early to familiarize myself with where everything is."

I opened my mouth and closed it again. "I didn't rearrange anything."

She crossed her arms and tilted her head. "Huh?"

"I didn't do any rearranging. I couldn't have. I was at the hospital with Jo till late last night. She went into labor, and little Addison Jade was born at 10:53 p.m."

"That's great," she said, "and we'll definitely circle back to that whole baby thing. But what do you call it when someone breaks into a place, doesn't steal anything, and just moves all your shit around?"

I moved past her and peered in the open cabinets, where pans were stacked so high and tight that it would cause an avalanche if you dared to move anything. Our ingredients were haphazardly crammed together, but there was at least *some* method to the madness. All of the flours were grouped together, including the extras we typically kept stored up top.

"Do you think Ella did it as some kind of going away joke?" she asked. "She *does* have a strange sense of humor."

"Ella would never mess with someone's kitchen." My

gaze climbed to the upper shelves, and as I looked around the room, I realized that every single one was empty.

"Well, *someone* did this," McKenzie insisted. "We need to check the security camera because the alarm didn't even go off. What do we do? Call the police and tell them we're on the weirdest episode of *Criminal Minds* ever—that someone has committed an act of psychological warfare by rearranging all our bakeware and stealing our step ladder?"

All the blood in my body rushed to my cheeks as I whirled on my heel. "What did you say?"

"Call the police? Psychological warfare? *Criminal Minds*?"

"The step ladder is missing?"

"Oh. Yeah. I was trying to at least put some of the stuff we don't need out of the way, but I can't reach it without the step stool. I've looked everywhere for it."

"Damn it, Dallas," I spat, letting out a guttural battle cry as I stomped my feet.

McKenzie's eyebrows shot up. "*Excuse* me?"

My ears were ringing, and the edges of my vision turned black. Jo had gone into labor, so I hadn't had a chance to talk to him after my epiphany at the support group meeting.

"It was him. I know it was."

"What? Why would he do that?"

"Because he's been up my ass constantly lately."

"What you and Tommy Lee choose to do in the privacy of your own home is none of my business, Katie."

I barreled on and ignored her quip, my fists balled at my sides. "Before Thanksgiving, I nearly fell off the step stool at home and he freaked out about it. I swear I can't so much as sigh too loudly in his presence anymore or he's ready to take me to the doctor. Ever since I started having another flare-up he's become obsessed, McKenzie. It started off innocuous enough, him telling me I needed to get more rest or making me dinner. But now I can't even cook in my own kitchen or put up my apparently-sad damn Christmas tree without him needing to *help* me, and his version of *helping* means doing every fucking thing and treating me like I might spontaneously shatter at any given moment, and I'm sick of it."

McKenzie frowned. "Why is your Christmas tree sad?"

"*That* is what you took from all of this? Seriously?"

She sighed. "So, Mr. Wonderful isn't so perfect after all?"

"That's the thing, though." I threw my hands up. "It's not like he's doing anything *bad*. Well, except for calling my Granny's old Christmas tree, that I happen to love, 'sad.' I know he means well, but it's making me crazy."

"Have you told him that?"

"No."

"Well... why not?"

I rolled my head back onto my shoulders. "I don't know what to say. Stop being so perfect? I appreciate how much you care, but could you try caring a little less? How do I tell him without seeming ungrateful or hurting his feelings?"

She shrugged. "I mean, I dunno. I guess you can just keep not saying anything and continue ignoring *your* feelings."

I thought about what Margot had said during the support group about her wife being a well-intentioned jackass. And like Margot, I wasn't willing to live half a life to ease his worries. This had to stop.

"You're right," I said finally.

"I know."

"Humble too."

"Never been accused of that," she said with a laugh. "Listen, you've got to tell him. I know I give Tommy Lee a lot of shit, but I do think everything he's doing comes from a place of love, even if he's a complete idiot about it. I was kind of like Dallas when my mom was diagnosed with fibromyalgia. Granted, I was a kid at the time, and what I did to 'help' didn't actually help at all..." She paused and pursed her lips. "So, I guess what I'm saying is I was *exactly* like Dallas. I just wanted to make her life easier, but all I did was make her feel like she was incapable of taking care of herself, let alone me. He needs to learn to let you ask for help."

"Ain't that the truth."

She twirled a finger at me. "And *you,* Miss Ma'am, need to learn how to *ask.*"

"I can't ask if he never gives me the chance. And right now he has nothing else to do but be up my ass."

"Well then, Pammy." Her lips quirked. "I guess you and Tommy Lee need to have a little chat."

"I guess so, but until then let's organize what we can, and we'll finish the rest tomorrow morning after I find the step ladder."

I still didn't know what I was going to say or how I was going to say it, but this couldn't go on any longer. I had to talk to him tonight.

I'D COOLED OFF A LITTLE BY THE TIME I GOT HOME, AND I was fully prepared to give Dallas a piece of my mind. But when I walked through the door and found him waiting with a homemade chicken pot pie and an early Christmas gift of a custom hand-stitched chef's coat in the lilac color I'd chosen as our primary decor color for the restaurant, my frustration waned.

"So, how did the day go with the new setup?" he asked as we finished our dinner. He rubbed his hands together, beaming proudly.

"Actually, I wanted to talk to you about—" I began, but he cut me off.

"I know I should have asked you first," he admitted. "But after I left from visiting Jo and Derek at the hospital yesterday evening, I got to thinking about ways I could make things a little easier on you and prevent anything from happening like it did the other night."

"Dallas, that wasn't a big deal."

"Just hear me out," he said, holding up his hands. "It's been weighing on me that what if next time, it *is,* and I'm not there? So, I tried to put things as close to where I got them as possible, just within reach so you're not having to get on a ladder to get anything."

I tried to maintain my composure. "Everything is kind of crammed together now, though."

"Already thought about that. So, I was thinking, what if I had a custom storage cabinet built to put back there, where everything could be easily accessible?"

"That's... very thoughtful. But it's really unnecessary. If I'm having a tough day I can ask you or McKenzie or one of the others to grab things down for me," I said, trying to appeal to his worries.

"But what if you're there alone?" he pressed. "I don't want you having to climb up there and risk falling."

"Right." I took a deep, steadying breath. "Okay. A storage cabinet would be great, but I wish you would have asked me and not moved things around until we could get one installed."

His cheeks flushed. "That's kind of why I didn't ask. I was

afraid you wouldn't agree to it, or that even if you did something would happen between now and when we got it put in."

He means well. He's being overprotective because he cares. Don't freak out.

"I'm sorry. You're right. I should have asked." His shoulders hunched forward. "Are you mad?"

Yes. "No. I know you only did it because you want to keep me safe, but I swear I'm not as fragile as you think. Can you just... ask next time?"

"Yes," he promised. "Of course. I'm sorry."

"It's okay." And it would be.

Maybe this would convince him to relax a little and stop treating me with kid gloves. Maybe it didn't even have to be some big discussion. If I could just be patient, the problem might sort itself out.

"Is there anything I can do to make it up to you?" he asked, pushing his chair out from the dining table and leaning toward me.

My lips curled into a salacious smile, the hint of a plan forming in my mind. Dallas needed a reminder I was still the strong, sexy woman he'd fallen in love with.

"Actually, there is." I disappeared from the room for a moment, returning with a bottle of whipped cream in my hands.

He might not listen to me about the bakery or storage cabinets, but I would show him I could still be in control.

TWENTY-EIGHT

Dallas

"Are you sure this is okay?" I asked again as she knelt in front of me. "Do your knees hurt?"

"I'm fine," she insisted. "Would you just enjoy this, please?"

I was trying. I willed my mind to focus on the fact that my very hot and *very* naked girlfriend was squirting whipped cream on my dick with the intent of licking it off. Literally every guy's dream. But all I could think about was whether her knees were hurting, if this position was comfortable for her, or if her hands were cramping up.

Her tongue flicked over the tip of my cock before she took me in her mouth. My eyes rolled back in my head.

Fuck. That feels good.

I tangled my hands in her hair as she worked her mouth along my length, watching the way her pink lips slid up and down my skin. But my focus kept drifting to the rest of her body and wondering if she'd really tell me if holding this position was hard on her.

"Why don't we move to the bed?" I asked between pants. "I don't want you to be uncomfortable."

She responded by sucking harder, but I couldn't even appreciate how good it felt. All I could think about was how this might make her hurt later.

"Come on. Let's just go to the bedroom."

She released me and rose to her feet, wiping her mouth with the back of her hand.

"That's it," she said, gathering her clothes off the floor. "I'm done."

"Are you okay?" My brows knitted together. "Are you hurting?"

"I'm fine, Dallas, but I can't do this anymore."

"Do what?" I asked, scrambling for my pants.

"*This*," she spat as she pulled her panties onto her hips and her sweatshirt over her head. "This thing where you treat me like I'm a paper doll and *any* sudden movements might cause me to split in half."

I yanked my shirt over my head. "Katie—"

"No. I've had enough," she shouted. "I've tried so hard to not lose my shit, Dallas. Because I know you mean well. Really, I do. But you've got to stop."

"Stop what?"

She tossed her hands in the air. "Everything. Hiding the step ladders, rearranging *my* business, cooking dinner all the time, putting up my Christmas decorations, asking me if I'm okay every five damn seconds. We can't even have sex without you asking me a million questions. You couldn't make me feel less sexy if you tried."

My throat turned to sand, and I gulped. "I just wanted to help."

"I know, and I appreciate that. But what I need is for you

to back off." She clenched her fists at her sides. "You are my favorite person in the entire world. You're the kindest, most loving man on the planet, *but you are driving me crazy.* My MS isn't going to be what does me in. You suffocating me *will.*"

Her words slapped me across the face. She thought I was *suffocating* her?

"But I... I wasn't... I didn't mean..." I searched for the right words to explain my behavior, but there were none.

Maybe I had been a little overbearing, but it was because I worried about her. Because every time her symptoms flared, I feared that meant her disease was progressing or that something bad was going to happen, like it had on the Fourth of July.

"Yes," she said, firmly. "I know. But that doesn't change how it makes me feel. I can't be a bystander in my own life anymore. I can't. I won't."

"Katie, I never meant to—"

"But you did. And part of this is my fault because I let you do it. I let it go on this long because I didn't want to hurt your feelings or seem ungrateful. I still don't." She gave me a sad smile. "Do you remember what you said to me after I got diagnosed? You said you didn't want to fix me. So what changed?"

Nothing. Everything. I hung my head. "It's not *you* I want to fix. It's everything else. I want to make the world easier for you. I want to take away everything that causes you pain."

"And that's noble of you, but it's also not possible." She dropped her hands to her sides. "When you do that, you're leaving nothing for me. I don't get to have a life or even figure out what my limitations actually are, because you've already set them."

"Fuck. I'm sorry." I scrubbed my hands down my face. "I don't know what's wrong with me. I guess I've just been scared. Seeing you hurting and in pain… It terrifies me."

I hadn't considered the possibility I was actually making everything so much worse.

She nodded. "Then you need to decide if that fear is too much for you. Because I can't keep on living half a life to make you feel more comfortable with my illness. I won't do it anymore."

"I'm sorry. I'm *so* sorry." My stomach roiled. "Please. Give me a chance to make things right. I don't want to lose you."

"Right now, I feel like *I've* lost me."

My heart began to race, and panic clawed at my chest. "What can I do? I'll do anything."

"I think you should go back to your place for a couple days. I need some space to clear my head. Let me and Emilia have a girls' night tonight. I've got to make a few things to take to Jo's tomorrow evening anyway."

Anything except that. I swallowed hard.

"Okay," I said, almost inaudibly.

"Thank you."

I nodded. "Before I do, is there anything you need—"

She peered at me through slits. "If the next words out of your mouth were going to be you asking me if I need anything, I'm going to ask you to think twice before finishing that sentence."

Heat rose up my neck and to my earlobes. "Right. Sorry."

"It's fine. Everything is going to be okay. *I'm* okay. I just need a breather."

I forced a smile. "I understand."

But I didn't actually understand at all.

When I woke the next morning, the condo felt colorless without the splashes of light and warmth Katie's presence brought in. I'd spent much of the night staring at the ceiling through the darkness, the sheets unnaturally cold against my skin without her tangled in them with me.

After sunrise, I gave up on getting more sleep and tried to watch a show on the couch to distract myself, but my lap felt empty without the weight of Katie's feet, so I clicked the tv off.

I paced around the living room, playing the last few months over in my mind. How had we gotten here? She'd breathed new life into me, but all I'd managed to do was make her feel suffocated.

My thoughts kept going back to the Fourth of July when I'd watched helplessly as she'd slipped into unconsciousness and I'd been powerless to stop it. All I could do was catch her before she hit the pavement. That same feeling had resurfaced when she'd gotten diagnosed with MS. It became this invisible threat, a serpent that could strike at any given moment, and all I wanted to do was protect her. Was that really so bad? I had to gain some clarity and figure this out. How could I take care of her and keep her safe without her feeling smothered?

Unable to sit with my thoughts any longer, I called Derek to check in.

"How are Jo and little Addison this morning?" I asked when he answered.

"Both mom and baby are doing great," he said, and I could hear the smile in his voice. "They're discharging us this afternoon, so we'll see you when you and Katie bring the food over."

It was as though someone wearing heavy boots had stepped on my chest. When Katie had mentioned the night before about making something to take to their house, I definitely hadn't been included in those plans.

"Oh, um, actually, I don't think I'll be coming with her."

"What? Why not? I thought you'd want to see the baby."

"I do. Of course I do." I cleared my throat. "But Katie... She asked for some space."

"Hang on," he said, before I heard him tell Jo in a muffled voice that he would be right back.

"What did you do, man?" he asked when he came back on the line. "What's going on?"

"Wait, why do you assume I did something?" I countered.

"Well, you've been known to lose your temper on occasion. I thought maybe—"

"I didn't lose my temper," I snapped before realizing the irony of my statement and the way I'd said it. "Sorry. I'm just kind of freaking out right now."

"Tell me what happened," he said.

So, I did. I told him about the conversation we had the night before and what Katie had said.

He paused for a moment. "Dallas, can I be honest with you?"

"Yeah. Shoot." I steeled myself, bracing for whatever criticisms he was about to bestow upon me.

"It sounds like when you decided to quit music that you made taking care of Katie your job. You're an 'all in' type of guy, and that's not necessarily a bad thing. You're devoted, and you care a lot, but that can be a little intense, especially if it's all focused on one person. I think you found yourself with all this time on your hands, and you kind of channeled that energy into doing everything for her."

Was he right? *Had* I done that? "It never felt like that to me. I was only trying to help."

"Of course you were," he said. "I know that, and I'm sure Katie knows it too, but maybe it would be helpful if you could channel some of that energy somewhere else."

"But... where?"

"I know you planned to step back from music, but maybe you should keep doing sessions or something."

I shook my head even though he couldn't see me. "I don't think that's something I want to do."

"Well, you're helping Katie once she takes over the bakery, right?" he asked. "Is there something you could do to get things going there?"

"Yeah." I gave a half-hearted sigh. "Maybe."

But what? I felt self conscious and a little embarrassed. I'd said I would help Katie, but what real experience did I have? Had I been kidding myself in thinking I could even be useful to her?

"Maybe just showing her you have some sort of life that's independent of her will help you guys regain your equilibrium again."

"Yeah," I said again. "Maybe you're right. But listen, this is the last thing you should be thinking about. I was just calling to check on you guys and here I am making it about me. I'm sorry. I didn't mean to dump my shit on you."

"I asked, remember?" He chuckled. "Besides, I'm here for you. You know that."

I smiled. "I know. I can't believe you're a dad now, man. Wasn't it just yesterday we were listening to *my* dad's old records in the garage after school?"

"Eating Doritos and Funyons."

"God, no wonder we couldn't get girlfriends back then," I joked. "It doesn't seem possible. In so many ways I've still seen you as my little brother, even though you've obviously been grown up for a long time. I've always felt protective of you, you know? I wanted to look out for you and keep you safe, and now look at you. You have a little one of your own to look after."

"I love you, man. I probably don't say it enough, but I appreciate that you've always been there for me. Even when you didn't know what I was going through, you still made me feel safe. Thank you for that."

My throat became thick, and emotion prickled behind my eyes. "I love you too, brother. I'm so fucking proud of you. And you... You're going to be an amazing dad, Derek."

"You know I owe some of that to you, right? My dad certainly didn't teach me what it meant to be a good person. It was you, Dallas."

I lifted the neck of my shirt to wipe my eyes. "Geez, kid. You didn't have to go and make me cry," I said with a laugh. "Thank you, though. I think I needed to hear that."

"This thing with you and Katie is going to work itself out. You'll see."

"I hope so, but I feel like I can't get things right, you know? I'm fucking this up." I blew out a breath and raked my hand over my face.

"Don't be so hard on yourself. Hell, look at us. We went through a rough patch not too long ago, remember? You were being so protective that you overstepped a bit, and yeah, I was pissed at you, but we got through it," he said. "Once you realized you'd messed up, you did what you could to make it right, and you'll do it again. That's what you do when you love somebody."

"You're right. I've got to figure out how to make this better."

"I don't know, but I think you start by honoring her need for space. Don't push it."

"Me? Be pushy?" I feigned offense. "Never."

"Uh-huh. *Right*," he teased. "But anyway, you two will work this out. Just give it some time."

"Thanks, man. I'll let you get back to Jo and Addie. Tell her Uncle Dallas will be by to see her later this week. Give her a kiss for me."

"I will," he promised, before we ended the call.

I flopped back on the couch and considered what he'd said. As tempting as it was to text Katie to check on her, I knew it was a bad idea. Derek was right. I needed to respect her wishes and give her the space she asked for. But I also needed to find a way I could help without making her feel suffocated or she wouldn't want me to be a part of Katie's Kitchen after all.

I needed a plan, and there was only one person who could help me come up with one.

LATE THAT AFTERNOON, I ARRIVED AT LIVVIE CAKES, SOON TO be Katie's Kitchen, and let myself in the back door like I had dozens of times.

"Knock, knock." I announced myself, and McKenzie looked up from where she was tidying up the center island.

"Tommy Lee," she said, barely flicking her eyes up to

look at me. "Katie's already gone for the day. I think she was going to Jo's."

I shoved my hands in my pockets. "I know. I'm actually here to see you."

She lifted her brows. "If you're looking for Christmas gift ideas for Katie, I think Jo would be better suited for that conversation. I don't know if you've noticed or not, but I'm not exactly a jolly little elf."

I chuckled. "No, I've got Christmas covered, but I was hoping to talk to you about something else."

"I don't know." She squinted at me. "I'm still kinda pissed at you."

"What? Why?" The words popped out before I could reel them back in. "Oh. Right. Yeah, I'm sorry about that." Of course, she'd been mad. When I'd rearranged the kitchen, that had affected more than just Katie, even though that was bad enough. I hadn't even thought about what that would do to McKenzie.

"Fine. 'Tis the season for giving and shit." She tossed the towel in her hand on the counter and folded her arms across her chest. "What do you want?"

"It seems I've made a mess of things."

She snorted. "Ya think?"

I rubbed my hand along the back of my neck.

"Sorry," she said. "Look, I know you mean well, and if it makes you feel any better, Katie knows it too. But you've *got* to get your head out of your ass, dude. You've got to relax."

"I'm starting to see that," I said, forcing a smile. "I just worry about her. I don't want her to overdo it and be in pain. What if her condition worsens?"

"Look, I get that you're concerned, but you have to understand this isn't about you." She huffed out a breath and rested her elbows on the butcherblock. "My mom has some chronic pain stuff too, so I do understand where you're coming from. But you've got to let Katie decide what she can and can't do."

"But what if she does too much and—"

"*And*? You know what's going to happen if she does?" she asked. "She's going to figure out what her limits are, and she'll know how to better prepare herself for the next time."

"I guess you're right."

"I hate to break it to you, Tommy Lee, but Pammy got along fine before you came into the picture, and she didn't get MS overnight. These symptoms have been present for a while now and somehow she managed then. She'll figure it out, but you've got to let her do it. She's tough."

"She is, and that's the problem. I'm afraid she won't ask for help when she needs it."

"And she might not. But that's not your problem. Give her room to breathe and set her own boundaries—with herself *and* with you. You're doing too much."

"That's just it. I don't think I am," I said with a sigh. "I mean, yes, I'm doing too much as far as Katie's concerned, but I'm not really *doing* anything. I left music and basically have put my entire focus on Katie. I want to help her if she needs it, but more than that I want to be... I don't know... useful. To her and just in general. I want to find a way I can help that's actually benefiting her and not stepping on her toes. I need a sense of... purpose."

She blinked. "So, let me get this straight. *You* want to talk to *me* about your life's purpose? What about me makes you think that's a good idea?"

I gave an awkward laugh. "Well, when you say it like that, I guess it's not. But I just thought you know this business inside and out, and you work well with Katie, and you clearly care about her. I guess I was hoping you might have some insight on how I could help. Without getting in the way."

Her face softened. "Oh."

I suddenly felt self-conscious. This was a stupid idea. McKenzie hardly knew me, and after my little stunt in the kitchen, I was sure the last thing she wanted to do was deal with me. I was about to apologize for wasting her time when she spoke again.

"What if you took some cooking classes?" she asked. "You've got something a lot of people don't have—time and I'm assuming money, unless you've squandered it away on a secret obsession with collecting rare Troll dolls that'll be unveiled on an MTV special with Dr. Drew."

I choked on a laugh. "No. No Troll collections."

She grinned. "So, use the resources you have. I know she's taught you a lot and you've practiced some on your own, but it might help you to figure out where you fit in this whole thing if you got out there and learned something new. Maybe it would help you understand more about how a kitchen really works."

I don't know why the idea had never occurred to me. I did love to cook, but all my training came from Katie and a few YouTube videos. If I went to school for it, I could bring some new skills to the table and become a true partner to Katie instead of trying to do everything for her.

She'd awakened my love of food, but that didn't mean I couldn't explore that interest outside of her. Just for the love of it. Just because I enjoyed it. Even if I never used what I learned for Katie's Kitchen, I could still use it for me.

The idea made me kind of... giddy. Excited, even.

"But I don't know," she said with a shrug. "That's just a tho—"

"McKenzie, you are a genius." I cut her off by folding her into a bear hug, but she swatted at my chest.

"God, what is *with* you people and your hugs?"

"Sorry." I jumped back and held up my hands. "Got a little over excited."

"You have big Golden Retriever energy, Tommy Lee." She wrinkled her nose as though she smelled a wet dog. "It's unsettling."

I smiled. "Doesn't everyone love dogs?"

She shrugged. "I'm more of a cat person."

"Fair enough. Okay, no hugs. Will you accept a fist bump?" I held out my hand.

She bit back a grin. "If I do, will you leave?"

I nodded. "I'll even wag my tail on the way out."

She rolled her eyes and touched her fist to mine.

"I'm growing on you, McKenzie," I said as I backed away toward the door.

She smirked and went back to cleaning. "You sure are. Like a really bad rash."

By the time I got back in my car, I felt better. Focused.

And like a bad rash, I wasn't going to give up easily.

TWENTY-NINE

Katie

HAVING my house to myself was luxurious. It was like the first time Granny left me alone for the night when I was sixteen. She and one of her friends had gone to Memphis, leaving me with the house all to myself for a full twenty-four hours. I loved Granny, of course, but there was something nice about having some time alone to stay up late and watch tv or eat ice cream for dinner. Though I'd skipped the Rocky Road this time, there'd been no one to suggest I go to bed earlier, and I got to have my kitchen to myself while I made some goodies to take to Jo and Derek.

I'd found the missing step ladder hidden in my basement at home, so McKenzie and I spent the next morning at work putting the kitchen back the way we'd had it. In just a matter of a few short hours, I felt like I'd regained some of my independence.

After dinner that evening at Jo's, Derek took Addison to the nursery for a nighttime feeding giving us a moment alone in their living room over some Earl Grey tea, where I filled her in on what was going on with Dallas.

"Even if he does mean well, that's seriously annoying," she said, scrunching up her nose. "When are you going to see him again?"

"Soon," I answered. "It's not like I don't want to be around him at all. I love him. I just need some room to breathe, you know? A hard reset. He was acting kind of crazy."

"You could throw him in a bowl of rice," she suggested with a grin, taking a sip of her tea. "It worked for my iPhone when I dropped it in the bathtub."

I laughed. "If he keeps this up, I may have to."

She dropped her voice. "Derek said he talked to Dallas this morning. He was pretty down and seemed to be feeling a little nostalgic." She paused for a moment and chewed her lip. "Even if stepping back from music was the right thing for him, it's still a huge deal. I know he's going to be helping you with the restaurant, but that hasn't really started yet."

"But even with that I just... I need him to not be on me, asking if I'm okay every five seconds," I said. "It's like he's forgotten I existed before him just fine."

"From my own experience with Dallas, it seems like he's always based his entire identity on outside things. I saw that firsthand when he thought I was trying to Yoko Ono the band. His whole life was the guys and their music, so it rattled him when they split. I think he needs to reconnect with himself and find some sort of... I don't know... self-fulfillment."

"Exactly, and it can't just be taking care of me."

"And I know seeing you in pain is hard, but he can't cope with that by micromanaging your entire life."

"That's what I'm hoping to get across to him."

"But I *do* think maybe some of his concerns are valid."

She held up her hands as though blocking a preemptive punch.

My eyebrows shot up. "How so?"

"It's just… you're not always the best at asking for help. And that's *not* an excuse for how he's acting. You're a caretaker, and I love that about you. You're the first person to make soup for someone when they're sick or if they just had a baby." She grinned. "When I first came back to Nashville you did everything you could to make me comfortable. Remember our little spa night in?"

I smiled at the memory.

"You're the most thoughtful, generous person I know." She reached over the center cushion of the sofa to touch my knee. "All I'm saying is you *do* tend to put everyone else's needs ahead of yours. But it's okay to accept support too."

"I do," I said. *Don't I?*

She narrowed her eyes at me. "I think you acquiesce to it when the people who care about you kind of force your hand. And maybe that's why Dallas is being so pushy."

"But I don't *need* help. And it's not like he's given me the opportunity to ask, anyway. He anticipates every possible need and then some."

"Okay." She held her hands up in surrender. "Anyway, speaking of needing help, how are things going with Katie's Kitchen?"

"I take over after the first of the year, but we aren't doing our official launch until spring," I answered, glad for the change of subject. "I'm still trying to decide on a few menu items."

"Are you changing the entire thing?"

I shook my head. "I want to keep all of Liv's original recipes and the coffee bar, of course, and we'll still do catering and wedding cakes and things like that, but we're expanding the menu. I want it to feel like the old meat and three places Granny used to take us to—like a real country kitchen."

"She would be so proud of you, Katie."

"Yeah," I said with a smile. "I think she would. It still feels so surreal that this is actually happening. Like a dream I might wake up from at any minute."

"It's real, and it's going to be incredible." She paused for a moment and glanced down at her mug. "And how are you feeling?"

"It's kind of a day to day thing," I admitted. "The cold weather has made me feel worse, but I'm keeping up with my massages, taking my meds, and doing everything I can to manage my symptoms when Dallas isn't hounding me to go to bed early."

"And... how do you feel about things, you know... emotionally?" she asked. "Aside from when you first got diagnosed you haven't really talked much about it."

I opened my mouth but shut it again before I could respond with an automatic 'fine.' How *was* I feeling?

"Well, I went to a support group for people with chronic illnesses, and that was nice. There was this lady there—Margot—she has MS too, and she and her wife went through a period like what Dallas and I are having. So, that made me feel good, I guess. To know I'm not alone. And it was just kind of cool to see people like me leading their lives. Not being held back by their illnesses. Like Margot. She was a runner before she got diagnosed with MS, and she still is."

"That's great."

"Yeah," I said, but my mind drifted. In some ways, I wished I'd never gotten the diagnosis because that was when things had started to change with me and Dallas. I didn't often allow myself to think about my MS and the ways it had changed my life, but at that moment, I felt kind of... mad.

"Hey, are you okay?" Jo asked, interrupting my thoughts.

"Yeah," I said, forcing a smile.

"You know you can talk to me, right?"

I pulled the sleeves of my sweatshirt over my hands. "I just worry this whole thing is going to become the way people mark every achievement I make. Anything I do—like opening the restaurant—will inevitably become this great MS success story. It'll be about how I accomplished it in the face of MS, completely ignoring how hard I've worked to get here."

"And I suppose on the flip side of that, any bad thing that happens becomes a cautionary tale."

"Exactly. Not every good thing happens in spite of my illness, and not every bad thing happens *because* of it. Some things just... *are*." I pulled one of the plush throw pillows onto my lap and clutched it to my chest. "I guess this thing with Dallas has me worried because my illness is the only part of me he can see right now. What if that becomes all *anyone* can see? What if that becomes my singular personality trait? Katie: the sick friend."

She studied my face a moment before speaking. "I wish I knew what to say or how to keep people from doing that, but I don't. I do think this is going to be a bit of a learning curve for you and for everyone that cares about you. Because those that love you are going to ask how you're feeling and want to help any way they can, but I can see where that can cross a line and become too much, like it has with Dallas."

"And I don't know how to navigate that," I said with a resigned sigh. "Obviously."

She reached for my hand. "Look, I know I can be a little

too much of a mother hen sometimes. I'll try to keep myself in check, but if I slip up, please don't be afraid to tell me. I want to support you however you need me to."

"Thanks, Jo." I squeezed her hand. "There *is* something that I think would help."

"You name it."

"I'm going to need unlimited access to baby snuggles."

She grinned. "Deal."

I ENJOYED STAYING UP A LITTLE TOO LATE WATCHING *GILMORE Girls,* but as I curled up in bed with Emilia beside my head, I missed Dallas. I wished I could warm my cold feet against his legs and rest my head on his chest.

Emilia perked up and sniffed at Dallas' side of the bed before glancing back at me as though alerting me that our bed was missing a very key component to her slumber.

"I know, sweet girl," I said, stroking the tip of her ear. "I miss him too."

I reached for my phone on the nightstand and illuminated the screen. There were no missed calls or messages. Dallas had heard me loud and clear when I'd said I needed space. I opened his text thread and stared at our last exchange. It was quick. Similar to ones we'd sent to one another many times before. Me letting him know I was headed home. Him telling me he loved me and to drive safely. We always let each other know when we were coming or going and that we'd made it to our destination. It was such a simple gesture, but it made me feel protected and loved.

His overzealous attempts to 'help' me lately had overshadowed some of the things I loved most about him. Like the way he paid attention to the little things. He knew how I took my lattes and that when I was sad, I only wanted my Granny's recipes. He'd taken care to study her faded notes that were written inside the margins of her cookbooks and made the exact adjustments that she did. Every recipe of hers he'd made for me tasted just like Granny herself had prepared it.

How had we gone from *that* to *this?* Dallas was one of the most thoughtful people I knew, and he felt things in a big way, sometimes to his own detriment. And I guess mine too. He'd been known to let his emotions get the better of him, and when those emotions were good, it was *great.* But when he was acting out of anger or, in my case, fear, it could be disastrous.

I remembered how mad I'd been at him earlier that year when he'd said some hurtful things to Jo out of fear of losing the band. Things that led her to making the decision to leave Nashville, me, Derek, and the life she'd built here. He'd realized quickly how wrong he was, but it had been too late. She'd already gone to New York. But in true Dallas fashion, he'd set out to right his wrongs and flew to her on the eve of Midnight in Dallas' last show together. He'd missed every bit of press and was completely absent from some of the last photos ever taken of the band so he could make things right with Jo and Derek. Then he'd driven Jo all the way back to town and played the last concert with the band.

Dallas didn't do anything half-assed, and it made sense that he'd applied that same energy to helping me. My MS diagnosis had freaked him out so much it was like he'd forgotten to ask me how *I* was feeling. Not physically, but emotionally. He'd lost sight of the fact that with MS or not, I was still *me.* And I still needed the freedom to *be* me.

Dallas had taken the first step in making things right by

giving me the space I'd asked for, so I wanted to be the first to reach out, and I couldn't wait a minute longer.

My fingers flew across the screen.

Katie: Hey... are you up?

It was only a few seconds before the bubbles returned to let me know he was typing.

Dallas: I am. Everything okay?

Katie: Yeah. I just miss you.

His reply came almost instantly.

Dallas: I miss you too. How's Emilia?

Katie: She's okay. Misses her dad.

Dallas: Give her a kiss from me.

I smiled down at my phone.

Katie: Why don't you come give her a kiss tomorrow yourself?

Dallas: Really???

Katie: Yes. ☺

Dallas: Are you sure? I know you needed some space, and I respect that.

Katie: I'm sure. How about I cook us dinner tomorrow night? And we can talk?

Dallas: I'd like that.

Katie: Then it's a date. ☺ **I love you, Dal.**

Dallas: I love you too. Good night, Butter Bean.

The words danced across my screen, and a grin spread across my face as I tapped out another text.

Katie: Hey wait...

Dallas: Yeah?

Katie: What are you wearing? 😉

"I missed you." Dallas folded his arms around me from behind and kissed my neck as I finished drying the last of the dishes I'd allowed him to wash. "And your delicious cooking."

We'd been so happy to see each other that we'd agreed to put off our talk until after dinner. He'd arrived with two dozen long-stemmed red roses for me and a plush donut for Emilia. We'd bantered while I finished making the risotto, and as we polished off our glasses of Cabernet, I told him about McKenzie nearly losing it on a bachelorette party that had popped into the bakery earlier that day, already drunk at eleven a.m.

"You could have had my cooking any time you wanted, but you wouldn't allow me in my own damn kitchen," I teased as I tossed the dish towel on the counter and turned to face him.

"I know, and I'm sorry." He dropped his gaze and hung his head. "I was so stupid, Katie."

I scrunched my nose and held up my thumb and forefinger less than a quarter inch apart. "Just a little bit."

He chuckled. "I don't know how you tolerated me."

"It is a mystery, isn't it?"

He pressed a kiss to my forehead. "I want you to know I was listening to everything you said. I just had to pull my head out of my own ass long enough to be able to *hear* it. And someone gave me a little help with that."

"Yeah, I heard you talked to Derek."

"Actually, that's not who I'm talking about."

"Oh?" I tilted my head. "Who was it?"

"McKenzie," he answered.

"*Really?*" I'd been working with her all day and she hadn't said a word.

He nodded. "She helped me realize what a selfish idiot I've been. I made everything about me. Helping you was my way of dealing with my own fears, and I didn't stop to ask if you even wanted or needed my help."

"Yeah," I said, placing my hands on his chest. "It was a lot."

He pushed his hand through his hair. "I was one bakery break-in away from having a Netflix documentary made about me."

I laughed. "It was intense. I'm keeping Netflix on speed dial just in case you forget."

He grinned and cupped my cheek with his hand. "I promise that going forward I'll only help when you ask me to."

"Thank you," I said. "Look, this MS thing is new for both of us. We're still figuring it out. There were bound to be a few bumps in the road. And I also should have communicated with you before blowing up at you the way I did."

"You shouldn't have had to tell me I was being an idiot, though. I should have realized how ridiculous I was being. I'm sorry."

"Me too." I stood on my toes and kissed him.

"So," he said, rubbing the sides of my arms. "I have some kind of exciting news to share."

"Oh really? And what's that?"

"McKenzie also helped me realize I needed to *do* something. Obviously, I want to help you with the restaurant, but aside from what you've taught me and my YouTube education I don't know a lot about cooking or how the business side runs."

"McKenzie should start charging by the hour." I lifted my brows. "So, what does this mean exactly?"

"I went to a couple really nice restaurants in town yesterday and sat at the bar just asking questions because honestly, I didn't know where to start," he began. "I ended up at The Maple."

I gasped. "What do you mean you *ended up* at The Maple? That place is booked out till the end of time."

Their head chef was something of a celebrity in the culinary world. Willam Deveraux, one of England's most beloved chefs, had Michelin Star restaurants in cities like London, Paris, New York City, and Los Angeles. He'd only opened The Maple in Nashville about six months prior, but they had a waitlist as long as one of Granny's old Yellow Pages phone books.

He grinned. "Well, it turns out that Will and his son were big Midnight in Dallas fans."

"Will? As in Willam Deveraux?" I gripped him by the shirt. "*The* Willam Deveraux?"

He raised his chin. "The very same one."

"No way." I slapped his chest lightly. "He was *there*?"

"Apparently he stays on board for the first year at every place he opens to make sure all the kinks get worked out."

"And you're just, like, on a casual nickname basis with him now?" I gaped at him. "I… don't have words."

"I was telling him about you and Katie's Kitch—"

"He knows I *exist*?" I covered my mouth with my hands. "He knows about Katie's Kitchen?"

"He does." He pried my fingers from my face and laced them through his. "And I was telling him about how I wanted to learn more both in the kitchen and on the business side of things, and he offered me an apprenticeship for the next three months. Basically, he's going to give me the Will Deveraux crash course."

"An apprenticeship? Are you kidding me right now? This is incredible."

"Now, I *did* offer him some very exclusive Midnight in Dallas memorabilia in exchange for his time. A couple of MTV Video Music Awards and one of my drum sets for his kid."

I blinked. "You're giving him your drums?"

"I'm keeping my favorites. This is just my practice set. It'll make a pretty sick Christmas gift for his son, *and* it'll help me clear out some stuff I don't need." A smile tugged at the corners of his mouth. "For the first time since the band split up, I feel genuinely excited about doing something."

I could tell by the way his eyes sparkled as he spoke that he meant it.

"Dallas, this is great. It's more than great. This is amazing." I beamed at him with pride.

"*And* he said he'd love to have you in sometime. I told him you're already a pro in the kitchen, but if there are any French pastries you'd like to learn more about, he said he'd be happy to —"

"*Yes!*" I shrieked. "Oh my God. Are you kidding me? He studied at Le Cordon Bleu. He could offer to teach me how to make toast and I would soak up every word."

"And there's one more thing."

I clutched my hand to my chest. "I don't know if my heart can handle much more."

"I told him I'd been an idiot and that I wanted to make it up to you, and—"

"You're taking me to The Maple Room. Are we going? We're going right?"

"This Saturday night at seven." He wrapped his arms

around me and lifted me off my feet. "So, do you think you can forgive me?"

"I think that can be arranged." I crushed my mouth to his.

He squeezed me tighter and spun us around. "God, it's good to hold you again. Feels like home."

THIRTY

Dallas

KATIE and I had a relaxing Christmas and New Year's together, which was good because once my apprenticeship started, I barely had time to catch my breath. It turned out that while Will was a nice guy, he was also a beast in the kitchen. Figuratively *and* literally. He worked circles around everyone else, and if you screwed up, he had no problem letting you know. He didn't go easy on me because he was a fan of the band. The first month had consisted of a lot of late nights and him telling me, in his very distinguished British accent, that my cooking was shit.

I loved every second of it, and by the middle of February I'd graduated from 'shit' to 'mediocre at best,' which I'd learned was a compliment coming from him. Music had come easily to me, but *this* I had to work for, and it felt good. Every day was a new challenge, and I loved getting my hands dirty in the kitchen and trying new things. Will wasn't afraid to humble me or remind me I was a novice, and I was better for it.

"Anyone can bang on a drum, but few can make the

perfect soufflé," Will said late on the last Thursday of the month as he separated egg whites from their yolks with his bare hands, placing the thick yellow blobs into the bowl of a stand mixer. "It's an art."

The Maple Room was closed, but our class was still in session. Will was an excellent teacher. Thorough, too. Wherever he was, I was always a couple feet to his left, because he didn't like when people stood on his dominant side. There was no task too small for him to teach me. We worked on basic things like knife skills and even picking the best produce at the market. Then there were nights like this one.

"Okay, but why not use an egg separator for this part?" I studied the way the translucent goop slipped through his fingers.

"Because, you wanker." He glanced at me from over his thick black frames, his salt-and-pepper hair catching in the overhead lights. "This keeps *me* in control."

Will was nothing if not always in control of every detail of his restaurant. At first, I thought it was just an ego thing, but I quickly learned it was so much more. His restaurants were known for their creative yet unpretentious menus, but they were also well loved for the experience. Each had their own distinct vibe and flavor, and he wanted to evoke certain feelings for his customers from the second they stepped inside one of his establishments.

The Maple Room was a love letter to his Nana, Maple, who had taught him to cook as a young man. The menu was a Southern take on the foods she'd made for him back home in Oxford. He'd even decorated the place with some of her things, like the old piano he said used to be in the family room of her cottage and the photograph of her younger likeness that greeted guests when they first walked in the door.

Once he'd placed all the egg whites into a small bowl on the counter, he turned to me.

"Now, you do it," he said with a nod toward the uncracked eggs in front of me. "I haven't seen Katie around here in a couple weeks. You're not still licking your wounds after she kicked your arse during our lesson on French macarons, are you, old chap?"

I laughed as I cracked the thin shells gently against the counter as he had done and began the process of sliding the slimy whites through my fingers and into the mixing bowl in front of me. Will had instantly bonded with Katie. Like her, he'd been raised by his grandmother, and from the very first time they'd met when we had dinner at The Maple Room, they'd hit it off.

"Trust me, I know she kicks my *arse* at everything. If I can become even half the chef she is, I will have succeeded."

He leaned over my shoulder, inspecting my work. "Right you are on that, my friend. And how is our golden girl? Is she feeling well?"

"I don't know that I'd say '*well*' exactly," I admitted. "I'm worried she's spreading herself too thin."

He tutted. "I'm sorry to hear that."

"She's been so focused on the restaurant that she's not taking care of herself the way she probably should." It was killing me to not step in, but I'd heard her concerns loud and clear. I had to give her room to draw her own boundaries. If I asked whether she needed help and she said no, I backed off and let it go. Unfortunately, 'no' was always the answer. "The soft opening is next week, but there's still a lot of kinks to be worked out. You know how it is."

"I certainly do. And when is the grand opening?"

"The first Saturday in April."

He beamed like a proud father. "Well, I can't wait to see what she's done with the place."

The time that I wasn't at The Maple Room was spent at Katie's Kitchen. My chest still tightened when I saw the familiar dark circles that framed her eyes, but I didn't push. And if I even looked like I was about to, McKenzie was quick to smack the thought out of my head with a cutting side-eye. Or a literal smack to my head. Katie's hands had been giving her trouble, likely a combination of MS and overuse, and she was even more exhausted than usual, but she was a machine. When it came to her dream, nothing could slow her down.

"She took your advice and brought in some of her Granny's things," I said. "We hired someone to restore her old china cabinet and brought in her Granny's old Victrola record player."

There were still a few things to be done before the grand opening. Jo and McKenzie had also been accompanying Katie to thrift stores and consignment sales nearly every week for the last month, searching for everything from flatware and plates to mismatched dining sets. She was having the space freshly painted and the floors polished the next week, and her front signage was scheduled to be installed on Wednesday.

I didn't know how she'd done it, but she'd managed to keep the heart of what Liv had started while making it all her own. Walking into Katie's Kitchen felt like slipping on a well-loved sweatshirt or sinking into your favorite chair. It felt like the woman I loved—like home.

"We also framed some of her Granny's original recipes and hung them up," I continued. "She loved the idea. Thanks for the suggestion."

"I'm glad." He leaned against the counter and cleared his throat. "Dallas?"

I sighed as I gently placed the last yolk into the bowl of my mixer. "I fucked it up already, didn't I?"

His throaty laugh started deep in his belly. "No, no. It's not that." "I was actually going to say I've never had a pupil be able to completely separate the white from the yolk by hand on the first try before. Well done."

"Excuse me, Will." A sly smile crept across my mouth. "Is that a *compliment* I hear?"

"Let's not get ahead of ourselves, shall we?" he teased. "We've yet to actually *make* the soufflés. There's still plenty of time to fuck it up. Now, let's get to work."

"YOU GUYS!" KATIE BOUNCED AND POINTED TO THE SIGN. "That's my name. That's *my* restaurant."

"It looks so good," McKenzie said.

"Yes, it does," I agreed, squeezing Katie's shoulders.

We were standing outside Katie's Kitchen the Wednesday before the soft opening admiring the new signage. The name was written in a simple flowing script over a weathered white background. It was the perfect mix of cozy and classy, just like Katie. With only one more day left before the soft opening, everything had finally come together.

"Oh my God." Katie stared up at it, her hands covering her mouth. "I can't believe it."

When she turned to me, her eyes were glossy.

"We did it," she said, reaching for my hand.

"*You* did," I reminded her, threading our fingers together.

"But I couldn't have done any of it without you." She pulled McKenzie into a side hug. "Without *both* of you."

"Me more so than him though, right?" McKenzie teased, but it was true. McKenzie had been her right hand through everything. I'd helped as much as I could, as much as Katie would allow, but it was McKenzie who had been there day in and day out.

"Definitely," I said, smiling at her over the top of Katie's head, and she waved her hand as though it was no big deal. But it meant a lot. She'd been the one who'd sparked the idea that ultimately led me to train alongside Will, and she was always looking out for Katie. McKenzie was a tough nut to crack, and I still wasn't sure if she liked me or just tolerated me most days, but she would always be cool in my book.

"Let's take a picture of you with the sign for Instagram to announce the soft opening." McKenzie pulled her phone out of her pocket and readied the camera.

"Not by myself. This was a group effort," Katie said, looking up at me. "You have the longest arms. You take it."

McKenzie shrugged and handed me the device.

"Alright, pile in," I said, stretching out my arm to fit the three of us plus the sign into the frame. "Say cheese."

"You're supposed to say money. It makes your smile look more natural," McKenzie corrected, and I glanced back at her and arched a brow. "What? I overheard one of those bachelorette influencer girls say that last week. Whatever. Money is better than cheese, anyway."

"Okay, then. Here we go," I said, resuming my position. "One... two... three..."

"Money," we shouted in unison as I took the photo.

"Let me see." Katie reached for the phone and scanned the screen. "We look good."

"Are you ready to share it?" McKenzie asked as Katie gave it back to her.

She nodded. "Ready."

McKenzie's fingers flicked across the screen with lightning speed, and a moment later she turned it so we could see. There, on the Katie's Kitchen Instagram page that had once belonged to Livvie Cakes, above the caption that read 'New Beginnings' was the picture of us.

"It's official," McKenzie said. "Katie's Kitchen is open for business."

"SHIT, SHIT, SHIT." THE MORNING OF THE SOFT OPENING, I woke to the sound of Katie cursing from her kitchen. "What is wrong with me?"

I got out of bed, careful not to disturb Emilia who was snoring softly beside my head and stumbled into the room, stifling a yawn to find her already dressed and slamming the lid on the coffeemaker. Her empty travel mug sat on the counter in front of her. "Everything okay?"

She startled when she registered I was standing there. "Sorry. I didn't mean to wake you. I just forgot to put coffee in here last night, so I brewed us a delicious pot of hot water. For the third time this week."

"You're exhausted." I rubbed the sleep from my eyes as she poured out the water and filled the filter with ground coffee. "You've been burning the candle at both ends trying to get things ready. Cut yourself some slack."

"Shit." She huffed out a breath as she filled the basin and started the brew. "I just remembered I have to stop at the store on the way in. I need more rhubarb for the tart McKenzie's making. We ran out yesterday."

"I can go by on my way in."

"No, it's okay. I can do it." She shook out her hands, and I reached for them, rubbing circles into her palms.

"They're still giving you trouble, huh?" I asked.

She shrugged. "It's not a big deal. I've definitely felt worse."

"What day is your next infusion? It should be soon, right?"

"Crap." Her head fell back on her shoulders, and she groaned. "I forgot to schedule it."

"Hey." I pulled her into my arms. "It's okay. I know you're swamped. Do you want me to give them a call for you?"

"I'll call tomorrow."

I paused. "Tomorrow's Saturday, Butter Bean."

"Right." She sagged against my chest. "Monday, then. Don't worry. I've got it handled."

McKenzie's words from months before rang through my head like they'd done so often recently. I had to give Katie the room to figure out what she needed and to set her own boundaries. If she said she had it handled, I needed to trust that she did and let her do things her way.

"Okay," I said, rubbing the sides of her arms. "It's going to be okay. Don't stress. I'll be there as soon as I pick up the stuff from the florist."

Even though it was the soft opening, Katie had spared no expense in making sure everything was perfect. She'd had some small mismatched centerpieces made for each table that looked like they belonged in a cozy cottage.

She nodded. "Thank you for doing that, by the way."

"Of course. Is there anything else you need me to do?"

"Nope. I've got everything under control."

"I'm so proud of you, Katie. Today is a big day. One

you've worked incredibly hard for. Don't forget to take a second to enjoy it."

"I won't." She reached up and gave me a quick kiss. "I better get going. I want to get to Whole Foods before all the good rhubarb is gone."

I grinned. "Is there usually a run on rhubarb before eight a.m.? Or at all?"

"You never know," she sang as she moved past me to go to the bedroom to get her things.

"Want me to pour you some coffee to go?" I asked as the pot beeped.

"I'll get it," she called. "But thank you."

I filled a mug for myself and was opening the fridge to find the creamer when she returned, giving me a quick peck on the cheek.

"I'll see you soon," she said. "Love you."

"Love you too. Drive safe," I replied as she rushed out the back door.

I finally put my hand on the half and half and poured a steady stream into my cup before placing the carton back in the fridge. When I turned back around, Katie's travel mug was still there, empty on the counter.

THIRTY-ONE

Katie

McKenzie was getting out of her truck when I pulled in behind Katie's Kitchen. She waved as I got out of my car and shut the door.

"Today's the big day," she said. "How do you feel?"

I smiled through a yawn, cursing myself for forgetting my coffee. "Exhausted. But excited."

She fell in step beside me as I headed toward the door. "I'm gonna get started on that strawberry rhubarb pie as soon as—"

"SHIT," I blurted out, clenching my fists. "I forgot. I forgot to stop at the store." How could I have forgotten the freaking rhubarb? Dallas and I had *just* had an entire conversation about it. It was why I'd torn out of the house so quickly to begin with.

"Oh. Well, that's okay," McKenzie said with a wave of her hand. "You know what? We have plenty of strawberries, so it'll just be a strawberry pie. Not a big deal."

"Right." I forced a smile. I'd wanted to have strawberry rhubarb because it was one of my Granny's favorites, but

McKenzie was right. This wasn't a huge deal. It was a small oversight and part of businesses ownership and life was being able to pivot. And that was exactly what we were going to do.

"You know what? Scratch the pie." I pulled out my key and unlocked the door. "We can jazz up those strawberries a bit by doing a galette with a toasted almond crumble."

"Oooh." Her lips formed an 'o.' "That sounds amazing. See? Crisis averted."

We got inside and went to work preparing for the day. Within minutes, Sydney and Jacob arrived along with a couple of our new hires, and Katie's Kitchen was in full swing.

When Dallas got there just before ten with the flower arrangements, there was already a small line waiting outside the door.

"Look at that," he said as he helped me set out the centerpieces. "Your first official customers."

I swallowed hard when I recognized some of the faces as regulars of Livvie Cakes, people who'd been excited to find out I would be taking over and expanding the menu. A pit swelled in my stomach. I was grateful these customers had come out to support me, but it also felt like a lot of pressure. They'd loved Livvie Cakes, but what if they didn't love the changes I'd made?

"Okay." I clasped my hands in front of me. "Is everybody ready?"

I looked around to make sure everyone was in their places. Sydney was running the register and taking orders while our new hires, Abbey and Grant, would be filling coffee and bakery orders. In the back would be Jacob, Dallas, McKenzie, and me.

"Ready," Sydney said, giving me a thumbs up as Abbey and Grant exchanged eager smiles.

"I'll head to the kitchen so I can jump in and help," Dallas said, giving me a quick kiss on the cheek and starting toward the back.

"Okay, y'all." I squared my shoulders and took a deep breath. "It's showtime."

The first hour flew by, but my body was feeling every second of it. My feet ached, and I'd already had to stifle more than a few yawns, but my dream was a reality, playing out in front of me. I didn't want to miss a second. As I made my rounds happy customers stopped me to rave about the new menu, ask about the eclectic decor, and just to say hello.

Everything was moving along with ease. Well, everything except me.

I stopped by the table where Margot, Caesar, and a couple of others from the chronic illness group had gathered to show their support.

"Hey y'all," I said, putting on my best smile. "Thanks for coming out. How is everything?"

Caesar held up his hand. "Katie, I know we haven't known each other very long and you have a boyfriend, but will you marry me?"

"Not if she marries me first," Margot teased.

"Seriously, this is phenomenal." Caesar dropped his head back in a dramatic sigh. "These gluten-free crepes are to die for. Literally, I am already dead. I'm speaking to you from beyond the grave."

"I'm glad you like them," I said with a laugh. "And no

cross-contamination worries here, either. You taught me how important that is."

He kissed the tips of his fingers, then splayed out his hand. "Chef's kiss, baby. Amazing."

"Everything's really good," Margot added. "How's the day going so far?"

"It's been great," I answered. "We've had a steady stream of customers with a short line outside since we opened the doors. It's crazy."

"Buckle up because I fully expect that line to grow once word gets out about how great this food is," Caesar said before digging back into his crepes.

I glanced back and saw a handful of new customers had just walked in.

"I should let you guys get back to enjoying your food," I said, "but I'm so glad you came."

"Our pleasure," Margot said, grabbing my arm before I could walk away. "And Katie?"

"Yeah?" I asked.

She dropped her voice so only I could hear her. "I know you're busy taking care of your customers, but don't forget to take care of yourself too."

"Oh, I know," I said, waving her off. "I am."

"Are you sure about that?" She narrowed her eyes. "You're looking a little like I did the day I ran the Boston marathon."

I tilted my head quizzically. "But that went great, didn't it?"

"It did until I fainted after I crossed the finish line." She chuckled. "All I'm saying is don't hesitate to take a break if you need one. It's okay to ask for help."

"Of course." I nodded and smiled before saying my goodbyes and moving on to the next table. Margot was right, but I didn't need help. I had everything under control.

"It's perfect, Katie," Liv gushed early that afternoon. She and Jax had brought the kids and their head of security, Brady, in for lunch. "You've thought of every little detail, and it shows. It's beautiful."

"Really? You like it?" I asked. We were standing off to the side watching Chloe and Jonathan devour their cupcakes. I'd been both excited and nervous for Liv to see the finished product because even though she'd given the place to me, it had still been her baby first. Her approval mattered to me.

"I knew it was going to be amazing because it's you, but it's even more than I could have imagined." She peered at me through glossy eyes. "And thank you for continuing to donate to the foundation. You didn't have to do that."

"I wanted to."

Jax and Liv had created The Deanna Slade Foundation in honor of Jax's birth mother who lost her life to addiction. They provided mental health care and drug rehabilitation for unhoused men and women, and Liv had committed twenty percent of the bakery's profits to the organization. It was important to them, so it was important to me to carry on the tradition.

She blinked back tears. "Your heart is in every square inch of this place, and it shows."

"Thanks, Liv. I wish everyone could have been here together." I gave a wistful smile as I looked out at the full restaurant where Jo, Derek, and baby Addison were seated at the table next to Jax and the kids. "I miss them."

"I know. Me too." Liv pulled me into a hug.

Ella and Antoni had sent a beautiful arrangement of peonies and roses that I'd placed front and center near the register. It was a great reminder that they were with us in spirit, but there was one other person we were missing.

"Have you guys heard from Luca?" I asked when we parted.

She shook her head and frowned. "Sometimes he doesn't even respond when Jax texts or calls him, but I know Luca likes his space. What about you? Have you or Dallas talked to him?"

"Not really," I said with a shrug. "He sent me a text to say congratulations when I let him know about the soft opening, but he said he wouldn't be in town."

"I hope he's okay. I worry about him sometimes."

"Me too," I said. "But I'm so glad you guys could be here. It means a lot."

"Wouldn't have missed it for the world." She squeezed my arm. "By the way, can we talk about Dallas for a second and how freaking cool it is that he's studying with Willam Deveraux? Incredible."

"He loves it too. I feel like this apprenticeship really helped Dal find his passion. He seems happy," I said. "And did I tell you Willam taught me how to make French macarons?"

She gasped. "What? No. Oh my God, tell me everything. What's he like?"

"He's the best. Such a kind person. He was raised by his Nana, so we have that in common. Actually, he's the reason I incorporated so many of my Granny's favorite things in the decor here. He did that at The Maple Room, and it just made the place all the more special. He suggested I use some of

Granny's stuff here, and it really does make me feel like she's getting to be a part of it in some way."

"Of course she is." She fixed her warm green eyes on me. "Because she's a part of you. And she would be so proud of you."

My throat tightened, and I nodded as the front door bell chimed. I did a double take when I saw the person who'd entered surrounded by a buzzing entourage, her platinum hair flowing behind her. If it had been last summer, I wouldn't have known who she was, but since Dallas had introduced me to her music, I'd added a couple of her songs to my playlists, much to his dismay.

"Is that... Prose Gold?" Liv whispered.

"It is," I said.

Liv's eyebrows shot up. "Um, this is huge. People are calling her the next Billie Eilish."

A few of the patrons exchanged hushed whispers amongst themselves, clearly shocked they'd found themselves at what had become an almost impromptu red carpet event. People came to Livvie Cakes hoping to catch a glimpse of Liv all the time. But today they were getting an extra special treat with Jax, Derek, Dallas, and now, Prose Gold. In true Nashville fashion, though, they were pretending to ignore the famous customers.

I glanced over to the counter where Grant was staring at Prose, wide-eyed.

"Excuse me." I lowered my voice so that only Liv could hear. "I better go take care of her myself."

THIRTY-TWO

Dallas

"SHE WANTS A *WHAT?*" I asked. It was after-hours at Katie's Kitchen the following Wednesday evening, and we were gathered at the tables out front. Katie had just informed everyone that Prose Gold wanted us to cater her album release party at the end of the month. I just could not shake this girl.

"You heard me correctly," Katie said, stifling a laugh from where she stood before us. "A six-foot tall T-rex cake."

McKenzie snorted. "Don't forget the tiny human arms, though. That's the best part."

"Is this girl okay?" Sydney asked warily.

"No," McKenzie and I answered together.

"Regardless, she's still our client, and a very high-profile one at that," Katie continued. "It's our job to make her wildest culinary dreams come true, and that is exactly what we're going to do. The notes in front of you are what we'll be working off."

We studied the sheets of paper Katie had passed out, and I exchanged a wide-eyed glance with McKenzie.

"This thing is two pages long." I balked as I scanned over the notes about everything from the 'vibe' of the venue to what Prose Gold wanted and what she definitely *didn't* want.

"Dessert mac-n-cheese?" Jacob wrinkled his nose. "What even is that?"

"Gross," Grant said. "That's what."

"She wants, and I quote, 'two main dishes—one that conjures feelings of the magic of first love and another that contains the essence of sadness.'" I rolled my eyes. "What does that even mean?"

"I don't know," McKenzie said. "But the idea of ruining mac-n-cheese makes me pretty sad, so I'd say we're halfway there."

"A blood fondue fountain?" The color drained from Abbey's face. "Like real blood?"

"No, she just wants it to *look* like blood," Katie explained as though that made any sort of sense. "She wants it to *actually* be cheese. It's supposed to represent the death of her haters."

McKenzie slapped the pages on the table in front of her. "Am I the only person who thinks this chick is cracked?"

"Nope," I replied as the others shook their heads.

"I know she's a little... unconventional," Katie said evenly. "But we need to make this work. We have to. This event is going to give the restaurant a *lot* of publicity. It could really put us on the map, and with our grand opening happening the following weekend, we need this."

"Alright." McKenzie sighed. "How many people are we talking?"

Katie hesitated a second before answering. "Four hundred."

"Can our staff even handle that many?" Sydney asked.

Katie's silence told us it was happening regardless.

"So, is this going to be buffet style?" McKenzie asked. "Because we definitely don't have the staff to wait on that many people."

"No buffet," Katie said. "Prose was clear she wanted it to be a sit-down affair."

I turned to McKenzie. "What do you think Prose's real name is?"

She rested her head on her hands. "Karen, if I had to guess."

I stifled a laugh.

Abbey's eyes were wide with fear. "We can't possibly serve that many people ourselves, though, can we?"

"Absolutely not," McKenzie said. "We'll have to outsource and hire some extra people through a private company."

"Right." Katie nodded. "But we don't need to worry about the logistics yet. Today's all about brainstorming the menu."

I pressed the heels of my palms to my forehead, trying to ward off an oncoming headache.

"So what foods are sad besides dessert mac-n-cheese?" Grant asked.

Katie steepled her fingers. "You're thinking too literally here. She wants foods and smells that evoke feelings of magic and sadness."

"I think you might be giving her too much credit," McKenzie said. "The woman wants a T-Rex cake."

"Okay, that part I can't explain," Katie went on, refusing to be sidetracked. "But think about it. What foods make you think of falling in love?"

McKenzie held up her hands. "Yeah, see, I don't do that, so I have no idea." She looked around the room. "Any takers? Tommy Lee?"

Katie swayed slightly on her feet and steadied herself by gripping the edge of the table I was seated at.

"Are you okay?" I clenched my fists together to stop myself from jumping up to help her. My eyes darted over to McKenzie, who mirrored my concern.

"I'm fine," Katie insisted. "Just got a little dizzy is all."

McKenzie cleared her throat and spoke softly. "Maybe you should sit do—"

"I said I'm fine," Katie snipped before giving us a tight smile. "Anyway, where were we?"

"How did the soft opening go?" Will asked later that week at The Maple Room as I smoothed icing over the cake I'd made, spreading it evenly just like he'd taught me.

"It went well." It was our first session in several days since I'd been working more at Katie's Kitchen, and I'd baked his Nana's carrot cake, a recipe that had been in his family for generations. "We had a great turnout, and she seemed really happy."

"Hmmm." Will pursed his lips. "Then why does your face look all pinched and pouty?"

"I'm worried, Will," I admitted as I set down the spatula. "I feel like I'm watching a plane about to crash. She's taking on too much."

In an effort to make sure everything was perfect for Prose Gold's party, Katie had forgone passing along any big tasks to her staff, deciding instead to tackle each detail herself. She'd designed the cake, the entire menu, and had taken on securing any additional things we'd need. She'd even insisted on doing all the ordering and shopping for the event.

"Have you talked to her about it?" Will asked, peering at me over his thick frames.

I shook my head. "I need to let her figure out her own boundaries and limitations. It's hard, though, when I see the path she's on. When one of us offers to help or take something off her plate, she refuses and insists on doing it herself."

"Oh dear."

"It's almost like she's got something to prove."

"And maybe she does."

"But why?" I asked. "Everyone who knows her sees how incredibly talented she is."

"I agree," he said, folding his arms over his chest and leaning against the counter. "But maybe it's less about proving something to other people and more about proving it to herself."

"Maybe you're right." The way I'd acted before had made her feel that I thought she was fragile and incapable. It hadn't occurred to me that maybe part of her shared those concerns.

"While I understand Katie is still learning how to navigate MS, she's also learning how to be a business owner." Will studied my cake, turning it on its pedestal. "When I first started out I nearly ran myself into the ground. And do you know what happens when you don't delegate because you think you're the only person who can do things right?"

I raised my brows. "You wear yourself out?"

"Well, *that*, and you inevitably fuck it up. We can't do bloody everything and expect to do it all perfectly. That goes for everyone—chronic illness or not. She has to learn that leaning on others doesn't make her weak. It makes her a better leader."

I wished there was a way I could help her see that.

"But that's for everyone to figure out for themselves," he said, as if reading my mind. "At least, it was for me. My situation was a bit different. I was a conceited bloke. Didn't want other people to do anything because I thought surely I was the most competent person to ever hold a whisk. Boy, what a rude awakening I had." He chuckled and removed his glasses, cleaning them with the hem of his shirt. "But Katie is as humble as they come. I don't think her stubbornness stems from thinking she's better than anyone, but more so a desire to not feel she's any less capable because of her illness."

"It's like she's trying to prove she's a superhero. And if you ask me, she is one."

"Right you are. That girl can work circles around me. But even Batman had Robin."

I gave a small smile. I'd be happy to be her sidekick, the one to always have her back, if she'd let me.

"Now, let's try this cake of yours, shall we?" He held out a knife to me. "Care to do the honors?"

I took it from him as he retrieved two small dishes and forks. Once I'd sliced and plated the cake, I watched as he took the first bite. He closed his eyes for a moment and chewed, nodding his head slowly.

A smile tugged at the corner of his mouth. "Tastes just like Nana made it."

"What? Really?"

"I think you've officially graduated from the Willam Deveraux Cooking School of Hard Knocks."

"A compliment from *the* Willam Deveraux." My chest

swelled with satisfaction. "So, do I get a diploma or something? Maybe a celebratory parade?"

He chuckled. "No, you nitwit. You get to do the dishes."

"Ah, there's the Will I know and love."

"Well done, my friend," he said, clapping me on the back. "Well done, indeed."

THIRTY-THREE

Katie

"I mean this with the utmost respect for you, but that is really creepy." McKenzie wrinkled her nose at my handiwork. It was well after closing, three days before the Prose Gold album release party. We were getting down to the wire and McKenzie was peppering me with questions to make sure I'd ticked everything off our to-do list.

"It's… something," I said with a laugh as I attached fondant-covered crispy treat arms to the T-Rex torso on the island in the back of Katie's Kitchen. "That's for sure."

Due to the fact that the cake was six-feet tall, I'd have to transport the pieces separately and put it together on site. Needless to say, I was more than a little nervous. There were too many things that could go wrong, so I'd been laser-focused on making sure everything would go off without a hitch.

"It looks so… so *real*." She studied the arms. "What do you think she was going for with this? Did the dinosaur eat a small child and steal its arms?"

"I can't begin to imagine the thought process that went into choosing this."

"Anyway." She shook her head as though she were trying to shake an image from her mind and returned to the checklist in front of her. "The blueberry ricotta mac-n-cheese?"

"I'm prepping that tomorrow."

"The stuffed mushrooms?"

"Picked up everything for those this morning." In honor of Prose Gold's request that the meal evoke feelings of a first love, I'd gone with my own take of the 'Marry Me' chicken recipe the internet had lost their minds for, with every side and fixin' imaginable.

"Got it," she said. "What about the fountain of death?"

"Yep. I used beets to turn the cheese red. It's... unsettling."

"Gross," she said. "Jacob and Abbey are working on everything that goes with it tomorrow. Basically anything you could ever want to dip in cheese will be there."

"Oh!" I pointed toward the list. "Make sure everything is bat-shaped."

"What? I thought it was moons and stars?"

"That was last week. She sent over an email this morning changing it to bats."

"Fitting. Since she's bat-shit crazy." She snorted. "I'll let them know. Moving on. Set up time?"

"Confirmed."

"Plates and flatware?"

I huffed. "Confirmed. McKenzie, really. Everything is done. There's nothing to worry about. I've been over that list at least a hundred times."

Her brows knitted together. "But—"

"I promise. I've got everything under control." I gave her

a reassuring smile. "Now, I've got to paint the detailing on these hands so it can dry overnight. Why don't you go on home and get some rest? We've got a busy few days ahead."

"Are you sure?" she asked. "I could stay and help you clean up."

"I'm positive. Lock the door on your way out though, will you?"

She lingered for a few seconds more, but I pretended not to notice.

"Okay then," she said finally. "I'll see you tomorrow."

"Good night," I replied as she gathered her things and left, clicking the lock as I'd asked.

I appreciated McKenzie and her willingness to help, but it felt like she and everyone else were underestimating me. Like I somehow wouldn't be able to do or remember everything on my own. This party might have been the biggest event I'd ever done, but it certainly wasn't my first rodeo.

The list she'd been working off of taunted me from the counter. I'd been over it dozens of times, making adjustments here and there as Prose came up with yet another strange request. There hadn't been a single detail left unthought of.

I took a deep breath and let it out, taking a moment to stretch my tingling fingers before tossing the list into the trash.

The day of the party was a whirlwind. It started before the sun had even risen when I left for the restaurant to place the finishing touches on the T-Rex head. The rest of the staff arrived at a more reasonable hour, and the kitchen buzzed with excitement.

We closed a little early so we had plenty of time to change and get to the event to begin setting up. Though some of the food was already made, some of it would be prepared on site in the kitchen at The Arthur, the stunning Victorian-style mansion Prose had selected as her venue.

"You know, now that I see the place the blood fountain kind of makes sense. It's giving major vampire vibes," McKenzie said as we carried in our second of many loads a little after five that evening. "Like if Posh Spice were Dracula."

I shushed her, but couldn't help a giggle. She wasn't wrong. The exposed brick and high ceilings were balanced by ornate chandeliers, heavy drapes, and gothic accents. A beady-eyed gargoyle statue stared at me from the roof, causing me to shudder.

"Dallas and the others will be here in about an hour with the rest of our things," I said as we began unloading our stuff in the enormous kitchen. "They got held up because Jacob spilled some cheese blood on his shirt."

McKenzie gestured around at the dark fixtures. "He should have just left it. It would have fit the aesthetic."

I chuckled. "I figured we could get a head start on prep and then I can assemble the cake."

"Roger that. I'll get going on the mushrooms."

"Perfect."

We worked alongside each other, preparing the food to the soundtrack of a string quartet practicing cover songs in the next room. Together we were in our element, moving around one another like skilled dancers. Once I'd gotten the chickens in the oven, I set out to assemble the cake. McKenzie helped me wheel in each piece on a cart loaned to us by the venue and then went back to the kitchen to keep an eye on things.

Thirty minutes later, the T-Rex was assembled with everything but its head. I climbed onto the step ladder I'd brought and had the head hovering over the rod that would hold it in place when a sharp gasp startled me.

"OMG!" Prose Gold shrieked out each letter from the ground beside me. "It's perfect."

I held my breath as I teetered on the ladder, dizzy from the movement.

"*This* is a work of art," Prose gushed, while I regained my footing and plunked the head onto the rod. "It's magnificent. Here, let me help you."

She extended her slender hand to me, tipped in long, black points. I let out a sigh of relief as I climbed down.

"Thanks, Prose." I plastered on a smile. "I'm so glad you like it."

"It must've taken you ages to make it."

"It didn't take too long at all," I said with a wave of my hand.

With both feet on the ground again, I was finally able to take in the full image of Prose Gold. Her long, previously platinum hair had been dyed a gorgeous shade of what could only be described as rose gold, and had been separated into several sections and spiked. She wore heavy, black eyeshadow and white contacts that were a bit unnerving.

"Oh, you like my dress?" she asked, clearly aware I was staring, though it was impossible not to. "It's vintage. My stylist just made a few alterations."

"I do. It's very unique." And it was. She wore a smoky-emerald green Steampunk corset dress with a lace skirt that had been cut dangerously short. She'd paired the ensemble with some beaded medieval-looking platform heels. It was gorgeous and something only Prose Gold could pull off.

"Thanks." Her fuchsia painted lips curved into a smile. She turned to look over her shoulder, and I had to duck to keep from being impaled by her hair. "Libby! Get in here and look at this cake."

A woman with sleek black hair hurried into the room and rushed to her side. "OMG. It's, like, stunning."

"Isn't it such a vibe?" Prose asked.

"*Such* a vibe," Libby echoed.

"Hey, Katie," McKenzie's voice called from behind me. "Sydney just texted and said they're five minutes OUUU-UOHMYGOD. What happened to your eyes? Do you need a doctor?"

I turned to find McKenzie gawking at Prose with a horrified expression on her face, and I pinned her with a please-stop-talking glare.

Prose and Libby giggled.

"No, silly. They're contacts," Prose said. "Aren't they cool?"

McKenzie gulped. "That is certainly a word you could use to describe them."

I gripped her arm and turned back to Prose. "We should get back to the kitchen and finish up."

Prose clasped her ringed fingers together in front of her. "Yes, the party will be starting soon, so I should go hide. You know I *have* to make an entrance."

"You *are* the guest of honor," I said as she turned on her heel, nearly taking out McKenzie's eye.

"I'll have Libby bring the check to you in a bit," she called over her shoulder.

"Thanks," I said as I pulled McKenzie back toward the kitchen.

"It wouldn't surprise me at all if she rode in on a bed of

nails," she whispered. "Or a headless horse or something equally disturbing."

"She's definitely a little... eccentric," I said, peeking in the oven at the chicken. "Looking good. We're right on schedule."

I beamed with pride as I poured myself a goblet of water and took a sip. The food was looking and smelling great, and once Dallas arrived with the cheese fountain and everything that went with it, we'd be all set.

"Awesome," McKenzie said, washing her hands. "What time do the waitstaff get here? I would have thought they'd need to be here by now."

The blood drained from my body as my grip on the glass in my hand slipped, sending it falling to the floor in what felt like slow motion.

Oh no. No no no. My bottom lip trembled, and I swallowed hard as the glass shattered, taking my dreams along with it.

McKenzie jumped at the sound, then rushed to my side. "Are you okay? I'll get a broom."

But I closed my fingers around her wrist before she could move. "They're not coming."

"But they *have* to." Her tone was shrill, bordering on a scream. "What do you mean... Why aren't they coming?" The panic on her face settled into a grim understanding. She knew before I spoke the words out loud.

"Because I never hired them."

McKenzie was on my heels as I tore through the mansion in search of a bathroom. My ears wouldn't stop ringing, and I was suddenly unbearably hot.

"In here." McKenzie's voice sounded far away even though she was right next to me, grabbing my arm. She tugged me inside a bathroom that was easily the size of my living room and wrenched some paper towels from the dispenser.

"The party starts in half an hour," I choked out as she dampened them and rang them out. "What am I gonna do?"

"You're not going to do anything. *We* are."

"I have to tell Prose."

"Sit," she instructed, gripping me by the shoulders. She led me to the tile wall and helped me lower myself to the floor. "We're not telling Wednesday Addams anything. At least not yet. Not unless we have to."

"But… we don't have servers," I cried as she draped the cool towels across the back of my neck. "She explicitly said she didn't want a buffet."

"It's going to be okay. We can fix this." She crouched in front of me. "We'll figure something out."

"This is all my fault." I buried my face in my hands. "You tried to go over that stupid list with me the other night, and I brushed you off. I was so hellbent on doing everything myself. What is wrong with me?"

"I need you to listen to me." She pried my hands away from my face. "All of that might be true, but it's not going to help us figure out how to get ourselves out of this. We can learn our life lessons later. Right now, we're going to find a way to fix this, okay?"

I nodded once as her phone pinged from the pocket of her pants, and she pulled it out.

"That's Sydney. They just pulled up." She blew out a breath. "Here's what's going to happen. I'm going to go fill them in, and you're going to stay right here in this spot. Don't move, and *don't* for any reason talk to Prose Gold. Alright? We *will* fix this."

"Okay," I said softly as she sprinted from the room.

The door closed behind her, leaving me alone with my thoughts.

Why had I been so stubborn? Why hadn't I let McKenzie help me? Or literally *anyone*. This event could make or break a new business. The visibility could be a blessing, or in this case it could be a curse. If Prose Gold decided to tell everyone how badly I'd screwed up, Katie's Kitchen could be closing its doors before it ever really opened them.

THIRTY-FOUR

Dallas

WE WERE ABOUT to unload the cheese fountain from my car when I heard someone frantically shouting my name. I turned to find McKenzie running toward me, red-faced and out of breath.

"What's going on?" I asked, jogging the last few feet to intercept her. "Is Katie okay?"

She leaned forward with her hands on her knees, panting. "Dude, that is a *loaded* question."

"You're freaking me out, McKenzie," I said, attempting to quell the alarm in my voice. "What is it?"

"Hey," McKenzie shouted to the others, ignoring my question. "Go ahead and unload everything and head to the kitchen. The guys at the door will show you where to go. I need to talk to Dallas for a minute."

"You got it," Sydney called, and they set to work as McKenzie grabbed me by the arm and yanked me toward the building.

"So, we've hit a small snag," she said once we were out of earshot of the others. "And by small, I mean colossal."

"Spit it out, already."

"We don't have servers."

"What do you mean *we don't have servers*?"

She stopped walking and looked at me. "Are you being facetious or do you really not know what I mean when I say we *literally* do not have fucking servers?"

"I don't understand. How can we just *not* have servers?" I asked. "Did they run out of gas on the side of the road? Did they all come down with the flu? What the hell happened?"

"Katie forgot to hire them."

Fuck. I rubbed the back of my neck, and my pulse quickened. "What do we do?"

She let out a nervous laugh. "Well, Tommy Lee, I was hoping you might have some ideas. Otherwise we have to tell Prose Gold that her party of A-listers are going to have to serve themselves like they're dining at the Golden Corral."

Prose Gold wasn't exactly my favorite person, but I knew how important this party was for Katie's Kitchen. Negative press, especially from someone like Prose, could be catastrophic for an existing business, let alone a brand-new one.

"And I don't know about you, but I don't want *any* part in that conversation," she continued. "So do you know where we can find, like, twelve people who wouldn't mind dropping whatever they're doing to come right this second and serve for Vampire Barbie?"

Think, Dallas. I pressed the heels of my palms to my forehead. Normally, I would call the guys and Liv and Ella and Jo, but that wouldn't work this time. Ella and Cash were in California. Antoni was in Nebraska. Luca was… God only knew where. I could maybe get Jax and Derek, but that still wouldn't be nearly enough.

An idea stopped me dead in my tracks, and I nearly dropped my phone trying to extract it from my back pocket. I found the number I was looking for and hit send.

"Who are you calling?" McKenzie asked as the person on the other end answered the call.

"Hey, it's Dallas. I really, *really* need your help."

"KATIE?" I CALLED AS I ENTERED THE BATHROOM MCKENZIE directed me to.

She looked up from where she sat on the floor in the expansive room, propped against the wall.

"I guess McKenzie told you about my epic failure." She gave me a weak, sad smile, and as I got closer to her, I saw how puffy her eyes were. "I really screwed up, Dal."

"It was an honest mistake," I said, sitting next to her. "An oversight."

"It wouldn't have happened if I'd just let you guys help like you tried to all along. And it's not like I didn't *know* I was forgetting stuff. I knew, but…" She sighed and trailed off, shaking her head.

"But what?" I asked softly, reaching for her hand.

"I didn't want to feel like I needed help because of my illness."

"That's the thing though—you don't. *Everyone* needs help sometimes, Butter Bean."

"I know, and I don't know why I got so in my head about it. I felt that if I could do everything on my own, people would look at me and think, 'wow, she's a badass,' instead of viewing me as some chronic illness sob story." She rubbed her forehead with her fingertips. "I managed to make everything I did about my illness even though that was *exactly* what I was trying to keep other people from doing. Nobody could have pulled off an event like this on their own."

"It was a huge undertaking," I said. "And maybe we all should have pushed a little harder when you said you didn't want help."

"I think that would have just pissed me off and made me try even harder to prove I could do it on my own." She dropped her chin to her chest. "I had to see it for myself."

"But look at all you accomplished. The cake, the menu, everything. Don't diminish that because you forgot one small thing."

"It's not a small thing, though." She glanced up at me, her mouth drawn into a frown. "I guess I need to face the music and tell Prose her four hundred guests won't have servers."

A grin crept slowly over my face. "But they will."

"We don't have enough people. There's no way we can manage it all."

"And we won't have to."

Her mouth fell open. "What? But… *how*? Who's going to wait tables?"

"I called Will after McKenzie told me what happened," I explained. "He and a few of his employees are on their way right now. It'll be tight, but if we can sacrifice having a couple of us in the kitchen, we'll have enough servers."

"Are you serious?" She steepled her hands in front of her mouth, tears springing to her eyes. "They're really coming here?"

"They are. But we should probably get back out there and have everything ready to go for when they arrive." I rose to a stand and extended my hand to her. "So, what do you say? Are you ready to kick this event's ass?"

"You better believe it," she said, allowing me to pull her to her feet. "Thank you. For not pushing me even when I was being stubborn. For saving the day and having my back."

"I love you, Top Chef Katie." I kissed her forehead. "And I'll be the Robin to your Batman any day. Every superhero needs a sidekick."

"WHAT ON GOD'S GREEN EARTH IS WRONG WITH THAT PROSE Gold girl's eyes?" Will asked as he entered the kitchen with a horrified expression on his face and several staff members on his heels. "Has she been possessed or something?"

I furrowed my brow. "Wait, what?" Prose was an odd bird for sure, but I'd never noticed anything strange about her eyes.

McKenzie registered the look on my face and snorted. "Just you wait. Talk about a jump scare."

Katie rushed to Will's side and pulled him into a hug. "Thank you for doing this."

"Of course, darling." Will kissed her cheek. "Anything for you."

She waved at the smiling group standing behind him. "Thank *all* of you for being here. I'm so grateful."

"Now, where do you want us?" Will asked. "Put me in, Coach. I'm here to work."

Katie straightened her shoulders, holding her chin high as she moved to address us at the front of the room. "This is a high-profile event, and some of the clientele might be a little… different."

"She means demanding," McKenzie corrected.

"So, let's keep the food moving quickly. If you have any issues, don't hesitate to find me or McKenzie."

"What?" McKenzie asked, pressing her palm to her chest. "Why me?"

Katie raised her brows and grinned. "Well, you *are* our manager and second in command."

McKenzie smiled, and I nudged her with my elbow. "Congrats, boss," I whispered.

Her cheeks turned pink, but she stuck out her fist to bump mine.

"Okay, everyone," Katie continued. "Prose wants the hors d'oeuvres and desserts set up on either side of the bar to encourage mingling, so Sydney, I'm putting you in charge of the blood fountain."

"I'm on it, Chef," Sydney said, heading for her post as Will and his people exchanged worried looks.

"Don't worry, it's not actual blood," McKenzie piped up. "Just blood-colored cheese."

Will grimaced. "And that's supposed to make me feel *better* for some reason?"

"Will, I'm going to have you in the kitchen with me, Dallas, McKenzie, and Jacob. Grant, you're going to be on the floor serving," Katie instructed. "Abbey, I want you on the dessert table. Make sure *nobody* touches that cake but me when it's time to cut it. Go—guard it with your life."

"Yes, Chef." Abbey nodded and left the room.

"Does anyone have any questions?" Katie asked.

"No, Chef," I answered with pride, as everyone else echoed my response.

She clasped her hands together. "Alright, everyone. Let's do this."

The evening was a huge success. Will's employees were top-notch, and everyone from Katie's Kitchen had brought their A-game. Katie shined as a leader and kept the dinner service running smoothly. She passed the baton to McKenzie after Prose Gold came back to the kitchen looking for Katie. Apparently, her friends had been raving so much about the food that she wanted to introduce them to the woman behind it all. Somehow I'd managed to fly under Prose's radar completely. I guessed 'Dalton' hadn't made much of an impression on her, and that was alright by me. After years of being in the spotlight, I was enjoying working behind the scenes.

I peeked out into the grand room where Katie was chatting animatedly with someone who had his back to me. She caught my eye and waved me over. I wasn't sure why until the mystery individual pumped their fist in the air and let out a wild howl I'd recognize anywhere. I shook my head and laughed as I made my way over to them.

"Deacon," I said, clapping the lead singer of The Slacks on the back. "How are you, man?"

"Dallas, my guy. How are ya?" He pulled me into a hug. "I can't believe this. Small world. Your girl here is a brilliant chef. I want to bathe in that blueberry ricotta macaroni and cheese. I'd never even *heard* of dessert mac-n-cheese before."

"She's incredible, isn't she?"

Katie beamed as I wrapped my arm around her shoulders.

"A goddamn sorceress is more like it."

"I was just telling Katie that I'll be needing someone to cater my birthday party this summer," Deacon said, holding out his hands. "This is perfect."

"Katie!" Prose called from several feet away, motioning for her.

"Excuse me," Katie said with a smile. "I believe Prose wants me to meet someone else. It was great to see you again, Deacon."

"I'll be in touch about my party," he said as she walked away. "Hey, do you think she could make a life-size cake that looks like me?"

I laughed. "I think Katie can do pretty much anything."

"Amazing."

"Deacon, listen, I hope there aren't any hard feelings about—"

"No way. You had to do what was best for you. Honestly, I think things worked out exactly how they were supposed to." He lowered his voice and leaned closer. "It's not public knowledge yet, but the band is splitting up, and I'm going solo."

"That's huge, man."

"Yeah." His lips curled into a smile. "It is. At first, I hated the idea. I couldn't imagine not being with those guys all the time, you know?"

"Actually, I know exactly what you mean. I felt like that when Midnight in Dallas broke up," I admitted. "Life definitely looks a lot different these days, but those guys are still my brothers. I'd do anything for them."

"That's how I feel too. I love these dudes." He nudged me in the arm. "Did you hear Knox is gonna be a dad?"

"Seems like I did hear something about that," I answered, not wanting to give away that I'd been one of the first to know.

"He and Kira want me to be the godfather. Me." He

pounded his chest. "Can you believe that? I'm gonna spoil the shit out of that kid."

"As you should," I said with a chuckle, patting him on the back. "You look happy."

"I am. What about you? Have you been happy since you left the music scene?"

"Yeah, I have." I caught Katie's eye from across the room, and my heart swelled when she smiled at me. "I've never been better."

"Well, you look great, man. I'm so glad I got to see you."

"Me too," I said, holding out my hand to shake his. "I better get back in the kitchen, but tell Knox I said hi next time you see him."

"I will." He ignored my hand and hugged me instead. "You take care, brother."

I returned to the kitchen with a bounce in my step and was settling in at the sink to wash dishes when McKenzie sauntered over, depositing a stack of dirty plates on the counter.

"You did good tonight, Tommy Lee," she said. "You really came through for us."

I didn't look up from the pot I was scrubbing. "A fist bump and a compliment all in one night. McKenzie, if I didn't know any better, I'd almost think we're friends."

"Well, good thing you know better." Out of the corner of my eye, I saw her smile. "I want those dishes spotless, Tommy Lee."

"You got it, boss."

THIRTY-FIVE

Katie

THE DAY of the grand opening, the line for Katie's Kitchen was wrapped around the block. Prose Gold had made so many posts on social media about her party and how much she loved our food that we became inundated with customers and calls to book us for catering.

"Welp, that's it," McKenzie said, hanging up the phone in the kitchen about forty-five minutes before closing. "We're officially booked for catering until December."

"Holy shit. It's only April. I think it's time we consider hiring a few more people," I said, pulling the last blueberry ricotta mac-n-cheese of the day out of the oven. It had been added to our menu by popular demand after Prose gushed about it online.

Dallas opened the door that led to the front of the restaurant. "Hey Chef, there's some customers out here who really want to talk to you."

I plopped the dish I was holding on a rack to cool.

"Are y'all good for a minute?" I asked McKenzie and Jacob.

"Yep," McKenzie answered, and Jacob nodded.

I wiped my hands on my apron and followed Dallas out front, tears springing to my eyes when I saw the customers that awaited me.

"Surprise," Ella cried, throwing her arms around me. Right behind her was Cash with Betty on his hip and Grace with her boyfriend Sam.

"You guys," I said, dabbing at my eyes. "I can't believe you're here."

"You didn't think we'd miss your big day, did you?" Grace asked, as I moved to wrap her in a hug. "Congratulations, Katie."

Cash looked around, taking in the space filled to the brim with customers. "The place looks spectacular."

"You did good." Ella's eyes brimmed with tears as she squeezed my arm. "It's perfect."

The front door chimed and a chorus of disgruntled groans just beyond the entrance filtered inside.

"Cool your jets. We're friends of the owner," a familiar voice shouted, and my heart leapt.

"Antoni!" I shrieked as he and Nate walked in.

"Heavens to Betsy," Antoni said, embracing me. "I thought they were going to start a riot out there."

I stood back, looking at my friends in disbelief. "I didn't think y'all were going to make it."

Grace beamed. "We wanted it to be a surprise."

"Best surprise ever," I said, glancing back at Dallas who was making Betty giggle.

"We saw Derek and Jo," Nate spoke up. "They were circling the block looking for parking."

"And Liv and Jax will be here soon with the kiddos," Ella added. "It'll be like an impromptu Sunday dinner."

"Any word from Luca?" Antoni asked.

Dallas cleared his throat and shook his head. "I tried to reach him."

My smile faltered.

Ella propped her hand on her hip. "We'll just have to FaceTime his butt."

"I get the feeling he wants to be left alone," Dallas said quietly.

"Oh." Ella frowned.

"Doesn't he understand that's not how this family thing works?" Antoni asked. "We get on each other's nerves and in one another's business. That's how it is. Those are the rules."

Dallas and I exchanged a worried glance. I was concerned, but how could we reach Luca if he didn't *want* to be reached?

Sensing the shift in my mood, Ella put her arm around me and gave me a silent squeeze.

"I need to get back in the kitchen, but y'all go ahead and put your orders in," I said. "We'll have them ready just before closing so we can all sit down together."

My heart sank a little on that last word. Though I was thrilled most of my friends had shown up, I was still concerned about Luca.

The bell dinged again, and my eyes darted toward the door, my chest filled with hope. But that hope was squashed when I saw it wasn't Luca who'd entered.

"I have a delivery for Katie Kelley," the florist announced, approaching with a gorgeous spring bouquet.

"That's me," I said, waving her over.

"Here you go." She nodded and handed me the arrangement.

"Dal, do you mind holding this?" I asked, and he took it so I could open the small envelope attached.

I swallowed down the lump in my throat as I read the words printed on the card.

Katie,

I'm sorry I can't be there today, but know I'm thinking of you. Proud of you.

x

Luca

"I'M ZONKED," I SAID THROUGH A YAWN AS WE TRUDGED INTO my house late that night. "You want to order a pizza and just eat it in bed?"

"Are you talking dirty to me?" He winked. "What do you want? Our usual?"

I nodded. "Yes, please. Anything that doesn't require me to think or make any more decisions today."

Emilia looked up from her food bowl in the kitchen and wagged her tail before toddling over to us in a ducky printed diaper.

"Hi Emilia. Did you miss me?" I cooed, and she licked my face.

"I'll order dinner. You go get comfy." He reached for Emilia. "Hand over the floof. I'll take her for a quick potty break and meet you in bed."

I gave him the pup and yawned. "You don't have to ask me twice."

Not even ten minutes later, Dallas returned inside with Emilia and as promised, joined me in the bedroom. He placed her gently on the mattress, and she rooted around beside me on the blanket, wagging her tail. She took after me—the girl loved to get cozy in bed.

Dallas kicked off his shoes before flopping down next to me.

"Finally." He stretched his arms over his head and moaned. "It feels good to be home."

Home. I raised up on my elbow and gazed at him, taking him in. My throat felt thick as I reached for his hand.

He threaded his fingers through mine. "What's that look for?"

"Nothing," I said. "You said it felt good to be home, and it just makes me feel good to know you think of this house as home."

"I do. I love it here." He kissed the top of my hand. "But anywhere you are is home to me, Katie. You know that."

My stomach fluttered, and my pulse thudded in my ears.

"Move in with me," I said softly.

He studied my face for a second, a slow smile spreading across his mouth. "Really?"

I nodded. "Really. I'm so happy, Dallas. I have you, Emilia, the restaurant, the best family of friends I could ever hope for. But us living together—officially—that would make life as close to perfect as it can get. I love this house so much, but it doesn't have to be here. I know it's old, and honestly, it needs to be renovated for it to last so—"

He cupped my cheek and covered my mouth with his thumb. "This house is perfect."

My eyes stung as he rose to place a tender kiss on my lips.

"Tell you what," he began. "We can keep my condo for a while. Rent it out as an AirBnb or something temporarily. That'll give us some time to figure out what we want to do as far as renovations go, and when we're ready for that step, we'll have a place to stay while the work is done. Then we can sell the condo. What do you say to that?"

"I say yes!" I smiled through my tears and launched myself at him, sending us both toppling back on the mattress.

"She said yes!" Dallas announced to no one but me and Emilia, and we collapsed in fits of laughter.

I would have lived with him anywhere because he was my home too. But he knew how much this place meant to me, how special it was. This house was already bursting at the seams with memories like an overstuffed suitcase, but I had a feeling it had room for many, many more.

"Would you like some more fried chicken, Caesar?" I asked, holding the platter out to him.

"I couldn't possibly eat another bite," he said, taking the dish anyway and plopping three more gluten-free fried chicken strips on his plate. "Have you gotten rid of that boyfriend of yours yet?"

"You know I can hear you, Caesar." Dallas raised an eyebrow as he picked up a couple of the empty serving dishes from the tables we'd pushed together.

"I'm just joking." Caesar turned toward me, shielding his face with his hands so only I could see his mouth, 'No I'm not.'

Dallas smirked. "I'm still here, Caesar."

Caesar feigned innocence, pressing his hand to his chest. "What?"

The entire chronic illness support group and Dallas laughed as he went back to the kitchen.

"I know I've said this a hundred times tonight, but this sure beats that drafty old basement," Margot said, polishing off her mashed potatoes. "How's business been, Katie?"

"Insane in the best way," I answered. We'd only been open for a month, and our staff had already doubled in size so we could start taking on more catering gigs without always having to shut down the restaurant.

"And how are *you*?" Margot asked. "Are you taking care of yourself?"

I nodded. "I had my second infusion last week, and I'm trying to be more intentional about taking time to rest."

"That's great," Sarah, the group leader, said. "Rest is so important."

"And I trust you're doing better about asking for help?" Margot gave me a knowing look.

After the ordeal with the Prose Gold party, I'd confided in her about what I'd done, and she'd agreed to help hold me accountable so I didn't fall back into trying to do everything myself. It was easier for me to hear from Margot because she understood firsthand what I was going through.

"I have," I replied. "Promise."

Margot patted me on the arm. "Good."

"Is it too soon to ask what's for dessert?" Caesar tossed his napkin on his plate.

"It's never too soon for dessert," I said, rising from the table. "I'll be right back."

I disappeared through the door to the kitchen and returned a moment later with a tray full of chocolate soufflés.

"Oh my goodness," Margot purred. "Those look amazing."

I placed a dessert in front of each person.

Caesar's eyes went wide. "I have died and gone to heaven."

"That's like the fifth time you've died tonight," Margot pointed out.

Caesar dug his spoon into the soufflé. "Did you hear that crunch? This is going to be good."

"Of course it's going to be good. Katie made it," Margot said as he took his first bite.

"Actually, I didn't." I beamed with pride. "Dallas did."

"Really?" Caesar asked as everyone started to eat their desserts with contented sighs.

I nodded.

"Dallas," Caesar yelled. "Will you come out here?"

"You bellowed, Caesar?" he said, pushing through the door into the dining room with a dish towel slung over his shoulder.

"Will you marry me?" Caesar asked through a mouthful of soufflé.

Dallas chuckled. "I thought you wanted to marry Katie?"

"Well, I won't tell if you don't," Caesar teased.

I folded my arms over my chest in mock indignation. "I'm standing right here, Caesar."

The group erupted with laughter before going back to chatting amongst themselves.

Dallas moved to stand beside me, reaching for my hand.

"I'm going to head out so I can take care of Emilia," he said, kissing me on the cheek. "See you at home?"

My heart fluttered, and I squeezed his hand. "See you at home."

Epilogue

Dallas

"I think that's the last of it," I said, wiping the sweat from my brow. It had been about a month and a half since Katie's Kitchen officially opened, and life had finally settled down enough that we had some time off.

Katie peered at me from behind a stack of boxes in the living room. "Whenever we do get around to renovating, bigger closets will definitely be a top priority."

"Definitely," I agreed as she closed the distance between us and wrapped her arms around me.

"So, where should we start?"

"You mean we have to unpack it too?"

She laughed. "We have the entire day off. Might as well make use of it."

I waggled my brows at her. "I could think of some things that would be a lot more fun than this."

She giggled. "There will be time for that later."

"Fine," I pouted. "Want to start with the kitchen stuff?"

"You read my mind." She skipped past me. "You did remember the French press, didn't you?"

"Did you want me to move in or my French press?" I asked, trailing behind her.

She looked at me from over her shoulder. "Is it wrong if I say both?"

"Yes." I bit back a smile. "Yes it is."

Together, we started going through the boxes, putting away the kitchen supplies, occasionally tossing extras of things into a box we'd designated for donations. Emilia toddled around near our feet, curious about what we were up to. Once we'd cleared the kitchen, about an hour later, Katie's shoulders sagged as she yawned.

"I need a break," she said. "How about some lunch?"

"I like lunch. Why don't you and Emilia relax and keep me company while I make it?"

"Okay, but only because Emilia's been working so hard." She scooped the pup off the floor and winked at me.

"How about a tuna melt?"

"Sounds good," she said, leaning against the counter with Emilia cradled in her arms.

I got to work gathering what I needed to make the sandwiches and set a skillet on the stove to warm.

"By the way, I forgot to tell you, your buddy Deacon called the restaurant after you left yesterday."

"About his birthday party?"

"Yep." She pursed her lips. "Did you really tell him I could make a cake that was a life-sized replica of him?"

"Um. Well, I don't think I said those *exact* words." I

gritted my teeth. "I'm pretty sure what I said was that you could do anything."

She swatted my arm, but a smile tugged at the corners of her mouth. "Dallas!"

"Ow. What?" I chuckled, draining a couple of cans of tuna and emptying them into a bowl. "So, he really wants you to make him into a cake, huh?"

"Not only that, but now he's decided he wants the cake version of him to be wearing a spacesuit." She shook her head and sighed. "Is this going to be my thing? Weird cakes?"

"You kinda set yourself up for this when you agreed to do the T-Rex cake with those creepy baby arms."

"I'm going to need you and McKenzie to help me figure out how to make this one happen. He wants to meet with us next week to work on some ideas for the menu. I told him I'd have a sketch of what the cake would look like when he comes in."

I started chopping some red onion, a couple dill pickles, and a stalk of celery. "Note to self. Brush up on astronaut cakes. Got it."

She hesitated a moment before she spoke again. "I tried to text Luca again yesterday."

"And?"

"Nothing," she answered. "I haven't gotten a response from him since I thanked him for the flowers he sent when he said he was doing some traveling."

"He doesn't respond to me either."

"I'm worried about him. I know he can be kind of aloof and that he likes his space, but this seems like more than that, don't you think?"

"I do," I admitted. "If he wasn't traveling, we could just show up and pay him a visit in Kentucky."

"That's probably exactly why he's traveling. He knows us too well." She gave me a faint smile as she placed Emilia on the floor in front of her food dish. "It just makes me a little sad, you know? Ella and Cash won't be coming back to visit until at least Thanksgiving, and who knows when Antoni will get to come back? Jax and Liv are going back on the road before long, and Jo and Derek are bouncing between here and New York. Then Luca is... wherever he is. I just miss them."

"I know you do." I stopped what I was doing and folded her in my arms. "I do too."

"I miss Sunday dinners."

"Yeah. Me too." I pulled back so I could look into her eyes. "What if we started some new traditions of our own this year?"

"Like what?" she asked.

I shrugged. "What about a monthly game night? We could invite Will, McKenzie, and some of your friends from the support group. I could see if Knox and his wife would want to come. And Jo and Derek and everyone can come when they're around. I know nothing will ever take the place of our Sunday dinners, but it could be good."

"Yeah, it could," she said. "I don't know... I just don't want to let go of everything else. I don't want that to be over."

"I don't think it'll ever end. This will just be the beginning of a new chapter."

"A new chapter," she echoed, a smile spreading across her face. "I like that."

"Then let's do it."

I smiled and kissed her softly, knowing that no matter what chapter we found ourselves in we'd always turn the pages together.

Acknowledgments

As always, I would be lost without Jennifer Bottoms and Kate Oscarson. I couldn't do any of this without you.

Nicole Hazel, my best friend and medical consultant who happens to be one of the best nurses that ever existed. Thank you for the research you put into making sure Katie's journey was as accurate as possible.

Kayla Kleffman, I'm grateful every day that you turned up in my inbox.

Elle Maxwell, for making my characters come to life so beautifully.

Kia Clay, for still believing in me.

Ali Roller, thank you for becoming a reader so you can go on this journey with me.

Mrs. Ross, for being the first person to encourage me to use my voice.

Jen Malone, for helping to make this book shine.

Everyone at Parnassus Books in Nashville, TN.

Love and hugs to S.L. Astor, Reah, Jena, Lauren, Eve, Mia, Allie, Flavia, Marianne, Susana, Kerry, Kelsey, Leigh Ann, Sophie, Sammi Jo, Christana, Brooke. At one point or another, all of you have lifted me up during this process and I appreciate each of you.

Mom and Dad, who have not read these books. Please don't. Like ever.

My furbabies who definitely can't read but who happen to be the best writing buddies.

My husband and favorite love story. Let's go to Target. I love you!

And lastly, to you, my beautiful readers. I appreciate every post you make about my books, every message you send me, every book club you invite me to. None of this would be possible without you.

Melissa Grace is a freelance writer whose work has been featured in publications like *Medium, Thought Catalog,* and *The Mighty*. She resides just outside of Nashville, Tennessee with her husband and many fur children. This is her fourth novel.

Learn more and stay in the loop about Melissa's future projects at: www.melissagracewrites.com. Find her on social media:

twitter.com/heymelissagrace
instagram.com/heymelissagrace
facebook.com/heymelissagrace
tiktok.com/heymelissagrace
goodreads.com/melissagrace
bookbub.com/authors/melissa-grace

Made in the USA
Las Vegas, NV
19 July 2023